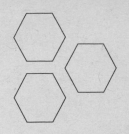

CURED

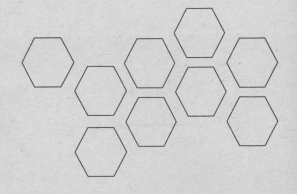

CURED

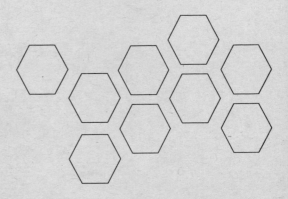

BETHANY WIGGINS

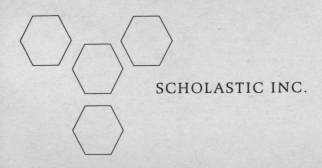

SCHOLASTIC INC.

ISBN 978-0-545-78241-8

Copyright © 2014 by Bethany Wiggins. All rights reserved. Published by Scholastic Inc., 557 Broadway, New York, NY 10012, by arrangement with Walker Books for Young Readers, an imprint of Bloomsbury Publishing, Inc. SCHOLASTIC and associated logos are trademarks and/or registered trademarks of Scholastic Inc.

12 11 10 9 8 7 6 5 4 3 2 1   14 15 16 17 18 19/0

Printed in the U.S.A.   40

First Scholastic printing, September 2014

Book design by Regina Flath

To my brother, Matt—childhood playmate, nemesis,
and partner in crime. Once you even rescued me.

CHAPTER 1

A person can survive on sixty pounds of beans and three hundred pounds of rice a year. Dinner in the Bloom home tonight is beans and rice for the 365th night in a row. And we ran out of pepper yesterday.

I stare down at my plate of food and frown at the brown bean juice seeping past the scoop of white rice. My empty stomach doesn't even rumble.

"Eat up before it gets cold," Dad says with forced enthusiasm. "And when you're done, you can bring a plate out to Uncle Rob."

I open my mouth to complain—

"And before you whine about the food, think of all the kids who are going to bed hungry tonight."

I sigh and put a bite in my mouth. As I chew, I stare at the framed embroidery hanging on the wall across the table from me: *Faith and Hope for the Future.* It is made with purple and red embroidery floss and has white needlepoint lilies with green stems sewn around the words. That's the first one Mom made.

I look at the empty chair below the framed embroidery saying, and my heart aches like it has a hole in it. The chair has been empty for almost a year and a half. Mom says time will make Dean's absence easier to bear—I'm surprised she hasn't embroidered *that* yet. Time hasn't helped. It has only made me miss my brother more—made the hole in my heart bigger.

I can feel Dad's eyes on me, and a wave of dread makes my hands cold. I set my fork down and look at him, wondering if he can tell that I am planning something dangerous. He wipes his mouth with a stained cloth napkin. "Your hair's getting too long, Jack. Maybe Mom should buzz it tomorrow."

I force myself not to sigh with relief and run a hand over my head. *Too long* means my hair is finally long enough to hide my scalp when I am standing in sunlight. It means it is finally long enough to stick up a little bit in the morning when I get out of bed. It means I am a little less ugly than normal.

"She's . . ." Mom clears her throat. "*He's* still good for a few weeks."

I gulp down another bite of beans and rice and stare at my plate. I won't be here in a few weeks. I won't be here *tomorrow.*

"But—"

"No one who looks at Jack will see anything but a boy," Mom says, cutting off Dad. "Sometimes even *I* forget what Jack really is."

"Yeah," Chris says. "I don't remember you *ever* looking like a you-know-what." He's eight. I stopped looking like a girl when he was five.

Josh nudges my ribs with his elbow, and the smell of rancid fuel settles around me. He and Steve spent the afternoon siphoning gasoline from abandoned cars and filtering it so it will run the generator. "You've got being a boy down so good I almost expect you to start peeing standing up." It is meant as a compliment, but my older brother's words flood me with shame. I bite my bottom lip and scowl.

It was the day Mom began embroidering things like Faith and Hope for the Future *and* Speed Is Better Than Strength *onto spare pieces of fabric and framing them around the house. It was the day I, Jacqui Aislynn Bloom, was seen for the last time in the real world.*

I knew something was wrong before I woke up. The sound was part of my dreams. Muted popping. Distant cheering. It was like the Fourth of July, and I was hearing it from inside my house. Only it was October.

I opened my eyes and the sounds didn't flit away like dream sounds do when you wake. The deep thump of an explosion rumbled my window pane. I looked out of it, at the pale outline of dawn shining down into the window well and lighting up the glass, and pulled my covers closer around me. I didn't have anything to wake up early for, since school had been canceled for nearly a year.

Upstairs, feet pounded through the house. Dad yelled. Someone came barreling down the basement stairs and my bedroom door was thrown open. I sat up and blinked the sleep from my eyes.

Dean, armed with Dad's Glock, stepped into my bedroom and closed the door behind himself. His blue eyes flashed with worry. "Under the bed!" he ordered, dragging me from my covers by the arm.

"Ouch! What are you—"

"Now!" he yelled, making my ears ring. Dean never yelled at me.

My bottom lip quivered and he glared. I fell to my stomach and clawed at the carpet, squeezing myself into the narrow space until I barely had room to take a full breath, with the bed pressing on me from above and the floor from below.

"What's going on?" I asked, voice muffled by the dusty carpet squished against my cheek.

"The gangs have finally made it to the suburbs. They are looting anything and everything. Some of the neighbors are joining forces with us, and we're going to try to keep them out of our neighborhood, to keep our families safe."

"Why do I have to hide? I want to see what's going on."

Something popped outside my window, followed by a woman wailing. Dean leaned his face down and looked at me. "Jacqui, they're looting things like food and guns. They're also taking women and girls. We love you too much to risk you getting taken, so just stay put. We're going to protect you. Even if we die trying."

Dean stayed in my room all day, an armed guard standing in front of my bed. I lay wedged under there until sunset, until my stomach was so empty I thought I might die, until the neighborhood grew silent again. That's when Mom came into my room.

"Quickly, Jacqui. Come here," she said.

I dragged my way out from under the bed like a beached walrus and screamed. Mom's long, thick hair was gone; her apron was gone, her wedding ring, her earrings, her nail polish—all gone. She wore men's clothing that hung loose over her ample body, and she was armed with the electric clippers that she used to trim my brothers' hair.

I stared at her peach-fuzz hair and stark scalp gleaming through. She plugged the clippers in and turned me so my back was to her. When the blade buzzed down on my forehead and into my hairline, I threw my hands in the way. The blade caught my skin and nicked it.

"Mom! What are you doing?" I wailed.

"Cutting your hair," she said, yanking my hands out of the way. "It's the only way we know how to keep you safe, so don't fight me! If only you were a boy," she added under her breath.

I sucked the blood from my finger and stood stone-still as the clippers buzzed off row after row of my hair, until the thick, dark mass of it was spilled in a pile around my feet. When she finished, I was too stunned to move. All I could do was stare at the thick, glossy, deep-brown hair that curled in smooth ringlets on the floor—the one thing I had that every girl coveted—and suck on my finger, even though it wasn't bleeding anymore. My head felt too light, and cold air breathed against my scalp. I had been stripped of the one thing that gave me the confidence to go out in the world and ignore the rude things people said about me. Now, I felt naked.

"Dean," Mom said, raking my hair up off the carpet with her fingers and stuffing it into the garbage can beside my bed. "Get the size-fourteen boys' clothes from the storage room."

Dean did what she asked, setting a plastic storage tub onto my bed. Mom opened the container and started sorting through the clothing. She pressed a pair of well-used but clean tighty-whities at me, followed by a pair of jeans and a gray sweatshirt. She rifled through my underwear drawer until she found the sports bra that I had never worn.

"Put those on," she said. "Quickly!"

There was such panic in her voice that I didn't wait for Dean to leave. I pulled my purple nightshirt over my head, rolled my underwear over my thighs and down to the floor, and then put on the bra and pulled on my brother's old underwear and sweatshirt. I could hardly get the pants up over my thighs, and then had to suck in my stomach to button them.

Mom crouched by my feet and rolled the hem of the pants one time. "Better." She dumped the contents of the storage tote onto my white bedspread, and then took all the clothes out of my drawers and stuffed them into the storage tote. "From now on you are Jack! And you're a boy."

I stared at her back as she hurried out of the bedroom. And then I ran my hands over my boot-camp hairdo and started to cry. Dean came back into my bedroom and wrapped his solid arms around me.

"It's okay, Jack," he said, his embrace strong and firm, his voice level. "But you've got to stop crying. Boys don't cry."

He let go and I looked up in time to see him wipe the tears from his eyes.

CHAPTER 2

We use the generator for only two things. First, the hair clippers. Because me looking like a boy is my family's highest priority. Second, the treadmill. Because my physical endurance might be the only thing that saves my life one day. Hanging on the wall beside the treadmill is a recently completed embroidery saying, *When in Doubt, Run.*

I peer up the stairs, see no one, and then run past the zooming treadmill to Dean's old room. Josh sleeps here now. I move the small table beside his bed and fall to my knees. The carpet is cool against my fingers. I pinch the fibers and lift.

A manhole covers the cement beneath the carpet. I slide it aside and the smell of damp earth oozes out around me. Dropping down into the hole, I look at the food we have stored down here and my mouth waters. Several cans of dehydrated ground-beef substitute and cornmeal are mixed in with countless barrels of beans and rice, but we are saving them for a special occasion—the day my brother comes home. We used to have lentils and barley, too, but we've eaten all of that.

Peering at the entrance to the storage room, I pull three bottles off a shelf and take them out of the storage room. With trembling hands, I replace the manhole, cover it with the carpet, and put the table back on top of it. And then, with the three containers in my hands, I dart to my bedroom.

I drag my backpack out from under my bed and unzip it, cramming the three containers of calorie tablets inside, right on top of my spare pair of boys' underwear, size fourteen, my toothbrush, and toothpaste. Next, I put a water purifier attached to a two-liter bottle inside. When contaminated water is put into the purifier, it is filtered into the two-liter bottle and comes out clean enough to drink. One purifier can clean roughly ninety gallons of water. A person typically needs two liters of drinkable water a day. One purifier should give me clean water for 180 days. I hope that will be enough. Dying of thirst is supposed to be slow and painful.

I fill all the remaining space in the backpack with bullets. Bullets that fit my dad's Glock. Because if I am going out on my own, I am taking the best gun. The Glock is smaller and lighter than a rifle and has a clip that holds nineteen bullets. I think Dad will understand. And Mom should embroider *that* onto a piece of fabric: *If You Go Out on Your Own, Take the Best Gun.*

I shove the backpack under the bed again and go to the still zooming treadmill. I am about to get on when I hear Mom's hushed voice drift down the basement stairs. I know this tone of voice. It means she is saying something she doesn't want me to hear. It is the voice that means I need to eavesdrop. Slowly, I creep to the basement stairs and look up. I can't see anyone, but Mom and Dad are obviously standing in the kitchen and holding a conversation.

". . . our granddaughter," Mom says. I frown and creep up two stairs. I can't be hearing them right, because they don't have any grandchildren.

"That's what he said," Dad answers. "But it wasn't just them. It was all the women. That's why he mentioned moving Jack."

Moving me?

Mom squeaks, and then she starts crying, audible sobs I can hear all the way in the basement. "Why?" she asks between sobs.

"You already know the answer to that, Ellen. It will be worth the risk. We have until morning to decide."

It won't matter what they decide because I won't be here in the morning.

"I'm going to go relieve Rob. You try and get some rest. Be content in the knowledge that the child will be safe."

I roll my eyes. I am *not* a child.

Dad walks by the top of the stairs and I press myself against the wall. When he's past, I go back down and get on the treadmill for the last time. As I jog, my plan runs through my brain over and over again, like water being filtered until the deadliest elements are removed. I hope my plan has been filtered to perfection. I really don't want to die yet.

To conserve energy, I run two slow miles instead of my

customary eight, and when I get off the treadmill, my brain is still going at top speed. After I call good night to my family, I go to my room, take off my sweaty clothes, and get dressed in a white T-shirt, boys' underpants, boys' green camouflage pants that have been taken in at the waist, boys' running shoes, and my tackle vest.

I lie down in bed with my ankles crossed and my hands behind my head and stare at the dark ceiling. My mind is still running. Still filtering. I do not sleep.

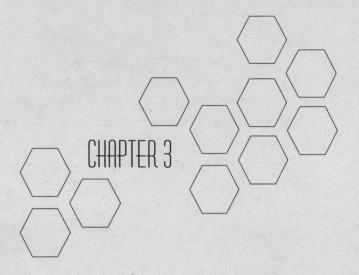

CHAPTER 3

The best kept secret is the one no one thinks to ask. At five a.m., I go upstairs, and then out into the backyard and up the ladder to the roof. Josh has Dad's gun up and ready, but when he sees it is me, he lowers it and pats the shingles beside him.

"How's it going?" I ask, looking at the dark world.

"Totally dead," he says, stifling a yawn. "It's been like this for two months—since they started letting anyone live behind the wall. All the Fecs went into the walled city to get the cure."

"I never thought the feces dwellers would leave. I keep expecting them to come back," I say.

They were like rats—sneaky, thieving creatures that lived in the sewers—but they made life interesting. "I'm glad they don't have to worry about turning into wild, savage beasts anymore. It's about time someone helped them."

"You've got to be glad the raiders are gone, though," I say with a shiver. I still have nightmares about the lawless gangs of men who ruled the streets and preyed on the weak and innocent—especially women. "Do you think they'll ever come back?"

"Not with everyone living inside the wall. The raiders don't have any Fecs to hunt anymore."

"Here." I hold a water bottle out to him, and he takes it without question. Josh is nineteen—two years older than me. He's short for a man but still several inches taller than me and has the same dark-brown, curly hair that all of us Bloom children have.

"So, you couldn't sleep?" he asks, unscrewing the lid and taking a swig of the slightly brown water.

I look down into the dark backyard, toward the well we dug. There is water everywhere, if you dig deep enough. After a year of drinking soil-flavored well water, I forgot what clear water tasted like. Now, more than three years later, I don't even mind the taste. And hopefully it will cover up the flavor of the drugs I put in the water bottle.

"Jack?"

I jump and look at him. "What?"

"You couldn't sleep?" he asks again, yawning.

I shake my head and study him, leaning in for a closer look at his face.

"Thanks for this." He holds up the water bottle and a surge of guilt makes me sick. "But you *know* Dad will flip if he finds you out here. You should probably . . . go back into . . ." His eyelids look too heavy for his eyes. He pats his cheeks a few times and blinks. "Wow. I'm so . . ." His eyelids crash shut like they're made of lead. I reach for his gun, but his eyes pop open again and he blinks at me. ". . . tired." His head lobs forward, his chin rests on his chest, and snores rumble from his throat. Holding my breath, I ease him down so he is lying on his side, then position him so he won't roll off the roof.

"Sorry, bro," I whisper. When he wakes up he's going to have a major headache, and he'll want to kill me. Hopefully I'll live long enough to give him the chance.

I ease the gun out of his hand and tuck it into the holster on my belt. Without making a sound, I cross the roof and shimmy down the ladder. Inside the house, I pause and listen for the sudden *click-click* of a rifle being cocked. I am greeted by silence. Sliding a folded square of paper from my pocket, I put it on the kitchen counter. There are only seven words on that paper, but it is the hardest thing I have ever written. It says:

I'm living inside the wall now.

I creep to the basement stairs and pick up my waiting backpack, then tiptoe to the front door and unlock all four deadbolts. Cool air swirls around my face.

Before I have the door half open, I dart onto the front porch and whisper, "Shh!" to the four dark forms in the front yard. The dogs wag their tails and walk toward me, their chains clanking. *"Sieda!"* I whisper. It means *"sit."* Our dogs speak Italian, not English. That way no one can give them orders—unless they speak Italian. The dogs whimper but sit, staring at me with eyes that reflect moonlight. *"Buoni cani!"* I whisper, and take four treats out of a pocket of my tackle vest. I toss them each a homemade dog biscuit—whole-wheat flour, salt, water, and ground rat, cooked until it's too hard to rot. The dogs snap their treats out of the air and crunch them. When the food is gone, they look at me with expectant, glossy eyes. *"Sieda, sieda."* They sit.

Dawn is smeared against the eastern horizon and barely illuminates the debris-filled road. As usual, the morning is completely silent, like someone has pushed an omnipotent mute button. No birdsong, no crickets, no car motors, no droning airplanes, no voices. Opening the top pocket on my tackle vest, I take out a silver *J*—my lucky charm—and press it to my lips before tucking it back into my pocket. I need all the luck I can get.

Careful not to rattle the bulging pack on my back, I tiptoe down the porch steps and slink over the dead lawn. When I get to the road, I pause. I am about to step over the line that I have been forbidden to cross. I take a deep breath, walk off my property, and start to run, chasing the silence away with the gentle slap of my shoes on dusty pavement.

When I have covered three blocks, I stop running, take Dad's gun from my belt, and point it at the silent sky. The gun recoils in my hand as the bullet rips toward heaven, rumbling like thunder.

The sound echoes off the mountains, devouring the silence. If my plan works, every person in my house—except Josh—will be waking up right now, able to protect themselves. They won't be sitting ducks. My dogs start barking, as if they knew what I was planning. *"Buoni cani!"* I whisper. *Good dogs!*

Movement catches my eye. My stomach drops, and I point my gun at a shadow standing frozen in the middle of the street.

His gloved hands are up, his voice quiet. "Please." That's all he says, but it's enough. I am aiming my weapon at the vagabond that wanders to my house a couple of times a month for food. I lower the gun and run past him. My destination? The city inside the wall. I need to talk to Fiona Tarsis.

CHAPTER 4

For three years I have trained for all worst-case scenarios. All worst-case scenarios include me running away from danger. I run and run. The sky slowly grows lighter, illuminating the tops of the Rocky Mountains. The golden glow creeps down their steep sides, and the world around me becomes visible. I gasp an involuntary breath. This is my first time off my property in two years, ten months, and sixteen days. Since the day I became Jack.

Silent, odorless, still, the dawn-washed world seems as if it is holding its breath. As if the oxygen has been stripped from it and everything exists in a vacuum. A city of black and white. The only bright color comes from the canary-yellow fliers nailed to power-line poles, poles that serve no purpose anymore except to hold the colorful announcements:

Cure!

My feet pump a rhythmic *thump-thump-thump* on the road, sending up little puffs of dust that float ghostlike above the cracked pavement, marking my path. A path where no other feet have trod for a long time. I push harder, run faster, wondering why running on pavement, out in the open, feels so different from running on the treadmill at home. It feels so easy.

The world continues to hold its breath around me, claustrophobic with silence as the sun's light creeps to the base of the mountains and paints the city. Abandoned houses? Gold. Broken-down cars? Gold. Rusted bikes? Gold. Glass skyscrapers? Gold. The tears in my eyelashes? Gold.

I swipe my eyes, blink away the tears that blur the houses on either side of the road into two long trains, and go faster, rushing through a world that breaks my heart. A world I've heard talked about for nearly three years but have never seen, except from my front yard. It is worse than I ever imagined. So empty. So abandoned. So dead.

By the time the sun hovers a hand span above the eastern horizon, I have passed through neighborhoods, business districts, industrial factories, and skyscrapers. I come to a jolting stop and stare up, and up some more, at a wall that springs skyward from the side of the road, as if it grew out of the sidewalk. It runs left and right with no door in sight. I turn left—south—and nearly trip. With hardly a thought, my hand is on my gun, finger trembling against the trigger. Slowly, just like I've practiced, I brace for the recoil and take aim at the man leaning against the corner of a building on the opposite side of the road.

Trust no one! That is the first thing I was taught about survival.

That, and *never get caught*. And then I have to wonder how this timeworn beggar, who was at my house when I left, is now here in front of me. His cheeks look hollow beneath his scraggly beard, and I know he's hungry. The first time I saw him I gave him an individual serving of applesauce in a plastic container, the kind with the foil lid you can peel back. It was one of the hardest things I've ever done, but he looked so ravenous—I figured I could live one more day without it. I wasn't sure about him.

"Please. I'm not going to hurt you," he wheezes, slowly lifting broad, gloved hands. He stares at me, eyes vibrant beneath bushy brows. A long, matted beard hides most of his face, and rags hang from his hunched body. What's visible of his face is flushed and damp with sweat, his chest lifting and falling fast beneath his tattered brown shirt. I swallow and keep my gun up and ready. "I'm not going to hurt you, Jack." Only his mouth and beard move, like a ventriloquist's puppet.

I swallow past the fear in my throat—I know this guy . . . sort of—and take a deep breath. I narrow my eyes. "Weren't you by my house this morning?"

The man nods, and the unexpected movement makes me jump and almost drop my gun. He flinches. "Your dad was supposed to meet me this morning at sunrise," he says. "Why don't you let me walk away from here? Before you accidentally shoot me." Slowly, he lowers his hands and takes a tiny step backward. When he's taken ten steps, he turns his back to me and keeps slowly walking. I stare at his back, at the torn, ragged, dirt-covered shirt straining against a pair of thick shoulders, and my knees go weak. I might be good with a gun. And I might know how to run. But without my brothers, Dad, and Uncle Rob, I am vulnerable. That guy would be able to snap me in half without even trying, and no one would come to my rescue. I wait until he's gone from sight to start running again, south along the wall.

After a few minutes, I slow my pace. They don't see me, the two guards who stand talking to each other at the wall's base, and I can't help but wonder how they've managed to stay alive if I can sneak up on them without trying. I clear my throat before I am too close so that they don't startle and shoot me. They both whip around, rifles aimed at my heart. I lift my hands and stop walking.

Their eyes dart over me and, despite the gun at my belt, they visibly relax. I don't blame them. I'm short, I'm too thin like everything else in this starved world, and they don't know that I'm a perfect shot. Without a second thought, they underestimate me. Being underestimated is an advantage, and yes, that saying is framed and hanging on the bathroom wall at home.

"What do you want?" one of them asks. His hair is sandy blond, cut short, with three lines shaved above his left ear. I take a few cautious steps closer, and his sun-bleached eyebrows furrow. "Aren't you the dentist's kid?" he asks.

I take a closer look at him. "Top left incisor," I say. "Root canal."

He grimaces, flashing the silver-capped fang my dad fixed, and lowers his gun. "That's right. Minimum numbing. What are you doing in this part of town?" He looks past me. "And alone?"

My family is well known. People come to us for doctoring

and tooth problems. They also think we never leave our property. But they're wrong about that. *I* never leave, and my mother and little brother never leave, but everyone else does.

"I'm looking for someone. I'm hoping you know her. Fiona Tarsis." I can't believe those words are coming out of my mouth. It has been a little more than two months since I have seen her. I thought I would never see her again.

"Fiona Tarsis?" He looks at me a little closer. "Everyone wants to get a look at her. Why do you want to see her?"

"I have a message for her."

Every time the dogs barked, my heart lurched inside my chest. I worried that one day it would lurch so hard it would stop beating altogether, and I'd be dead. I could think of worse ways to die. Lots of them.

It lurched tonight. So badly that I dropped my forkful of beans, and it splattered on my shirt. Everyone jumped up from the table and ran for their guns. I was last out the front door, since I had to put my vest on. Sometimes being a girl is so unfair.

I stepped out into the evening sunlight and for a split second was filled with hope. Hope that my brother would be walking down the street toward me, his barrel chest and heavy shoulders framed by the sunset. I put my hand up to block the sun, and my hopes were dashed to bits. And then dread smashed the bits into nonexistence.

My brother was not on the road in front of our house. It was a girl. A woman. With long blond hair and breasts that swelled gently against her clean white shirt. I wanted to call out to her, to warn her. If the raiders saw her . . . and that's when I realized who I was looking at. Fiona Tarsis. A girl I'd gone to school with until midway through seventh grade, when they shut the schools down because of the bee flu. Our moms were practically best friends.

"Ellen! Come here!" Dad yelled. Dad never had Mom come outside when there was a threat, and he never called her by her real name unless he was frazzled.

I heard the front door open, heard a foot scuff on the porch. "Dear Lord Almighty, that's Fiona Tarsis," Mom said. "If she doesn't have the mark of the beast, let her pass."

"Hold your hand up," Dad said. I watched as she lifted both of her hands up high into the air, like she didn't know what Dad was talking about. "No. Your right hand."

She turned her right hand and showed us the back of it, where the tattoo would be since she had been infected with the bee vaccine. Her skin was pure. Unmarked. "She's clean," Dad said, voice full of surprise. But I wasn't going to tell Dad the truth about her. I remembered her talking about how much she hated the shots. She might not have the mark, but she was infected. Slowly, I lowered my gun.

"Get on past here, Fiona," Dad said. Fiona started walking, her hips gently swaying, her long hair gleaming with sunlight. Her gaze locked on mine, and I could tell by the way her eyes grew round and her steps slowed that she recognized me despite my boy hair and the vest covering the only real curves I had, small though they were. "Get on past here," Dad warned, his voice mean. Fiona broke eye contact with me and started a weary sprint away.

I ran to the edge of my yard. "Fo—Fiona . . ." I didn't ask, just stuck my hands into her hair, twisted it, and shoved it down the back of her shirt. "Cut your hair off!" I wanted to say more—that if the raiders caught her, she'd be raped every day for the rest of her life. But I didn't have time. I reached into a pocket of my vest and pulled out the crackers I'd been nibbling on—savoring—for two days, and shoved what was left of them into her hand. Fiona's dazed eyes swept over me, over my house, over my little brother perched on the roof with his gun, and then she turned and slowly jogged down the road.

I stared after, wondering how long it would take for her to get caught. There was no way she would make it out here on her own. That thought hurt my heart. It made me want to scream with frustration, made me want to chase after her, made me want to do something to change the world we lived in. Instead, I held it inside, all those feelings, and funneled them into a space in my empty heart.

One of the dogs started barking. And then the other three joined in. They were all straining in the direction Fo had come from, their chains pulled so tight I wasn't sure if the stakes would hold. My two older brothers were in the yard again, guns up, beside Dad. My little brother, perched on the roof, stood and took aim. Uncle Rob came out of the house, still chewing his dinner, Dad's Glock in his hand. I looked down the shadowed street and my blood ran cold. Men were coming. Lots of men. Running. Armed.

Dad didn't wait. He shot a warning bullet into the air and the men stopped. There were fourteen of them. We'd held off more before, but it always ended with a lot of them dead on the street in front of our house, and Dad and Uncle Rob cleaning up the mess the next day. And I was always sent inside first.

"We don't have any business with you, dentist," one of the raiders called. "We just want to walk past here and catch up with someone."

Oh no. He meant Fo. They already saw her. I wanted to scream a warning down the street to her. She had to hide.

There was a long pause where the raiders' predatory eyes shifted *between Dad and the road Fiona just went down. I waited for Dad to tell me to lower my gun and let the raiders pass. Instead he said, "Jack. Go into the house."*

Without lowering my gun, I backed up to the front steps. I lifted my foot to step onto the porch, when a shot rang out. Lesson number one about guns? When you're being shot at, you get down as fast as possible. A flat target is a lot harder to hit than a standing one. But I didn't mean to take cover. My body just crumpled to the ground. A split second later, everyone else fell to the ground—Uncle Rob, Dad, Steve, Josh. The raiders ran. Raiders never run when they can fight. Never, at least, until now. Now that they have something they want more than a fight. Dad rolled to his stomach and fired a single shot at the raiders, but they were already fading into the dusky evening.

Everyone got up and watched them disappear down the shadowed road. Everyone but me. I lay half on the dead grass, half on the cement walkway leading to the front porch, and stared at the purple sky, wondering why my arm was wet. And then it hit me. I'd been shot.

CHAPTER 5

I blink and rub the jagged scar hidden beneath the sleeve of my shirt. It's still tender, two months later.

"You have a message for Fiona Tarsis?" The militiaman asks, snapping my attention back to him. "What kind of message? Is she overdue for a cleaning?" He starts laughing and elbows his companion, a black-haired man I have never seen before. "Get it? The dentist's son coming to tell someone they're overdue for . . . Never mind." He rolls his shoulders and scowls. "She's sort of busy today."

"It's a really, *really* important message. Life-or-death important," I explain.

Brow furrowed, he studies me for a moment before taking a walkie-talkie from his belt and saying, "Hey, Tommy. Tell Dreyden Bowen to come to the east side of the wall, exterior. Someone needs to talk to him."

"No way, man. He's busy today," a voice crackles over the walkie-talkie.

"I know he's busy, but it's a matter of life or death. Just send him out for five minutes."

I fold my arms over my tackle vest and tap my toe, studying the militiaman—Rory is his name. I never forget a name. "Rory, I need Fiona Tarsis. Why did you ask for Dreyden Bowen to come out here?" I know—knew—Dreyden Bowen. And he's definitely not the person I am looking for.

"Where Bowen is, she is." There's a yearning in Rory's voice, a tightening in his eyes. He clears his throat and I might as well have disappeared as his focus returns to the lifeless, silent city.

Dreyden Bowen takes his time coming, sauntering down the street with his arm around someone, and a rifle in his free hand. He's dressed in clean blue jeans and a long-sleeved pinstripe button-down shirt, and his dark-brown hair is brushed neatly to the side, barely covering a short patch of hair above his left ear. He sees me standing with one shoulder pressed against the wall, and his body tenses. His eyes quickly move over every millimeter of me, lingering momentarily on my gun, and then on the knife attached to my belt.

The person with him is wearing tan pants and a dark-blue blouse that does nothing to hide her curves. Her long, blond bangs are being held out of her face by a dark-blue headband and all I can think is, *She's so dead if the raiders see her!* She hasn't once looked at my face because she is too intent on my right hand. I glance at her hand, at her ten-legged tattoo, before flashing my tattoo-free hand at her. Finally, she looks at me—right at my face—and her brown eyes go wide.

"Jacqui?" she blurts.

I glare at her and clear my throat. "It's *Jack*," I growl, gaze darting to Rory and his partner to see if they've noticed. They have. Rory's eyes are traveling over my entire body, searching for the subtle signs that I am, in fact, female. His partner is doing the same—both of them squinting at my flat, vest-covered chest, like if they look hard enough, they might see something.

"Do you know this kid?" Bowen asks Fo.

"Yes! It's Jacqui Bloom," Fo says, grinning.

Bowen frowns and looks me up and down again, and then focuses on my face. "Jacqui Bloom!" He smiles and clasps my shoulders in his hands. And then he laughs and hugs me.

I stand there, rigid and confused, bulky pockets of my tackle vest digging into my bony ribs. This is the guy who used to steal my homemade school lunch because he was too embarrassed to tell the teacher that he couldn't afford to buy a hot lunch and too broke to make a bag lunch. I was so scared of him beating me up if I reported it that I started packing two lunches—one for him and one for me.

My mom used to leave a turkey—fully cooked, with all the trimmings—on his front porch every Thanksgiving afternoon. She would have Dean and Steve ring the doorbell and run. I was sworn to secrecy.

"Jacqui Bloom. How have you been?" he asks, pushing me to arms' distance. He is so happy to see me that I wonder if he knew it was my family all those years ago giving him Thanksgiving dinner.

"Um . . ." I have no words. *How have I been?* I've been a

prisoner in my own home for several years, pretending to be a boy, training to run for my life, living on near-starvation rations. I slide my hand over my buzzed hair and shrug. "I've been better."

"I almost didn't recognize you. You look like a boy. And you're . . . *thinner*," Bowen says.

"Yeah. That's sort of an inevitable consequence of living in a world without food," I say. He laughs. So do Rory and his black-haired partner. And then I'm being smothered with another hug—Fo. I put my arms around her and hug back. She's soft, a sign of being well fed. "I need to talk to you," I say, breathing in the floral smell of shampoo.

She lets go and looks at me. "Thanks for the peanut-butter crackers. I didn't know how big a sacrifice they were when you gave them to me."

Peanut-butter crackers. My mouth waters at the thought. "You're welcome. Where can we talk?" I glance at Rory in time to catch him checking out my butt. My cheeks flame. So do his. I grab Fiona's elbow and pull her away, and Bowen follows.

When we're out of Rory's earshot, I blurt, "So, you know your mom used to live inside the wall, right?"

Fiona glances at Bowen before nodding.

"Well," I continue, "when they kicked her out, she came to my family for help. She didn't know what to do or how to survive outside the wall. Dean said he'd help her."

The color drains from Fiona's cheeks, and her dark eyes lose focus.

"The problem is," I say past a lump in my throat, "my brother never came back."

"Your brother, Dean, agreed to leave your home to help Fo's mom survive outside the wall?" Bowen asks, studying me.

I nod. "He was going to take her out of the city and try to find a safe place for her to live. There are rumors of safe places."

The beginning of a smile tugs at Bowen's mouth and he looks at Fo. "Do you know what this means?"

She blinks slowly and takes a deep breath. "It means," she answers, voice trembling, "that there's a chance she's alive."

"And I'm hoping you will help me find them," I say, explaining the reason for my visit.

Bowen throws his arms around Fo and spins her in a hug. I stare at them and wonder how they can look seventeen when I look twelve. I don't want to be a little boy anymore. I want to be like them. Normal. Happy. Free. Myself—female. He kisses her, right on the lips, and my eyes pop open wider. Dreyden Bowen and Fiona Tarsis are *together*? A *couple*? I rub my nose and try not to look as shocked as I'm feeling. They're the last two people from junior high that I'd match up.

Bowen sets Fo down and she clasps my hand in hers. "I'll help you find them," she says. "But come inside the wall with us. We have something important we need to do first, and then we'll pack."

I shake my head. "I'll wait here."

"Are you sure?"

I nod.

"All right," Bowen says, tugging Fo down the street. "Give us three hours and we'll meet you here."

I watch them walk down the street, watch how Fo's hips swing when she moves, and call, "Fo, dress like a boy!"

"Are you sure you won't come with us?" she asks, looking at me over her shoulder.

"Positive." I will never set foot inside the wall.

My hair fell long, thick, and wavy over my shoulders. I wore my best dress. I filed my fingernails the night before and took a sponge bath. My teeth were brushed and flossed, my face was scrubbed, I wore makeup, and I held a plate of apricot scones made with dried apricots, since there was no more fresh produce.

"Remember to smile," my mother said, wedging Dad's Glock into the waistband of her floral-print dress. She straightened Chris's tie, then combed his hair away from his forehead with her red fingernails. She painted her nails only for special occasions. I guess this was a special occasion.

She turned back to me and tucked my hair behind my ears. Her hands were cold and damp. "Don't forget to hold the plate of scones out to Governor Soneschen!" she whispered.

I hardly heard her. I was too intent on the militia stationed at the south gate. A few of them looked really good in their brown uniforms and short hair, with stripes shaved above their ears. The new legal age to marry was fifteen. I was less than a year away from fifteen, and one of the militiamen— the one I'd been staring at the longest—was checking me out. And then I realized all of them were staring at me. Some of them started laughing. One man was trying to get others to bet on whether they'd let me and my mom inside the wall. No one would bet with him. They didn't want to lose their food rations.

My face started to burn. My soft, round fingers squeezed the plate of scones a little too hard and I crushed the corner of one. Little white crumbs spilled out around my polished black shoes.

"Careful," Dad said, brushing a few crumbs from my belly. He looked

at his watch and then looked through the open gate. People were inside the walled city, peering out at us with curious, guarded eyes. Green things were in there too, and hummingbirds darted past the entrance, their wings making a high-pitched buzzing noise. Dad combed his fingers through his thick black hair and then looked at his watch again. He frowned and took a tiny step inside the gate. The two militia standing guard stepped in front of him, blocking entry. "No admittance without the governor's approval. And no civilian guns inside the wall," one of the men warned, looking pointedly at my mom.

Dad stepped back, and the guards retreated to the sides of the entry, but they didn't take their eyes from him.

Inside the wall, two men flanked by four guards dressed in stiff, black uniforms were walking toward us. One man was tall, the other short. The short man saw my dad and smiled. His shoes clicked on the clean-swept pavement as he approached.

"Hello, Dr. Bloom. Thank you for coming to speak with me on this glorious Sunday," the short man called as they approached.

"Hello, Governor Soneschen." My dad put his hand on my shoulder and pulled me forward the slightest bit.

Governor Soneschen stopped at the gate's entrance, one tiny step away from being on the outside of the walled city, and smiled down at me like I was ten, not fourteen. "Who do we have here?" he asked. I played the part of obedient daughter and did just what I was told. I held the plate out to him and smiled my prettiest smile.

"This is my daughter, Jacqui," Dad said. I held the plate of scones closer to the governor, waiting for him to take it, and cleared my throat. He stared at me as if he didn't even see the food. "Remember we talked about my daughter last week?" Dad added after an awkward silence.

I looked at my dad. I didn't know he'd been to the wall before.

"Oh, yes. I do recall that." The governor blinked and let his gaze sweep quickly over me, but he ignored the scones.

"This is my son, and my wife." Dad took his hand from my shoulder and touched Chris's head, then put it on Mom's arm. Mom smiled and held her hand out to the governor. He didn't shake it. Dad leaned toward the governor and said in a quiet voice, "You said to come speak to you today, and to bring my wife, my youngest son, and my daughter. I talked things over with my three older boys, and they understand that there aren't enough resources inside the wall for them to live here with us, but they can fend for themselves. They just need to know that the rest of their family is safe. That is . . . I am hoping that you have changed your mind?"

The governor looked at me again, looked at my brother, and then looked at Mom. His lips thinned and disappeared, sucked tight against his teeth. "I absolutely have changed my mind," he said.

Dad whimpered and reached out for the governor's hand, clasping it. "Thank you, sir. I knew you wouldn't be the type of man to make my wife and children live out here. I am so grateful you've reconsidered."

The governor pulled his hand away from Dad. "This city has a great need for someone with your dental and medical background. We want you to live here with us and be the official oral surgeon. Your son is welcome to live here too." He ruffled my little brother's dark curls. "And, in exchange for your services to those of us privileged enough to live inside the wall, your daughter is also welcome to live here with you. Or your wife. Your choice."

Dad's body went taut. He took a step closer to the governor, so that his worn brown boots were on the line dividing the outer city from the walled city. The men surrounding the governor gripped their guns and leaned toward Dad. The militia guarding the gate did the same.

"But the gangs," Dad whispered, as if I couldn't hear him. "They're moving farther and farther from the city. It's only a matter of days before they make their way to my neighborhood! They're looting everything! Even the . . ." He looked at me and his bottom lip quivered. "Your city is the only place where my wife and daughter will be safe!"

"But we have rules, Dr. Bloom. If I break them for you, I will have to break them for everybody." The governor folded his arms over his chest. "And if I break them for everybody, we won't survive. Our survival is dependent on balance. If there are too many mouths to feed, the balance will be ruined, and we will run out of food."

"That's not true! If you have more people working, there will be more food produced, and more—"

"Your daughter and your wife"—the governor snapped, cutting off Dad— "do not meet our health requirements. They are obese. They will consume more food than others. They have a higher risk of acquiring diabetes. They have a much higher risk of stroke, heart attack, kidney failure. We can't afford to waste food on anyone who has these potential health risks."

Dad took another step forward, so that the toes of his worn boots were touching the toes of the governor's glossy brown loafers. The governor's guards swung their guns up point-blank at my father. He either didn't notice or didn't care.

"Waste food? This isn't about how much food they will or will not eat! They are not safe out here!" Dad yelled. Silence slammed the world. Everyone inside the walled city stopped what they were doing to stare at us. Behind me, the militia had frozen in place, their eyes riveted on my father. "The beasts are getting more desperate for food and are becoming more violent! The Fecs are all turning into beasts! The gangs are growing in number! They've moved from the inner city and are now raiding the suburbs for food, weapons, and women! My daughter . . ." Dad whimpered and a sob tore at his chest.

"Can I have a moment with you, Governor Soneschen?" The tall man said. I'd forgotten about him, standing silently one step behind the governor, blue eyes narrowed, with his arms folded across his chest.

"Not now, Dr. Grayson," the governor snapped, not even bothering to look at the man.

The doctor unfolded his arms, stepped forward, and loomed over the governor. "Yes, now, Jacoby. This is important! If I have more help taking care of the comatose beasts in the lab, if I have another person with an extensive medical background helping me do research, I might be able to find a cure for the beasts."

The governor slowly turned and studied the doctor. "There is no cure. There is no hope for the beasts and Fecs, and you know it. Finding a cure is just a fantasy! A waste of time! I will not risk this city's entire population's dying from starvation by letting too many people in just to appease your irrational fantasy."

"The entire population wouldn't die from starvation. We will only be letting four more people in!" the doctor yelled. "And it isn't a 'fantasy'! It's called hope."

The governor glared at the doctor. "Please don't make me order you to stand down, Charlie. It is imperative to our survival that we do not overpopulate! Look at these people!" His eyes swept over mom and me again. "They are obese! They will deplete our food supply! We cannot—"

"I'm leaving," Mom blurted, her voice choked. Dad turned to her, eyes startled. She pressed her soft hand to his damp cheek. "Take care of my babies. The boys will take care of me." She grabbed me and hugged me to her, squishing me against her full, dough-soft belly, pressing her tear-covered cheek against mine. She did the same with my little brother. And then she pushed the two of us forward a step, turned, and started weaving her way through the silent militia.

Governor Soneschen smiled and nodded his head. "Never underestimate the love of a mother. It looks like the decision has been made for you, Dr. Bloom." He swept his arm toward the city and stepped aside. "Welcome to our city."

Dad clenched his hands into fists, took a small step back, and glared at the governor and doctor. "There is no way I will help you and your privileged class of people. I will never leave any part of my family out here in exchange for a life inside your wall. My family is my life. We will never set foot inside your city!"

The governor blinked twice and his arm dropped. Dad grabbed me, jerking me backward, and the plate of scones fell and scattered over the ground. The militia started cheering as Dad dragged my brother and me toward my mother.

"Wait, Dr. Bloom," Dr. Grayson called. Dad ignored him.

That was the last time I left my home. That was also the last day my father's hair was black. When he woke up the next morning, it was as white as snow. Three days later, we cut off my hair.

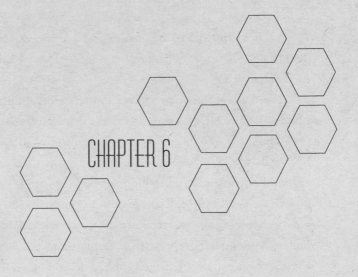

CHAPTER 6

I sit with my backpack between my feet and the wall against my back and wait, gun in hand, finger on the trigger. But no one is around. Even the two guards—Rory and the other guy—look half-asleep when they're not stealing glances in my direction. I shrug my tight shoulders and glance at my watch—2:15 p.m. Bowen said they would be ready to go in three hours. It has been four.

The empty streets are haunted with the memory of people and life, with cars stopped permanently at broken stoplights, and graffiti spray-painted on the sides of dark-windowed buildings, yet the city is utterly lifeless. I wonder how many of the abandoned vehicles belonged to people who died from the bee flu when it was spread from person to person, and how many people died at the hands of beasts—the people who were changed by the bee flu vaccine.

Another hour passes before life fills the vacant streets. Five lives to be exact. I stand and put my backpack on while I watch them approach.

Bowen is wearing the jeans he had on earlier, but he's traded his fancy shirt for an army-green T-shirt, and he has a backpack and a rifle. Fo has a rifle hanging from her shoulder and a backpack, too. She's wearing baggy tan pants with a fanny pack around her waist that helps hide the curve of her hips. She has on a white T-shirt that falls flat against her chest and an unzipped brown men's leather jacket. She's taken the headband from her hair so her long bangs hide half of her face, and there's a hint of a shadow on her jaw, like she's rubbed dirt on her skin, making it look like she needs to shave. She *could* pass for a boy . . . if you don't notice how she glides instead of walks.

Beside Fo is a woman with long, light-brown hair that has been braided crownlike around her head. She smiles at me, and I have the sudden urge to take off my tackle vest and wrap it around her—to cover her up. This woman is pretty. She's wearing pants that accentuate her hips. Her shirt does nothing to conceal the curve of her breasts. I look at her face and realize I am looking at Fo's sister, Lissa.

"Hi, Jack," Lissa says, stopping in front of me.

"She's not coming, is she?" I ask, looking at Fo.

"No. She and her husband came to say hello to you and good-bye to me and my brother."

I look at the fourth person and my eyes narrow. Dr. Grayson smiles at me but I don't smile back. He is Fo's brother-in-law. He brought Fo's mom to us when she was kicked out of the wall.

He *knew* there was a chance Mrs. Tarsis was alive, but based on Fo's earlier reaction, when I told her about her mom, the doctor obviously didn't tell her.

"How are you, Jack?" he asks.

I fold my arms and glare at him. "Why is it I'm the first person to tell Fo about her mom leaving with my brother, when you've known all along?"

Dr. Grayson looks at Lissa, and then at Fo, but he doesn't get a chance to answer because Fo blurts, "Lissa, You knew? You knew that Mom might be alive? You told me she was kicked out of the city. You made me believe she was dead."

"I . . . I couldn't tell you." Lissa looks between Bowen and Fo, and tears fill her eyes. "I knew if I did, you two would try and find her, and I'd barely gotten you back. I couldn't risk losing you again. Not when our brother was on the brink of death."

With those words, the last person in the group limp-walks out from behind Fo. He is wearing faded jeans and a gray hooded sweatshirt—hood pulled over his head—and the biggest backpack I've ever seen. He's tall—would be taller than Bowen if he weren't slouching. Despite his long-sleeved hoodie, I can tell that lean muscles cord his forearms and biceps and bulge in his shoulders, making the hoodie appear too small. He's not carrying any weapons, at least none that I can see. But with a body like that, he *is* a weapon.

My gaze stops on his hands and I gawk—they are covered with fine, pale scars, like he's wearing delicate lace gloves. My eyes follow his right hand as it slowly moves up to his hood. He has the mark—a black ten-legged tattoo entwined with thread-fine scars. He pulls the hood from his head and I gasp. His head is shaved, with a hint of pale stubble growing from a scarred and bruised scalp. One of the scars on his scalp is surrounded by suture scars, making it look like a long, pink caterpillar is crawling over his skin. The sun-tanned skin on his face is interlaced with intricate white lines, a shroud of white, lacelike scars. I look into his haunted eyes and take an involuntary step back. One eye is a deep, warm brown, the other a pale, colorless gray that's looking in the wrong direction.

"Jack, you remember my brother, Jonah, right?" Fiona asks, voice little more than a whisper.

I nod, not taking my eyes from him. He lifts his right hand and pulls the hood back over his head. I keep staring at his shadowed face, searching for the boy he used to be, but can't see any of the old Jonah. If Fo hadn't told me who he was, I would not have known.

"What happened to you?" I whisper. He looks past me, as if he didn't hear what I said.

"We need to go," Bowen says. "There'll be plenty of time to get reacquainted later."

Lissa hugs Bowen, then Jonah, and then Fiona. When she's done hugging them, she turns to me, wraps her arms around me, and squeezes. "So good to see you, Jack," she whispers. When she lets me go, tears are streaming down her cheeks. "Take care of my sister, Bowen."

"You know I will." Bowen turns to the two militiamen. "Hey, Rory. I need you to escort Lissa and Dr. Grayson back to the gate."

"Sure thing, Bowen."

"I love you guys," Lissa says. She dabs at her eyes. The doctor puts his arm around her shoulders and they walk to Rory.

Bowen turns to me. "First of all, we need to find my contact on the outskirts of the city before the sun goes down. We need to hurry."

"What contact?" I ask, annoyed that Bowen's already put himself in charge. "I've never heard anything about a contact on the outskirts of the city."

One of his eyebrows lifts, and he looks me up and down. "How many times've you been out of your house in the past four years?"

"I leave my house every day," I snap, thrusting my chin forward.

"And how many times've you left your yard?"

I frown and bite the inside of my cheek—a habit my dad has tried to break me of for years. Bowen nods and says, "That's what I thought. Now, let's get going."

We turn north, but instead of walking, Bowen whips his rifle onto his shoulder. On the road in front of us stands the vagabond, looking hungrier than ever. "Don't shoot!" I blurt, jumping in front of Bowen. "He's harmless."

"Do you need something, old man?" Bowen calmly asks, pushing me aside.

I cringe, waiting for the vagabond to ask for food—the one thing you can never have enough of in this world. The one thing I can no longer spare. "Do you have information about the cure?" he asks with a deep, rich voice. I stare at his mouth, wondering if I'm imagining things. His teeth look pearly white, the kind of teeth my dad loves—straight, clean, beautiful. They've never looked like that before. Usually they're brownish-green and so fuzzy they almost look plastic.

The vagabond's gaze travels from Bowen to Fiona and stops on Jonah, moving down Jonah's body and freezing on his right hand. He stands a little taller and his eyebrows—so covered with mud and dry grass that I can't even tell what color they are—crawl halfway up his forehead. "It's true. There's a cure," he whispers.

"Yes," Fo says, lifting her hand to show him her tattoo. "My brother and I are living proof."

The man sighs, his breath rustling his crusty beard, and then he laughs, white teeth gleaming, and looks up to the sky. Without another word he turns and wanders down a road that leads east.

A prickling feeling crawls up my spine and makes my buzzed hair stand on end. "That was weird," I say, my voice unnatural in the silent world. Silently, we start walking north down the vacant street, with the wall at our left blocking the sun and the view of downtown Denver. Jonah shuffles beside me, and whatever is in his bulging backpack sloshes with every step. When he puts weight on his right foot, his left foot folds sideways and drags. I wonder if he'll be able to run when we have something to run from.

A breeze blows against my face, whistling through the broken windows of abandoned buildings and cars, and I shiver despite the warm September afternoon. I take a look over my shoulder, peering back the way we've come, thinking the vagabond might be following us. A tumbleweed blows down the street, but nothing else moves.

CHAPTER 7

There are two hundred mountain peaks visible from Denver. By the time we reach the northern outskirts of the city, the sun is a little more than a hand span over one of them, and the air seems heavy with eyes and ears. Bowen senses it too, if the way he keeps looking over his shoulder is any indication. I peer toward the city for the tenth time, almost expecting to see the vagabond creeping along behind us, but don't see anyone.

We are walking in the middle of Interstate 25. It has been reduced to a crumbling eight-lane highway with nearly invisible street lines interrupted by the occasional abandoned vehicle. It is so wide, I feel like an ant crawling along a sidewalk. Everything is silent. Too silent. Too abandoned.

"Don't worry. The rumor inside the wall is, the raiders are gone," Fo says.

Dad says rumors are typically wrong. He worked on a man's teeth about a week ago, a man who tried very hard to hide the scars on his palms—northern raider markings. If the raiders were really gone, they wouldn't still be coming to my dad for dental work.

"Do you think it is actually true that the raiders are gone?" Fo asks, as if she's jumped into my head and plucked out my worst fear. Jonah, on my left, doesn't take his gaze from his shuffling feet—where it's been all afternoon.

"Of course they're not gone," Bowen says, his voice low. "They've just been lying low."

"Do you think they have watchers during the day?" Fo asks. I nod and rest my hand on my gun.

"They're always watching." Bowen stops walking and spins in a circle, eyes darting all around.

"What are you looking for?" Fo asks, her voice like quiet music.

"I'll know it when I see it." He gives her a hint of a smile, and then reaches out and cups her cheek in his hand. She looks right into his eyes and doesn't move, as if they're the only two people in the world. Embarrassed to be witnessing something so intimate, I avert my gaze. "Don't worry," Bowen says after a minute, his voice filled with emotion. "I'll take care of you and so will Jonah. Right, Jonah?"

Jonah grunts without looking away from his feet. I fight the urge to clear my throat and blurt, *Well, who is going to take care of me?* Because I already know the answer. Me. I'm the only one who will take care of me out here.

We walk for a few more minutes, past broken-down and abandoned cars; past pale bones stark against the faded black-top; past sun-bleached trash, empty water bottles, and faded beer cans that have been blown against the cement median. My gaze wanders over the world, soaks in the absolute bleakness of every-thing, and I realize how impossible it is that we might actually find my brother. There is nothing out here.

"There!" I jump at Bowen's voice. He is pointing to the near-est off-ramp, a ramp that leads to neighborhoods of oversize houses. We exit the highway. I follow a step behind Bowen and Fo, with Jonah at my side, toward a wooden building made to resemble a log cabin, with grimy windows—where the windows aren't shattered. It's a diner, and the weather-beaten sign that hangs above it says, "The Other End of Town."

"You guys hungry?" Bowen asks, gaze glued to the diner.

"Uh, Bowen, I don't think there's going to be any food in there," I say, feeling my stomach quiver at the mere thought of salty, greasy diner food. In this world, you need guns to survive more than you need food. Because if you can't protect your food, you starve. And if you starve, you die. Common sense. "Guns before food," I whisper, one of my mother's many needlepoint phrases.

"We're not *really* looking for food. It was a joke, Flapjack," Bowen says.

Flapjack. I roll my eyes at the name. In fifth grade I won the school's annual pancake-eating contest and earned the hated nickname. It didn't help that I was soft and round like a pancake and the shortest kid who entered the contest. The only person who came close to eating as many pancakes as me was Bowen. He ate eighteen. I ate twenty-one.

"Why don't you get your gun ready just in case," Bowen adds.

I stand tall and pull the gun from the holster on my belt. My heart rate accelerates as I lift the Glock and swing it from side to side.

A tan, square hand covers mine and calmly pushes the gun down. "Jack, calm down." Bowen's voice is gentle. "I don't actually think you'll need it. It's just a precaution. Have it ready just in case."

I take my trembling finger from the trigger and try to catch my breath.

"You're a jumpy thing, aren't you," he says, one eyebrow raised.

I glare. "Can you blame me?"

"No." He sighs. "You'd better be ready to fight too, Jonah," Bowen adds.

Jonah grasps the shoulder straps of his massive backpack and stares at the pink-and-orange-hued clouds glowing above the mountains, as if he's oblivious to our conversation. But then he takes a step closer to Fo, and she smiles at him.

"So, what's in your bag anyway?" I ask him. He looks at me and his bad eye reflects the fire-colored sky.

"Water," Fiona blurts.

"Yeah. Lots of water," Bowen adds.

"Didn't you bring a purifier? There are so many lakes and streams around here that water should be easy to find."

"Of course we did. It's just another precaution." Bowen rolls his shoulders as if *he's* the one burdened by Jonah's pack. "Let's go."

We walk to the diner and stop in front of the entrance. The dusty ground is disturbed here, fanned with the hint of footprints. I crouch down and stare at the ground, scrutinizing the markings, trying to discern whether they're going into the diner or coming out.

"Bowen," I whisper. "These prints are fresh. We need to leave while we have the—"

My head jerks up at the sound of a deep chuckle. A lone man stands framed in an empty diner window. I have my gun aimed at him so fast that Fo jumps. The man's foot whips out and kicks my gun. It clatters against cement, sliding away from me in a swirl of dust. I dive for it but my hand comes down on a worn, brown cowboy boot.

"Beat you to your own gun, Freckles," a deep voice says. I slowly look up and my gaze travels over a dusty pair of faded blue jeans, an empty gun belt, two beefy hands each gripping a gun, a button-down shirt; up to a weathered face; stopping on a pair of hard eyes shaded by a cowboy hat. "Kids 'n' guns aren't a good combination. Sort of like antifreeze and Kool-Aid. They're all kinda sweet but deadly when mixed."

I swallow and scurry backward, crashing into the solid mass of Jonah's legs. He loops his hands under my armpits and lifts me to my feet.

"You all mind showing me your hands? I can't have you coming in here pointing firearms at me." Without a word, the four of us lift our empty hands, and I fight the urge to look at the rifles looped over Fo and Bowen's shoulders.

"Much obliged." The cowboy holsters one of his guns and

picks mine up off the ground. He turns it from side to side, blows the dust from it, and then points it between my eyes. "That's a nice piece, Freckles. If your aim is good, you could kill nineteen men without reloading." I shudder at the thought. "Now, what do you kids want?"

"We want a hot bath and a nice meal," Bowen says. I turn and glower at him. Seriously? That's how he's going to answer this towering pillar of cowboy strength, who is aiming my own gun at me? I look back at the cowboy just as deep creases form in his weathered cheeks. It takes me a moment to realize he's smiling.

"You've come to the right place," he says, holstering his other gun. With the hand holding my gun, he waves us inside. I follow Fo and Bowen through the window frame and wonder if I am really, truly going to get a hot bath and a meal. With Jonah behind me, the cowboy leads us to a faded red vinyl booth. He sits. Bowen gives Fo and me a warning look before sliding onto the opposite bench.

The cowboy's eyes move over Fo, Bowen, and Jonah, studying them one by one. When he looks at me, staring deep into my eyes—so deep I worry he can see the secrets hidden there—he frowns. "So." His gaze goes back to Bowen. "What exactly are you aiming to buy?" He taps my gun against the peeling paint of the table.

"We need to get to Wyoming. Word in the city is you know the right path to take."

My spine goes rigid. "Wait. *Wyoming*? We never said anything about—" The cowboy glares at me and I swallow the rest of my sentence.

The cowboy's eyes narrow, and he looks back at Bowen, at the shorter patch of hair over his left ear. "Who told you I know anything about Wyoming, militiaman?"

Bowen's jaw pulses a few times before he says, "You're Randall Flint. You're the man who sells the map to Wyoming. I've been researching you for a while now."

The cowboy laughs. "Been researching me, have you? So you think you know all about me? Because you're taking an awful big risk traveling with a woman." My heart starts to race, but he looks at Fo.

"I don't know what you're talking about," Bowen growls.

"I'm just saying, if anything happens to you, I don't think a woman, a kid, and an unarmed mental patient are going to be able to make it on their own out here."

I don't see Bowen move, but somehow his rifle is off his back and aimed at the cowboy's chest. The cowboy puts his hands up, still holding my gun, and leans back against the red vinyl booth. "Whoa, boy. I was just trying to make a point. You could have been walking into a trap. The raiders are even more desperate than normal for women. Have you heard the latest news?"

"What news?" I speak without thinking.

"The raiders' women escaped seven days ago. Every last one of them. And with the wall open, and people protected, they haven't been able to catch any more. They're getting restless and desperate, and that makes them more violent, especially Hastings."

"Who is Hastings?" Bowen asks.

"The worst one of them all. He's got the shortest fuse. And

he's the one in charge. You've got to be more careful with her."
He nods at Fo. "Don't trust anyone beyond this point. You never
know when you're being swindled. Now, if you'd oblige me and
lower your gun, I'll give you what you want."

Bowen doesn't move. "Give me what I want and then I'll put
the gun away—after we've all four of us walked out of here. I'll
pay you, too. Four ounces for the information, if my sources are
right."

The cowboy smiles and holds out his hand. Bowen nods
toward Fo without taking his eyes from the man, and Fo opens
her fanny pack and removes a small jar filled with liquid gold.
Honey—a food product that is priceless because it is so rare.

"Four ounces of honey." She places it on the edge of the
table. "How can you tell I'm a girl?" she adds.

The cowboy takes a slow, long look at her, and his eyes light
up. "The way you move. Smooth as cream. Don't swing your
hips when you walk. Now . . ." He takes the jar and opens it,
dipping a filthy, callused finger into the contents. When he pulls
his finger out, a long trail of sticky gold streams off it, making
my mouth water. Careful not to spill a single drop, the cowboy
touches his finger to his tongue and nods. "That's good. Payment
accepted. But before I give you the goods, I have a warning. Have
you heard of Sirens?" He screws the lid back onto the honey and
wraps his grizzled hand around it.

"Sirens, like on a police car?" Bowen asks.

"No," I say. I have heard stories about Sirens, told by the raiders my dad worked on. "They're like the Sirens in *The Odyssey*,"
I say. Jonah nods. Bowen's and Fiona's faces remain blank, so I

elaborate. "The Sirens would sing to ships and seduce the sailors into coming close, but when the ships got too close, they would be dashed on the rocks and everyone would drown."

The cowboy nods. "Yep." He pushes up the brim of his cowboy hat with the barrel of my gun. "The kid's got knowledge. Beware the Sirens—seemingly normal, healthy people who will try to tempt you from the path I've marked for you. They'll tell you all sorts of lies to lure you to your death. All sorts of lies to keep you from Wyoming. They whisper about hidden colonies of people and unending food supplies. Don't believe them. Don't listen to them. Don't associate with them."

"How will we recognize them?" I ask.

"That's the hard part. I don't know who they are or what they look like, but they'll be after you. So be aware. And watch out for wolves, too. You ever heard about the wolves?" The cowboy looks right at me.

"They came down from Yellowstone when things changed and are infesting the mountains," I say.

The cowboy nods. "That's right. They're half-starved and feed on human flesh, so unless you want to get eaten, avoid the Rockies at all costs. Now, grab one of them atlases by the front door on your way out. Your path is already marked, courtesy of me, Randall Flint. There are water stations roughly every twenty miles, too, so you don't have to leave the marked path to get water from natural sources." He sets my gun on the table and slides it toward me. "You might need this, Freckles, in case you run into one of them Sirens."

I reach my hand toward the gun, and the cowboy winks and

smiles. Something flashes in his mouth. I freeze and take a closer look, and my skin crawls as a memory floods my thoughts.

I sat on the front porch, a crocheted wool hat keeping my nearly bald head warm, a rifle resting on my bent knees, and an open book resting on the rifle. The book, The Odyssey, *was taken from the library by Dean and given to me for my fifteenth birthday two weeks earlier.*

"The least you could do is read some of that out loud, after I went to the trouble of getting it for you," Dean said, glancing at me. He winked. I smiled and started reading to him.

He stood in the dead yard, between the dogs, watching the street. My uncle was on the roof. I was immediate backup. Normally we didn't use extra backup, but we were on edge because a group of beasts had passed through the day before.

I had read a few pages out loud when I heard a rattle and a click. Shutting the book, I looked up. Dean's rifle was on his rigid shoulder, and he stood deathly still. The dogs started barking, yanking on their chains. I jumped to my feet, knocking the book to the ground, and ran to Dean's side. My rifle was on my shoulder before I stopped moving, the crosshairs centered on a man. Something scuffled behind us, and I knew it was Uncle Rob up on the roof.

"Chest, head, chest," Dean whispered, reminding me how to most efficiently kill a man. My stomach dropped. I had never killed a human being, and I didn't want to. "And get in the house if it's a beast."

One thing was for sure. The stranger was too old to be a beast. A bushy handlebar mustache drooped down around his mouth. His gray hair looked wet and was slicked back so his bare, pale forehead gleamed above his suntanned face. But gray hair or not, the way this man walked toward us, toward three rifles aimed at him, gave me the willies. He didn't slow his pace. Not even a little bit.

"That's close enough, grampsy," Dean called when the man was standing in the middle of the road in front of our house. I sighed with relief, waiting for the man to stop, but he didn't. Dean didn't give him another warning. He pulled the trigger. Sparks flew around the man's dusty cowboy boots—boots that finally stopped walking forward.

"Where's the dentist?" the stranger called.

"Why do you need him?" Dean asked.

"I have a tooth problem."

"Jack." Dean's eyes stayed locked on the stranger. "Go wake Dad."

Clutching my rifle against my chest, I ran into the house. Dad was scheduled to take night watch, so he was getting caught up on sleep. I burst into his room, and he flew out of bed, his prized Glock aimed at me.

He lowered the gun. "What is it?"

"A man wants to see you. He's out front."

Dad rushed past me, barefoot, and went out the front door. I followed. The stranger hadn't moved. When he saw Dad, though, he took a step closer. Dad's gun was up in an instant. "That's close enough," he said. "What do you want?"

"I'm an old man," the stranger called. "One of my teeth is giving me a real problem and I can feel infection spreading into my face. Will you take a look?" Dad hesitated. The stranger took a step toward us.

Dean stepped between the stranger and Dad. "Before you come any closer to my father, show me your hands."

"What's that?" The stranger took two steps closer, his hands dangling at his sides, the toes of his boots nearly even with the edge of the sidewalk.

"Show us your hands and arms, old man. Now," Dean said, his voice intense.

The stranger frowned and stepped up onto the sidewalk, and my hackles bristled.

"I'm hard of hearing," he yelled, even though he was a mere five steps away from us. He took another step forward and paused, gaze darting up to the roof before focusing on me. His eyes softened and his mouth quirked up at the edges. He stepped onto the matted-down dead grass of the front yard, and his ankle wobbled and twisted to the side. The old man fell to his hands and knees and cried out in pain.

I didn't think, just acted. Three steps was all it took, though, before my brain overrode my impulse to help the man. But three steps were enough. I was one step beyond where the dogs could reach. Before I could get my rifle up and aimed, the old man was off the ground and leaping at me like a snake striking prey. Hard hands cinched around my head, clutching my forehead and chin. One firm yank and my neck would snap.

Right before the man grabbed me, I saw his palms. A quarter-size scar had been branded into each.

The dogs started barking again. Dean yelled something. My uncle had his gun aimed just above my shoulder. Only Dad seemed calm and collected, his gun held loosely in his hand and pointing at the ground. Everything seemed to slow down, like the universe had taken a deep breath and was holding it.

"What do you want?" Dad asked. The afternoon sun gleamed off his white, sleep-messy hair.

The man's hands tightened on my chin and forehead, twisting my neck to the side just a bit and pulling my back against the front of his body. *"All I want is for you to fix my tooth so I don't die from infection. If you agree* to that, I'll let your son go. But first I want your promise that I will walk away from here alive."

"Are you a raider?" Dean asked.

"Why else would I ask you not to kill me?" The old man took his hand from my forehead and held it forward, showing his branded palm. Dean cursed and gritted his teeth.

"We have helped raiders before." Dad's fingers twitched on his gun. "There is no need to hold my son's life for ransom."

"Word is," the raider said, "that one of my boys came to you for some work a little bit ago, but he never came back."

I shivered. I knew exactly who the old man was talking about. Dad paled. "He didn't give me a choice. If my patients cooperate, they walk out of here alive—that's a promise. But if they try to steal from me, or harm my family, we have no choice but to kill them. That promise stands for you as well."

The raider released me, and I fell to my hands and knees at his feet, too weak with fear to move. Air swished across my face, and the raider was on the ground beside me, eyes round with shock, and Dean straddling his chest. Dean shoved the barrel of his rifle into the man's mouth and put his finger on the trigger, his eyes flashing with rage. He looked insane.

"If you ever—EVER—touch my little brother again, you'll be eating my bullets, old man!" He shoved his gun deeper into the raider's mouth, making him gag and squirm. "Do you understand me?" Dean yelled so loudly that I flinched. The raider gurgled something. "Good. Because I don't feel like blowing your head off in front of him." He removed his rifle from the man's mouth and then jerked him to his feet.

"Put this on over your eyes," Dean said, pulling a red bandana out of his *pocket and chucking it at the man. The raider did what Dean asked. Guided by Dean and Dad, the raider walked into the house.*

A moment later, Josh came outside and helped me to my feet. Face grim, he brushed off my book and handed it to me. I sat down on the front porch and stared at Josh's back as he kept watch. I was too wound up to read.

Two hours later, the raider was escorted out of the house. On the front porch, he pulled the bandana from his eyes and looked at Dean. "If you ever get bored here," he said, "come and find me. I'm always looking for boys like you. I can promise you food and women."

"Get out of here before I break my dad's promise not to hurt you," Dean growled.

"Suit yourself." He winked and smiled at me when he passed, showing me a silver front tooth.

"You want your gun or not?" the cowboy asks, his silver tooth flashing.

I dart forward and grab the gun. It is warm from his hand. I stare at the cowboy and wonder if he recognizes me. His smile widens to a grin and he shrugs, showing me both of his open palms. They are scarred from one side to the other, with no visible circle brand. But I don't need to see the brands to know the truth: we have just walked into the enemy's hands.

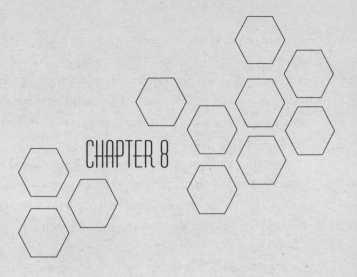

CHAPTER 8

I raise my gun and point it at the cowboy. He smirks and folds his arms over his chest, leaning back against the booth. His boot starts tapping against the floor. "I don't think you got it in you to shoot a man point-blank, Freckles." I swallow and try to hold my gun steady.

Bowen stands but doesn't lower his rifle. "Fo, get the atlas and make sure it's marked."

Fo hurries to the display of faded atlases beside the door and takes one, flipping through the pages. "It is marked."

"Good. Let's go." Bowen waits while I dash out of the diner, followed by Fo and Jonah, before slowly backing out.

"You all be careful out there," Randall Flint warns. The hair on the back of my neck bristles. "Remember what I said. Trust no one. Follow the marked path. And stay away from the mountains so the wolves don't gobble you up!"

The very moment my feet touch the road, I sprint in the direction of the interstate. The others follow and I am surprised that Jonah, his left foot clumsy beneath his large frame, can keep up with Fo and Bowen. I pull ahead of them all, my feet pounding, doing what I do best, doing what I've been training to do for more than three years—running.

Something hisses. My feet skid on pavement and I crane my head up, looking for the source of the sound. A white ball of fire is arcing across the sky, leaving a trail of pale smoke against blue. Two more fireballs follow, and then the evening is quiet again. For a moment.

A pink ball of fire bursts into the sky, crossing three fading trails of smoke. Bowen curses and puts his rifle on his shoulder. "He's shot off flares! They know we're coming, and they know we've got a woman with us! Get off the interstate!"

I turn left, west. Dread makes me faster than I have ever been before as I sprint the width of the interstate and hurdle the cement barrier. My feet come down on crisp weeds. Bowen lands beside me, then Fo and Jonah.

"Which way?" I ask.

Bowen presses a finger over his lips for silence, then points north and west.

I nod. "Follow me," I whisper, and run to the nearest paved road, leading us nowhere in particular. We run and we run with me in the lead, our feet slapping pavement. The farther we go, the quieter the sounds of the others become until I realize . . . I can't hear them anymore. I have outrun them.

I screech to a halt in the parking lot of an abandoned strip mall and wait for them to catch up. Drenched with sweat and panting so hard I can barely hear anything over my own noise, I stare in the direction from which I've just come. Evening shadows stretch over empty pavement, but nothing moves. I am about to retrace my steps when a lone figure finally appears. Thinking it must be Bowen or Jonah, I almost wave. But then I take a closer look. He has wide shoulders, a scraggly beard, and his clothes hang funny on him. And he is running toward me.

I drop to my hands and knees. The mall's shadow is stretched long across the parking lot, nearly hiding a lonely, dusk-colored car that sits on four flat tires. I crawl to the rusted car and press myself against one of the tires.

Slowly, carefully, I peer under the car and scan the street for feet. I frown. No one is there. A whisper carries on the silent air, and something rattles. Goose bumps dance down my arms and I rub my hands over my thin, wiry biceps. And then someone crouches beside me.

I open my mouth to scream, but a wool-gloved hand clamps down over it. Fuzzy fabric sticks to my tongue, and I am staring at a scraggly face I know but don't necessarily trust. I pull his hand off of my face and glare. "What are you doing here? Are you following me?"

"Look," the vagabond whispers. He nods toward the road, in the opposite direction I came from. I barely lift my head above the hood of the car and look.

Three men are walking slowly toward the strip mall, and one of them is leaning forward and studying the ground. When they get to the parking lot's entrance, the man staring at the ground pauses and crouches. He runs his fingers over the pavement, his eyes narrow, and a smile splits his face.

"They're tracking you," the vagabond whispers.

I duck behind the car again and shrink against the tire. "I wanna go home!" I whisper.

As the men walk into the parking lot, their voices carry to me. "Pink flare means a woman," one says. "When we catch her, think of the reward Hastings will give us. Look. Two sets of tracks go to that car and stop."

I focus on the parking lot. The pavement is covered with dust. Except where the vagabond and I have walked. "I'm so dead," I whisper. With those words floating on the air, the vagabond jumps to his feet and yanks me to mine. I stand in frozen shock for a moment, staring at the stunned raiders. The vagabond runs, leaving me. But then he stops running, turns back to me, and screams, "Come on!"

I don't have time to think, just react. I chase him across the parking lot and through broken glass doors, into the strip mall. Glass shards crunch beneath my feet and stick to the soles of my shoes, making it hard to run.

Gunshots thunder in the quiet air, and faded, plastic-wrapped rectangles of printer paper explode beside me. I scream and cover my head, but the vagabond yanks one of my arms down and wraps my hand in his, pulling me toward the back of the store. We stop in an aisle of rat-eaten computer chairs and office furniture, and the vagabond tugs me down behind a tipped particle-board desk.

"If we go out the back exit, there's a grocery store backed up against this mall," he says, panting. "We need to go into it if we want to get away."

I shake my head. "No. I need to find my friends."

"You can't find them if you're dead. Just trust me long enough to get us out of here alive, and then find your friends. Okay?"

I clench my jaw and firm my shoulders. He's right. I shake my head no but say, "Okay."

He squeezes my hand. "On the count of three, we run. One . . ."

A spray of bullets echoes through the store, and I can see three silhouettes framed in the store's front windows.

". . . Two . . ."

Footsteps thud on the gritty, warped linoleum, and my heart is beating so hard it's almost choking me.

". . . Three!"

He doesn't let go of my hand. I am yanked forward and dragged to the back of the store, to a door that leads into a sunset-bright world, with the back of a huge grocery store in front of me. We sprint over empty pavement and up a truck ramp that leads to the grocery store's delivery entrance. Before we set foot inside, the smell hits me like a wall. Sewage. Rotting food. Dead animals. We step through the missing delivery door and into darkness, and the smell nearly knocks me over. I cover my mouth and nose with my hand and pause. The quiet, indistinct hum of an air conditioner fills the building. It is a sound I never used to notice in the old world, but now that I am used to absolute silence, it sticks out like a warning. My skin crawls.

"I don't think we should be in here," I whisper.

"That's the point," he says. He rummages in his ragged clothing, and I get a whiff of something else that brings me back to the old world. Sunblock. And then it dawns on me. This vagabond, who is always filthy and covered with dirt and dead grass, does not stink. I look at him but can't see his face in the darkness. But I do see what he's holding in his hand, as it reflects the small bit of sunlight that is shining like a rectangular beacon from the door we just came in through.

"Where did you get a gun?" I whisper. In the year and a half that I have known him, he has never been armed. At least, I never *knew* he was armed.

"I always carry it with me." I gawk at him, and he squeezes my hand. "Don't worry—your father knew I carried it, and he never seemed to mind."

Shadows flicker in the store's rear doorway as three men cautiously creep up the truck ramp. They're each holding a gun. I reach for my gun, but the vagabond puts his free hand over mine. "You won't need that," he whispers. "We are going up."

Up? For the first time I look around. We're standing in a room lined with empty stock shelves that reach all the way up to the high ceiling. The floor is cluttered with stained egg cartons, mangled milk containers, torn and empty boxes, and lots and lots of lumpy stuff. I squint at the lumpy stuff and stop breathing. It is brown. And it stinks. I scan the room again and dig my fingernails into the vagabond's hand.

In the farthest corner of the room, in the direction of the air conditioner sound, is a mound of something that at first glance looks like a huge pile of old, dirty clothes. But there are arms and legs and tangles of matted hair mixed in with the rags. And if I squint really hard, I can see the pile breathing.

"There are beasts in here!" I whisper. "We have got to get out!"

He doesn't say anything, just starts pulling me toward a massive tower of metal shelves. "Go up," he says when we reach them. "Quickly!"

I put my hands on the cool metal and start climbing. The vagabond climbs up behind me, his feet softly clunking on the shelves. The sound seems to draw the raiders' attention. The three of them burst into the grocery store, guns ready.

I get to the top of the shelves—nearly two stories high—and lay down on my belly, peering down. The vagabond reaches the top and lies down on his stomach, with his head by my feet. He lifts his gun, takes aim toward the store's delivery door, and fires a single shot. One of the raiders screams and clutches his shoulder. The other two let loose and start firing in every direction but up.

Big mistake. The beasts in the corner of the room are no longer huddled in a sleeping mass on the floor. They are up and running for the doorway. And based on the way the raiders are shooting everywhere and nowhere in particular, they have no idea they are about to be hit with a dozen beasts. If they knew, they would be aiming all of their firepower at them.

"Run!" The word is shrieked, echoing above the noise of guns and beasts. I scream it so loudly, my throat feels raw. But I can't lie up here and watch a bloodbath. The thought makes me sick.

The gunfire stops. One of the raiders points to the beasts, and they start firing in their direction. Some of the beasts fall to the ground, but the others are almost at the raiders. The raiders stop shooting and run. The beasts follow them out the door, all but one little boy, with glossy black hair, who can't quite keep up. He goes out the door ten seconds after the others.

I rest my forehead on the cool metal shelf and just breathe. My body feels like unresponsive mush.

A hand clasps my ankle and gently shakes it. "We need to get out of here, Jack," the vagabond says. I don't move. "Before the beasts come back," he adds.

I gasp, swing my feet over the side of the shelves, and climb down as fast as I can. At the bottom, the vagabond takes my hand in his and leads me out of the stock room and into the nearly dark grocery store. We weave past trash and grocery carts left in the aisles, past empty shelves, and then go out the front doors.

The sun has just set. The evening star hovers above the pale purple silhouette of the Rockies.

"I need to find my friends," I whisper, pulling my hand away from the vagabond.

"I know. Follow me and be quiet."

I stay a step behind him and we quickly walk east and south, wading through the patches of dust and dead weeds that line the sides of the roads. When we get to a bend in the road, the vagabond crouches, running his fingers over the pavement. And then he points west. "They went that way," he says, and stands. But instead of walking in the direction he pointed, he pulls his shirt over his head and peels his arms from the long sleeves, revealing a dingy short-sleeved undershirt and muscular biceps.

Next, he takes the long-sleeved shirt and starts hitting it against the road. A cloud of dust billows up around the shirt, and I can't tell if it is coming off the filthy garment or from the road. He takes a few steps and does it again.

"What are you doing?" I whisper, glancing over my shoulder.

"Covering your friends' tracks. The raiders post trackers out here so that when Flint shoots off the flares, they have men who can find the runners." He looks at me. "You and your friends are runners."

"Why didn't Flint kill us himself?" I ask.

"He wants you alive. If he can't take the runners down on his own, he shoots off the flares. You guys were too tough for him alone, and he knew it." He hits the street with his shirt again.

"How do you know so much about the raiders?"

He glances at the shadowed world. "When you live with your enemy, your best chance of survival is knowing how they operate."

My mom needs to turn that into one of her needlepoint sayings.

He pulls me over to the side of the road, to a patch of dirt that used to be lawn. "Your biggest advantage right now is darkness. In a matter of minutes, it will be too dark to track you. Until morning, that is. So here's what you've got to do. Do not walk on the roads or sidewalks. Stay in the dead grass. Their trackers don't know how to track there. Look." He steps onto the dusty road and takes a few steps. Every place his feet touch, the dust is moved.

"Look over there." He points down the road toward a small

one-story house that probably wasn't in good shape *before* the bees died off. Now it looks like it might collapse if someone sneezes at it. "That's probably where your friends are. That's where their tracks lead."

I study the dimly lit road and can just make out a faint trail. "I'll cover the tracks," the vagabond says. "You get them out of there and find somewhere else to hide. The farther you get from here, the better your chance of surviving."

"Okay." Staying off the road and sidewalk, I take a step toward the house, but pause. I turn and watch the vagabond swing his shirt at the road for a moment before saying, "Thank you."

He stops swinging and looks at me. There is hunger in his eyes, and I wish I had some food for him. "You're welcome, Jack."

I turn and run.

CHAPTER 9

As I cross the threshold into the dark house, I hear the *click–click* of Bowen's M16 being engaged. I flinch and put up my hands. "It's me, Jack," I whisper. "Don't shoot!"

He curses under his breath. "I almost blew your head off! Never sneak up on me like that again!" Bowen, hardly more than a dark shadow, rises up from a corner of the house and lowers his rifle. "Where did you go?"

"I'll tell you later. We need to get out of here now," I say, not moving from the doorway. "The raiders have trackers. They're going to find us here."

"Trackers? How do you know?"

"They almost caught me." I don't mention the vagabond. I don't know what Bowen will think of him appearing again. I don't know what *I* think about him reappearing.

"How did you get away?"

"I ran into a group of beasts," I say, which is the truth. I just leave out the part about the vagabond leading me to the beasts and then intentionally waking them up. The thought of the beasts makes my knees knock together.

"Fo, Jonah," Bowen quietly calls into the next room. "We need to go. Now." Jonah and Fo come out and, without a word, follow me out of the house and into the deepening dusk. I wait for the buzz of mosquitos for a split second, and then remember there haven't been mosquitos for years. Bowen, rifle on his shoulder, walks down the driveway and out to the road.

"Wait," I whisper. "We need to stay off the pavement. That's how they tracked me."

Bowen looks at me. "All right, Flapjack. Why don't *you* lead the way to some shelter? But don't leave us behind this time if we have to run."

I nod and turn west and start the slow process of sneaking through yards, climbing over tipping vinyl fences, and ducking past abandoned cars. After nearly an hour, I find a rusting fifteen-passenger van that has been driven down a shallow ravine on the side of the road. I stick my head through a broken window and, using what little starlight there is, try to check the van for unwanted inhabitants. The bench seats are made of dark, cracked vinyl, and the remaining windows are tinted, making it nearly impossible to see anything else about the van.

"How is this for shelter?" I ask.

Bowen opens the sliding side door and steps inside. After a full minute of examining the van from front to back, he says, "Perfect."

We all get inside. Despite the broken windows, I lock the doors. Locked doors make me feel a little bit safer. Bowen shrugs his backpack from his shoulders and sets it gently on the van's floor, and then helps Fo get her pack off. Jonah, hunched over so he doesn't crunch his head on the ceiling, walks to the back of the van and peers out of the rear window. He stands unmoving, giant backpack still on his back as if he's oblivious to its weight. I take my backpack off. The sweat-damp spot it has left on my back makes me shiver.

"So," I say, looking at Bowen. "We're not really going to Wyoming, right? That was, like, to set a false trail or something. Right?"

Bowen sits on one of the bench seats and carefully sets his rifle over his knees. Fo sits and melts against him, so in the darkness they look like one entity. "Of course we're going to Wyoming," Bowen says.

"Haven't you heard about the settlement there?" Fo asks.

My eyes bulge with disbelief. "You guys can't be serious. Don't you know that the rumors of Wyoming are a raider trap?"

"What are you talking about?" Bowen asks, voice disbelieving. "How would you know, anyway? You've been cooped up in your house for as long as I've been in the militia. Longer, even."

"My dad's an *oral surgeon*," I say, as if that should explain everything. And, actually, it does if you think about it.

Bowen doesn't think about it. "And that means he fixes teeth. How does that make him an expert on Wyoming?"

"Do you know what nitrous oxide is?"

Bowen and Fo are silent. Jonah walks over to where we are and sits beside his sister. "Laughing gas," he says. His voice makes me jump—they're the first words I've heard him utter in, well, years.

"That's right," I say. "When people are inhaling laughing gas, they tend to get loopy. Sometimes, when my dad thinks he's got a patient that might have really important information, he ups the gas dose and pumps the patient for info about things. Like Sirens. And wolves." I think of what the vagabond said: "*When you live with your enemy, your best chance of survival is knowing how they operate.*" "I might not be that *big*, or that *tough*, but I have all sorts of information up here." I tap my head. "And Wyoming just happens to be one of the things I know about."

"Explain," Bowen says.

Evening sunlight was pouring in through the west windows of the house, making Dad's pacing shadow stretch long across the family room floor. "Where are they?" he grumbled, looking at me. I had no answer. The sun would be going down in a matter of minutes, and Dean, Josh, and Steve weren't back from their siphoning hunt yet.

"I'm sure they'll be back any minute," Mom called from the other room, where she and my little brother were hanging a load of clothes up to dry. We always hung the clothes indoors so they wouldn't attract thieves—we didn't want to shoot a person if he was merely coming into our yard to steal a pair of pants or a shirt. "When they're late, they usually have a good reason."

Last time they were late was because they'd found an abandoned dentist's office and had hauled tanks of laughing gas back to our house. The time before that, they'd found a convenience store that hadn't been looted as thoroughly as all the others and came home with two bags of candy bars. My mouth watered at the thought.

Still damp from my afternoon on the treadmill, I went out the back door and stood in the yard for a minute. Our cornstalks were growing. I couldn't wait for fresh corn on the cob. I took the pot of barley and lentils out of the solar oven. The smell made me want to puke. I was so sick of eating barley and lentils every other night. And on the nights we didn't have barley and lentils, we ate beans and rice seasoned with salt and pepper. I wanted meat. And bread. And anything sweet.

We did have a good amount of food stored in a secret room we dug below our basement. But we had to eat like food might never be grown again, so we were saving as much as we could. Because if the world stayed how it was now, we would run out of food in a few years.

I carried the food into the house and listened for my brothers, but the only sound was Mom humming while she hung the laundry to dry. I was hoping they'd be back by now, with some canned fruit or vegetables. Even canned peas were better than plain barley and lentils.

I set the lentils on the counter and lifted the hot lid off just as the dogs started barking. The lid slipped out of my hand and clattered onto the clean tile floor. My dad was past me and at the front door—Glock in hand—before the lid stopped spinning. Grabbing a rifle from the kitchen counter, I ran past Mom.

"Your vest!" she cried, and my feet screeched to a stop. Handing her the rifle, I yanked the tackle vest from a coat hook by the front door and thrust my arms through, hardly able to zip it with my trembling fingers. I took the rifle from Mom, then stepped out onto the front porch.

Uncle Rob was standing on the dead lawn between Bruiser and Duke, the rifle on his shoulder pointing northwest toward the bend in the road. All four dogs were barking, spit flecks flying from their jaws.

"Tranquillo," Uncle Rob said. The dogs went instantly silent, though they didn't relax a muscle.

"What have we got, Rob?" Dad asked, taking aim. I took my designated spot beside him and pointed my gun at a lone man slowly approaching the house.

"I'm not sure," Uncle Rob said. "I've only seen one, but there might be others. He looks like a raider."

"What do you want?" my dad called.

The man paused. He was thick, with arms like clubs and a chest like a cannon. "I got punched in the mouth and need my teeth fixed," the man called, his voice a deep, lisping baritone.

"Are you a raider?" Dad asked.

The man lifted his hands, showing round quarter-size brands on the palm of each. Raider. From the north side of the walled city. The raiders on our side, the south side, had four scars slashed across their forearms.

"Are you alone?" Dad asked.

"As you see," the raider answered.

Dad's rigid stance went even more rigid at the raider's nonanswer. "I need a yes or a no. Are you alone?"

"Yes."

In a quiet voice Dad asked Uncle Rob, "What do you think? Should we take him in or is it too much of a risk without the boys here?"

"We haven't had a northern raider for months. I can stand guard out here, Jack can help you. If I need backup, I'll call for Ellen," Rob said, voice barely above a whisper. "I think the chance at information from the north is worth the risk, and the boys should be back any minute."

Dad glanced at me. "I can do it," I said. I'd helped out lots of times before, just never on a raider. Plaque, blood, and gore didn't bother me.

Dad's lips thinned, and he took a deep breath before calling, "All right, Raider, come forward but keep your palms where I can see them." The raider, palms facing us, slowly walked up the road to our house. When he got to the yard, Dad handed me his Glock and disarmed the raider—a revolver and two sharp, blood-stained knives.

I squinted against the last rays of the evening sun, studying the man. His greasy black hair was a little longer than his ear lobes, and his clean-shaven face was younger than I expected it to be. His eyes, pale hazel, darted to mine, and he looked me up and down, sizing me up. I put my hand up to block the sun, trying to get a better look at the man, because there was something familiar about him, but Dad pulled a bandana over the man's face, blindfolding him. Next, Dad slapped a pair of handcuffs on him and led him inside. With Dad's gun tucked in my waistband, and my rifle aimed at the raider's head, I followed them into what used to be the master bedroom of the house but was now the work room. It got the best light.

"I need the generator on," Dad called. Feet thumped on the basement stairs and a moment later the generator filled the house with a gentle, throbbing hum. Dad guided the raider to a dental chair and had him lie down, unhooking the handcuffs to replace them with restraints we'd built into the chair.

"Is that really necessary?" the raider asked with a chuckle. I tilted my head to the side, listening to his voice, the way he formed his words, wondering why it seemed familiar.

"If you want your teeth fixed," Dad said, voice fierce, "you follow our rules. Now open up." Dad turned the exam light on and centered it over the raider's face.

The raider, still blindfolded, opened his mouth. The smell of infection and rot wafted out. I put a hand over my nose and tried not to gag. Pulling on a pair of latex gloves, Dad peered into the man's mouth and frowned. "This is going to take some work. Jack, get the laughing gas."

"Is it bad?" the raider asked.

"No, not bad," Dad answered, fastening a mask over his nose and mouth. "Bad doesn't even begin to describe your teeth. Your two front teeth are broken. It also looks like you haven't flossed in years. Have you been gnawing on raw meat?"

I smiled. That was Dad's dental humor. The smile was replaced by repulsion when the raider answered, "You can tell that just by looking into my mouth?"

Dad and I looked at each other and I felt the blood drain from my face. Sweat glistened below Dad's white hairline. "Jack, put the gas on him. And double the normal dose. This is going to take a while."

I put the mask onto the raider and cringed at the chunks of gray flesh stuck between his molars. The gas hissed. After a minute, the raider's body seemed to melt into the chair and he sighed. "Wow, that feels good." I flipped off the gas and removed the mask.

"So," Dad said, leaning over the man's mouth and starting the slow process of scraping his teeth. "Any news coming out of the north?"

The raider laughed. "Yeah, actually there is. But I can't talk about it. Top secret and all that." It was hard to understand him with Dad working on his mouth.

"What's top secret?" I asked.

Dad shook his head the slightest bit.

"Well, I can't tell you since it is a secret. But did you know that there are Sirens prowling the north?"

"Sirens?" Dad asked, pulling a chunk of something pale and squishy from the raider's teeth and wiping it on a paper towel.

"Yeah. We think they're just north of the city. We've tried to catch one but haven't been able to. Not yet, anyway."

Dad kept working, scraping away while the raider lay still in the chair. "Oh my, what a big cavity," he said after a few minutes. "I think we might need to pull this tooth. Jack, give him another dose of nitrous oxide."

I looked at my dad. It was too soon for another dose, but Dad nodded, so I put the mask back on the raider's face and turned on the gas. The raider sucked it greedily into his lungs. At Dad's signal, I removed the mask.

Leaning back in his chair, Dad folded his arms over his chest and pulled the mask down off of his face so it rested just below his chin. "So, what's the secret news coming out of the north?"

The raider laughed. "Promise you won't tell?"

"Promise."

"Wyoming. Have you heard about Wyoming?" the raider whispered.

"Yes, we've heard about the colony in Wyoming. What about it?"

The raider giggled like a little girl. "It's a lie. A trap. A piece of bait to lure people north. And then—hook, line, and sinker—we get them without even raising a finger. They walk right up to us, and the best part is, it's mostly women trying to flee to Wyoming!"

My stomach dropped and I gasped. I knew people who decided to try to relocate to Wyoming. We never heard from any of them again—always assumed they'd made it. Now I knew the truth.

Dad cleared his throat and wiped a sheen of sweat from his forehead. He put his mask back on and tapped the pick on the raider's chin. The man opened his mouth again.

"What's your name?" Dad asked.

"Don't you recognize me?" The raider's words were slurred from the pick and the gas.

The pick froze, and Dad's hand started to tremble. I thought he'd looked upset about the Wyoming news. I was wrong. Now he looked upset. "Recognize you?" Dad asked slowly.

"Yeah, Mr. Bloom. I'm Elijah Ashton. I went to school with your son, Dean. We were both on the football team. I was a linebacker."

Elijah Ashton. I remembered him. When I was eleven and Elijah was sixteen, he'd come over to the house almost every day. He'd stare at me and tease me and try to get me alone. He finally did get me alone once by following me into my bedroom, then said something about liking younger, bigger girls like me. When he tried to kiss me, I ran out of the room. Dad found out and banned Elijah from the house. Dad had to beg Dean not to beat up Elijah.

I stared down at the blindfolded guy restrained in the chair and took a step back. If he recognized me . . .

"Where is Dean anyway?" Elijah asked. "He was the toughest guy on the football team. Never afraid to take a hit. He'd make a good raider."

Dean despised the raiders.

"And what happened to your daughter? Is she all grown up and living inside the wall? Probably about to get married? I always thought she was a cute girl. And since when have you had a son named . . ." Elijah's blindfolded head slowly turned in my direction and his nostrils flared. "Wait a sec. Is that you, Jacqui? Jack?" He yanked on the restraints, making the dental chair lurch and the muscles in his neck bulge. Thrashing his head back and forth, the bandana slipped up onto his forehead and he stared right into my eyes. His breathing quickened and a leer tugged at the side of his mouth, exposing his cracked front teeth. "Jacqui Bloom." He growled deep in his throat, the wrist restraints snapped taut, and he started trembling with effort. Sweat popped out on his forehead and the restraints groaned.

"Nitrous now!" Dad shouted. "Full strength!"

I stepped up to Elijah and tried to put the mask on his face, but he struggled against it, eyes devouring me.

"Get your rifle," Dad ordered. I threw down the mask and grabbed my gun. I didn't need the scope to hit a target point-blank, but I pressed my eye to it anyway. Because if I was about to shoot a man, I didn't want to actually see it.

The door to the office flew open and I nearly dropped my weapon. Dean strode in, handguns in each of his hands. "Out, Jack," Dean demanded. My brain heard the order, but my legs wouldn't move. "Out!" Dean roared. I forced my legs to budge and ran out without looking back.

Elijah Ashton left later that night. He was in a body bag.

And we knew the truth about Wyoming.

Bowen curses and Fo gasps. "Do you realize what this means?" she says.

"Maybe Jack's wrong." Bowen says that, but I can hear the defeat in his voice. He sighs. "So, where do you think we should go, Jack? Where do you think Dean would have taken Fo's mom?"

I glance west at the black mass of the Rocky Mountains. "There," I say, pointing. When they don't respond, I realize they can't see where I am pointing in the dark. "We need to go west."

"West? Where the wolves are?" Bowen asks.

"Yes."

"Why do you think he'd go west?" Bowen leans forward and the bench seat creaks beneath his weight. "Do you have some inside information you'd like to share with us regarding the mountains?"

"No. We've never gotten any news from the mountains, which

is why we need to go there. Because if there is a colony located in the mountains, no one in their right mind would leave it to come to Denver, and the raiders wouldn't try to keep people away. Just think of it. That's the only place they discourage people from going."

Bowen hangs his head and mutters, "Why is nothing in my life ever easy?"

Fo wraps her arms around his shoulders. "Let's talk about this in the morning, after we've all had time to sleep on it," she says, voice soothing.

"Jack, do you mind taking first watch?" Bowen asks.

"No problem." I start gnawing on the side of my cheek, then practically hear my dad's voice—*Don't chew your cheek! You're going to wear down your teeth!*—and stop.

Bowen untangles himself from Fo's arms just enough to look at me. His face is nothing but dark shadows. "Do you know how to keep watch?"

"Yeah. Watch for raiders, beasts, wolves, Sirens, looters, or anything else that moves, and shoot it if it gets too close." I peer at the dark windows again. "Do you think it'd be all right if I sat on top of the van? I'll have a better view."

Bowen grunts. "You *do* know how to keep watch. Top of the van is where I'd go too. Wake us up if you see or hear anything." He lies down on the van's gritty floor, right in a patch of purple starlight. Without bothering to take off her fanny pack, Fo lays beside him, her head nestled in the crook of his shoulder, and sighs when his arms wrap around her. I try not to stare at them, but my eyes refuse to look away. I want that—to be held like that.

"Jonah, why don't you rest," Fo says.

"No, I'm coming out too," Jonah says. The sound of his voice makes me jump. I'd almost forgotten he was sitting right in front of me.

Fo lifts her hand up and Jonah clasps it. "Be safe," she whispers. He doesn't answer.

I climb onto the driver's seat and shimmy out the broken window, onto the top of the van. Jonah, still burdened with his backpack, follows. "Why don't you lose the backpack and grab a gun. You can help me stay awake," I say. Jonah looks at me for a long moment and then leaps off the van. He lands with a loud thud and a swish and strides away into the darkness. Slowly, the clomp of his footfalls fades to nothing and I am alone. "Or just go off by yourself," I whisper to the darkness.

As I turn in a slow circle, surveying the perimeter of the van, I hear Fo humming a quiet, sleepy tune that fills a small space of darkness with music. The empty world is hidden by the shroud of night. I look up at the starry sky and can almost imagine nothing has changed at all. I pretend I am the old me, soft and plump, with thick, dark hair, living for 4-H baking competitions, experimenting with bread and doughnut recipes, daydreaming about where I will go on my first date, what my prom dress is going to look like. . . .

Fo's voice grows drowsy and then fades to nothing, and I am left in a silent world with my silent thoughts banging around in my head.

CHAPTER 10

Cookies, Jell-O, cinnamon rolls, Doritos . . . I am in a world filled with food, and it is heaven. It *should* be, at least. But it is not. I stare at the tables covered with every edible luxury imaginable and take a step back. Eating will make my body change, make it turn soft and voluptuous. Voluptuousness is a death sentence. I have to hide behind my thin, childlike frame, like a child vampire, never changing, never maturing, never progressing.

"Hey, Jacqui." A hand shakes my foot and I blink sleep away. "Time to go," Fo says. I nod and tuck my gun, clutched in my hand, into my belt. "What were you dreaming about?"

I sigh. "Food. Do you remember when my mom taught us how to make cinnamon rolls? Do you know what I would *give* for a single cinnamon roll, fresh out of the oven, dripping with cream cheese frosting?" She nods. Of course she knows. I open my backpack and take out a bottle of tablets. One tablet has twenty calories and all the vitamins I need. Fo sees me put it into my mouth and her lips pucker. I shrug. "I didn't know what else to pack that I could carry over a long distance, so I get to eat these for now."

Bowen opens the van's sliding door and morning sunlight shines in. He reaches for his backpack, unzips it, and takes out a water bottle and the atlas with the marked Wyoming trail. He plops the atlas onto the peeling vinyl bench seat and opens it to the page with the map of the entire United States. I peer over his shoulder, at the red ballpoint pen showing a path from where we are, all the way to northern Wyoming. He turns the pages until he gets to our state and I snort.

"You've got to be kidding me. No one would be stupid enough to fall for that," I say, leaning in for a closer look. "All the cowboy did is highlight the main highway all the way to the edge of the state! That seems like the most dangerous route possible!"

"Look here." Fo touches the side of the map with her right hand. I stare at her tattoo and shudder with revulsion. My gaze moves from her hand to where she's pointing. Tiny words have been written in pencil.

Beware the Sirens. This is where they typically make a first attempt at contact. Stay wide of highway.

There is a line drawn from the writing to a point on the map. "I think this is just a couple of miles north of where we are," says Fo.

I look a little closer. The place with the Siren warning *is* a couple of miles north of us.

"Well, we won't be seeing the Sirens since we're not going north." Bowen takes the atlas and tries to tear it in two, but it is too thick. "I can't believe I paid four ounces for this piece of crap."

"I've been thinking." Fo looks between Bowen and me.

"What have you been thinking?" I ask, prepared for anything but hoping she suggests we turn back. I am beginning to doubt whether or not I should have left home.

Her eyes lock on mine. "If Wyoming is a trap," she whispers, "who do you suppose is trying to lure people *away* from the path to Wyoming?"

"Probably more murderers and thieves," Bowen snaps, chucking the atlas out of a broken window.

The atlas flutters in the morning air and falls to the ground like a bird with broken wings. I glance out the window, remembering the sound wings made, and frown. I lean my whole head out of the van's window and squint at the wide blue sky stretching overhead. Straight up it is as blue as a robin's egg. But west, a brownish haze frames the mountains.

"Bowen, Fo, come here." They come to the broken window and follow my gaze west. "Am I imagining things or does the sky look . . . *wrong*?"

"It looks weird," Fo agrees. She puts her fingers on her thighs and starts pressing, as if playing the piano. In time with the movements of her fingers, she hums a gloomy tune under her breath, and suddenly I feel doomed. More doomed than I've felt on this whole journey.

"It's just smoke," Bowen says, shrugging.

"Just smoke? But smoke means people! What if I'm wrong

about going west? What if we are being lured into the hands of more raiders?" I hug my arms over my chest. "We should turn back. This was a stupid idea. I don't think I can do this."

Bowen and Fo share a look. She rests her hands on the fanny pack that she wears over her stomach, like a woman resting her hands on her pregnant belly—as if there's something precious inside the pack. "You can go back if you want to, Jack," Fo says. "But I'm not."

"I go where she goes." Bowen nods at Fo. As if I didn't know that. "And not all fires are manmade. Everything is dead. Maybe lightning struck somewhere and there's a forest fire burning."

I bite the inside of my cheek once, hard. "Sorry. I'm just having a moment of weakness." Someone screams outside the van, a man-scream—deep and rough, like a growl mixed with a yell. "Please say that's your brother, Fo."

"Jonah!" she cries, and darts out the open door. Bowen follows, and I follow him.

Fifty yards away on the sidewalk in front of an elementary school, a man in a hooded sweatshirt is rolling on the ground with another person. Limbs are flailing. Dust is flying. I sprint past Fo and Bowen and reach Jonah first, staring in amazement as he grapples with a short, bone-thin, totally naked boy.

"Stay back, Jacqui," Jonah growls. The boy lunges away from Jonah, at me, and I leap out of his reach just before his small outstretched hand can grab me. A hand marked with the sign of the beast. He has nine marks. A Level Nine. Level Nines are lethal. I slowly back away. And then I step off the curb and fall flat on my back, the air whooshing out of me in one painful burst.

The beast jumps on me, his gap-toothed, olive-skinned face inches from mine. Glossy black hair hangs in his eyes. He whips the hair out of his face like a normal, rational boy, and then he opens his mouth for a bite—of me—and is pulled off by a pair of scarred hands. Jonah wrenches the boy's arms behind his back.

"Fiona," Jonah pants, slamming the beast onto the ground and resting one of his knees between the kid's sharp shoulder blades.

Fiona calmly walks up to her brother and the beast. "Hold him still," she says. The beast squirms beneath Jonah but can't get away. She unzips her fanny pack and removes a long, thin glass tube. I watch in silent fascination as she uncaps a syringe and jams it into the beast's bare butt cheek, injecting a clear liquid into him.

I scramble up onto my feet. "What are you doing?"

Jonah looks at me with pained eyes, but it is Fo who answers, "Injecting him with the cure."

CHAPTER 11

The cure? *The* cure?

I take a closer look at her fanny pack and a lightbulb goes on inside my head. She's carrying beast cure. And then another lightbulb goes on, nearly blinding my inner eye. Sure, she wants to find her mom and help me find my brother. But she also wants to spread the cure. Her eyes meet mine, and I'm awed at the silent determination I see there.

"How long does it take to work?" I ask, watching the child writhe beneath Jonah.

"It works in stages," Fo says. "After a couple of days, he will stop attacking things as long as he's well fed. But it takes weeks for a beast to regain humanity."

That's way too long. "We're not going to just hang out here and wait for him to be cured, and hope that the raiders don't find us, right?" I ask.

"We'll take him with us," Jonah says.

"You've got to be kidding me! What are we going to feed him to keep him from attacking us?"

"I'll cut my rations in half," Jonah says. He looks at me with his good eye. "You're pretty small. Do you have any spare clothes I can put on him?"

My face starts to burn, and I try not to start laughing at the insanity that my life has become. "Yeah, Jonah, actually I do. I brought a spare pair of boys' tighty-whities."

Bowen gapes at me, as if I'm the naked kid being pinned to the sidewalk by Frankenstein's twin. "Seriously?" he asks.

"Seriously. It's all part of pretending to be a boy. If I bend over and my shirt comes up and someone sees my underwear, what would they think if it was pink with lace trim?"

Bowen grins. "That you're a pretty twisted little boy." He laughs at his own joke, and I fight the urge to smack him.

Jonah pulls the sweatshirt over his head, and I forget to be embarrassed. His bare arms, up to the sleeves of his short-sleeved T-shirt, look like gold-and-white marble. Or cobweb-covered oak. There are teeth marks on his hand with fresh blood dripping from them. "What happened to you, Jonah?" I blurt.

Jonah looks at his hand. "The child bit me."

"No, I mean the scars." From the corner of my eye I see Fo cringe.

Jonah either doesn't hear me or chooses not to answer. He carefully forces the sweatshirt over the boy's head in spite of the way he's thrashing. Jonah maneuvers the hoodie down around the child-beast's torso, then ties the sleeves in a tight knot, straitjacket-style.

"I found him in the basement of a house a couple of miles from here, gnawing tin cans of beef stew open," Jonah says. Fo takes his hand and gently dabs the blood from his skin with the hem of her shirt. "We could go back to that house and spend a few days there while the kid adjusts. I think there's some food left."

The thought of beef stew perks me up a little bit.

"And I left my pack there," Jonah adds, looking at Bowen. For the first time I notice Jonah doesn't have his backpack on. I almost thought the thing was glued to him.

Jonah secures the beast under one arm and holds his hand out to Bowen. With a firm yank, Bowen pulls Jonah to his feet. "We'll get our stuff out of the van and you can show us the way."

I stand on what used to be a beautiful hardwood floor in an abandoned mansion, with giant windows that reach up two stories high, framing a view of the Rocky Mountains. The sun is being pinched between two peaks, and the smoke has thickened, turning the western sky a hazy pinkish-orange that has bled into the entire world as far as I can see.

We are somewhere around Westminster, a northern suburb of Denver. The house we're squatting in sits on the outskirts of a massive brown golf course encircling a mucky pond. White golf carts are rusting on the dead course, as if the golfers just up and left in the middle of their game. Or maybe they were attacked by beasts. Or raiders.

I spent the afternoon knee-deep in the pond, refilling my water bottle. Even filtered the water is slightly green. My hands still smell like moss. Fo and Bowen are scavenging the neighboring mansions for food, and I am alone with Jonah and the beast. At the sound of a muffled whimper, I turn.

Jonah sits on a weathered, cracked leather sofa beside a dark fireplace, cradling the sleeping body of the boy-beast. Muscles line Jonah's marbled arms, tensing and straining as the young beast thrashes and kicks in his sleep. He is so different from the Jonah I went to school with. He's a lot bigger, for one. Taller. Filled out. Not at all the thin, awkward Jonah whose greatest ambitions in elementary school were to make the girls laugh and to build *Star Wars* models out of thousands of tiny Lego pieces. He looks like a monster now.

Jonah's good eye meets mine, the eerie pink glow of sunset glinting off it, and he stares at me. After an uncomfortable minute he asks, "What?"

"What happened to you?" I ask, forcing myself not to recoil from his stare.

He holds up a scarred hand and inspects it. "You mean the scars?"

I nod, then say, "Yes," when I realize he isn't looking at me.

"They're worse on the inside," he whispers, closing his eyes and leaning his head against the sofa.

"It happened when he was a beast." I jump and turn around to find Bowen and Fo walking through the front door. "He's a Level Ten. He turned, and lived outside the wall for four years. He's still got all the physical leftovers of being a beast—like brute strength and the ability to heal at a rapid rate—but he has the mind of a human again," Bowen says.

"Why is he so scarred?" I ask in a quieter voice, as if Jonah isn't sitting in the same room. Fo's lips thin and she won't look at me.

"The people inside the wall used to watch beasts fight—pit fights—for entertainment, and Fiona was matched against Jonah—a sibling grudge match to really get the crowd excited. To get her out, I put a grenade on the pit's glass seal, and when it exploded, the glass cut Jonah to shreds as he shielded Fo from the blast. If you feel his skin, you can still feel some of the glass shards stuck in it."

I look at Jonah and shudder.

"It's a miracle he's alive," Bowen adds. "He nearly died to save his sister."

"Death would have been too easy," Jonah whispers. Fo hugs her arms over her chest and goes to her brother. She sits down on the sofa beside him and leans her head on his shoulder.

Bowen walks to the kitchen and sets his loaded backpack on a dusty marble countertop. I walk to the counter, eager to see what he's found. Surely the mansions in this neighborhood have good food left in them. Rich people probably ate well. And they probably had lots of canned food stored in case of emergencies.

But when Bowen unzips his backpack, I frown. It is filled to the top with flat, rectangular tins.

"Where's the beef stew?" I ask.

"The beast-boy ruined it all," he says.

"What is that stuff?"

Bowen grins and tosses a can to me.

I study it and grimace. *"Canned oysters*? People put *oysters* into cans?"

"Apparently. And crab. And lobster. And something called kippers." Bowen dumps his pack out, and by the light of the fading sunset I study the cans. All seafood, except one can of something called palm hearts.

"No wonder no other scavengers took this stuff," I grumble. "Do you think we will be able to get the beast to eat it when he wakes up?" My stomach rumbles, reminding me that I'm starving for something other than calorie tablets, and Bowen—mischievous grin plastered to his face—hands me a tin.

"Why don't you tell us how it tastes, Flapjack?"

I take the oysters and use the key on top to roll back the cover. The smell of the ocean overwhelms me, and not in a good way. The oysters are glossy, slick-looking brown lumps about the size of my thumb. Bowen watches, amused, as I stick my fingers into the oysters and pull one out, and then shove it into my mouth before I decide to chicken out.

It tastes . . . way better than I thought it would, like smoky, salty, tender fish. A little on the strong side—okay, a lot on the strong side—but a lot better than calorie tablets. I reach in for another oyster and Bowen laughs.

"If you can eat it, I think the beast will eat it," he says.

I devour the oysters in a matter of seconds, sucking the fishy residue from my fingertips and savoring the feeling of something filling the concave space beneath my ribs.

I go back to the window and watch the smoky horizon change from red to dark purple. "So, do you want me to take first watch again?" I ask Bowen. He's sitting on the sofa beside Fo, eating something fishy-smelling from a can.

"We need two people to keep watch at a time. I'll take the front yard, you take the back."

I nod, pat the gun at my belt, zip my tackle vest, and walk out the double doors that lead to a huge wooden back deck. The night is just dark enough that I can't quite see anything except the fading outline of the mountains. Holding the handrail, I walk down the deck steps, into the formerly landscaped backyard of the mansion and look around for a place to keep watch. At the edge of the yard is a hedge of dead bushes beside a vinyl picket fence. I head for the bushes and crawl into them so that I am hidden. Wrapping my arms around my shins, I rest my chin on my knees and watch the dark golf course.

The sky turns black and only the brightest stars shine through the haze. My butt seems to mold to the ground, sinking into it, and my eyelids grow deceptively soft. I imagine the buzz of mosquitoes and the chirp of crickets filling the quiet night, the sound of wind in aspen leaves, of an airplane droning across the sky. Car engines. Dogs barking. A stick cracks.

I lift my head and hold my breath. I was *not* imagining the snap of wood beneath a foot, yet I heard it. I think.

Slowly, I move my head from side to side. The golf course is dark. The house is dark. Everything is silent. Careful not to make a noise, I lower my chin back down onto my knees and listen. My heart goes from speeding to normal, and my breathing slows. I begin to wonder if I dozed off and dreamed the sound.

And then someone sighs, the gentle exhale of breath that can only be heard from close range. It came from the direction of the golf course.

CHAPTER 12

My blood curdles in my veins and I start to sweat. Sitting perfectly still, I start moving my eyes around, searching for the source of the sigh.

I glimpse something from the corner of my eye—a human-shaped shadow standing in the darkness on *my* side of the fence—and grapple for my gun. In one practiced move I slide it from my belt and put my finger on the trigger. My sweaty hand starts trembling so badly, the gun falls and bounces off my shoe. The ground rustles when the gun hits it, and the shadow drops out of sight.

Completely panicked, I fall to my hands and knees and run my hands over the ground, searching for my gun, but don't find it. I stand and pull the knife from my belt and unzip the bottom pocket of my tackle vest, removing a small flashlight. My fingers feel for the spot on the knife that releases the blade and it swings open. With the flashlight in one hand and the knife in the other, I spring to my feet and turn the light on, pointing it at the prowler. The shadow—a lone person—turns toward my light and starts running straight at me.

Full frontal attack. I have trained for this, trained to fight, fight, fight, and I am ready for his body to crash into mine, to use his own momentum to throw him off balance, to use both knife and flashlight as weapons. In half a heartbeat he's diving at me, hand wrapping around the top of the flashlight as if that is the only thing he's after, and everything turns dark.

Warm flesh contacts mine, and I lash out with my knife. He struggles against me, but I'm faster. I have learned speed over strength in a world ruled by physical prowess. With one practiced move, I whip him over onto his stomach and wrench his arms behind his back. The flashlight clatters out of his hand, the beam lighting up the bushes like bright, hopeful encouragement.

"The light!" my attacker gasps, struggling. I wrench his arms more tightly against his back, making his shoulder blades strain, making him whimper. "The light! Turn it off!" he says again, then adds a beseeching, pain-filled, "Please."

I glance between him and the light.

"You have just broadcast your location to a whole group of raiders. If you want a chance to run before they get here, let go of me and turn off the light!" he growls.

I am torn. If I let go, he might attack me. It's the perfect story to make me release him. He grunts and thrashes and manages to throw me off of him, and then dives for the light and smashes it into the ground. It goes dark as the glass shatters. And then he turns his back to me, falls to his knees, and puts his hands behind his back. For a moment, I stare at him, too stunned to react. Then I tackle him back to the ground, pinning his arms, but not quite as tightly as before. He lies perfectly still beneath me.

"What are you doing out here?" I ask, my quivering voice belying my rigid tone.

"I was getting water from the golf course pond." He says it like it should be obvious.

"What do you *want*?" I clarify.

"I can tell you what I didn't want," the stranger says, deep voice muffled by the ground. "I didn't want you to practically cut my arm off. Your bite is a lot worse than your bark. Here I am, trying to help you, and you cut the crap out of me! Every beast and carnivore within a mile is going to be coming over here to get a taste."

"What do you want?" I ask again.

"First off, featherweight, I want my pride back. You've got to weigh eighty pounds max, and you took me down." He makes a sound, a bumpy, weird sound from deep in his throat. It takes me a minute to realize what it is. Laughter. He's laughing!

I tighten my grip on his arms. "You're insane. Will you shut up before you blow my cover?"

His laughter stops. "Before *I* blow your cover? *Me?* First rule of desolation is *never use a light after sunset*! You can be spotted from ten miles away. You're the crazy one, my friend. Not me."

One of my dogs back home is a Rottweiler-hound mix.

When she senses danger, a Mohawk of fur rises on her back. The hair on the back of my neck bristles, and I let go of him, spinning in a circle, searching the darkness. "What have I done?" I whisper, and fall to my hands and knees, feeling around until I find my gun. Without waiting to see what the stranger does, I run.

The dead grass is smooth and even under my feet. At the house, I take the deck steps two at a time and burst into the family room with the leather sofa. "We have to go. Now!" I blurt. "I totally messed up."

Fiona stands up from the sofa and steps in front of her brother. Bowen walks through the front door. Behind me, footsteps pound up the deck stairs. I whip around in time to see the silhouette of a man cross the deck and stop at the back door. From inside the house, two guns click and I know precisely where they are aimed.

"Please don't shoot me. Please." The man lifts his hands, a gesture barely visible in the dark. "The kid cut me and I'm bleeding pretty bad. I was wondering if you could help me out real quick."

"Who're you?" Bowen asks.

"My name is Kevin. You've got about ten minutes before the raiders get here, since your watchdog was stupid enough to turn on a flashlight."

My face starts to burn with fury and embarrassment. The beast-boy grumbles in his sleep, and I can see the gleam of Jonah's good eye in the darkness.

"Jack? Please say you didn't turn on a light," Bowen says.

I don't reply because the room lights up with a rosy glow

that makes our shadows sweep across the walls. I look out the window as a pink flare arcs across the sky.

Bowen groans. "That looks close. Fo, keep your gun on Kevin. Let's get him to the master-bedroom closet where we can turn on a light. Jonah, come and get us if you hear or see anything."

"Got it," Fo says, voice gruff. Jonah doesn't say a thing.

"Jack, you lead."

Without a word I walk past Bowen, with Kevin hot on my heels. The master bedroom is on this level, past the kitchen and down a wide hall. The master closet is massive, with tattered clothes hanging on wooden hangers above rows and rows of rat-eaten shoes. I can't see any of this in the dark, but I memorized everything about this house during the day—just in case.

Inside the closet, Bowen shuts the door and turns on a flashlight, shining it in the stranger's face. He flinches and covers his eyes. There is a tattoo on the back of his hand—the *mark*. But there are no lines drawn through the circle, no recorded doses of vaccination.

"Show me your palms and arms," Bowen demands. The man holds out his arms and hands, palms up, and Bowen moves the light over them, searching for raider marks. I don't look for the marks because my eyes are riveted on the stranger's left arm. It is covered with blood that is dripping onto the hardwood floor. Bowen moves the flashlight to the source of the bleeding—a gaping gash, exposing muscle, two inches above the man's elbow.

Bowen's eyes meet mine. "Not bad," he says. I shrug.

"Do you have coagulant?" Kevin asks, gently prodding the wound. Compared to me, he's tall, but not nearly as tall as

Bowen. He looks right at me and I almost gasp. He's not quite a man. He's young. And surprisingly handsome.

"We have coagulant, but we don't have much. I don't think we should waste it," Fo says, still aiming her gun at the guy.

"Waste it?" Kevin looks at his wound again. "It's not like I did this to myself. Your little watchdog did it. I can't be bleeding like this and wander around out there."

I take a closer look at the gash. I've seen worse. I've also fixed worse. "I can suture it."

Fo, Bowen, and Kevin all turn and stare at me.

"My dad does this sort of stuff all the time. Only, I'll need water. To clean it out first and to wash my hands. I'll go get Jonah's pack."

Fo and Bowen look at each other, as if communicating a silent message. "We don't have any water to spare," Bowen says. I keep quiet, but I have to fight the urge to remind him that we have a backpack loaded with water. More than enough.

Kevin glares at Bowen and Fo, then turns his fuming, accusatory gaze on me before rifling through the clothes hanging in the closet. He stops rifling when he gets to a white cotton button-down shirt. Taking it from the hanger, he holds his right hand out to me, palm up. "I need your knife," he snaps, brows furrowed.

"Why?" I ask, wary.

His jaw tenses and releases, and then he shoves the shirt at me. "Please cut me a large triangular bandage."

Aha. Now I understand what he is doing. I take the shirt and, without putting it on the filthy ground, do my best to cut a large triangle. When I am done, Kevin holds his arm out. I wrap the fabric around his biceps and pull it tight to slow blood loss. He gasps as I knot the bandage into place.

"Sorry," I say.

The closet door swings open and Jonah, still holding the sleeping child-beast, strides inside. "Someone is coming," he says. "A big group. They're on the far side of the golf course. We need to go. Now."

"How many?" Bowen asks.

"I don't know, but they're carrying weapons. They're reflecting moonlight."

"Where should we go?" My voice trembles. I don't want to be doing this. I want to go home. I want to be safe. I close my eyes and mentally push my fear aside. A warm hand comes down on my shoulder, and I open my eyes and find myself staring at a close face. Kevin's.

"It's going to be okay," he says, his voice filled with gentle reassurance. "Don't be scared."

"I'm not scared," I snap.

"I am," Bowen says, looking at Fo. "We need to find somewhere to hide. Somewhere safe."

"I have a safe place a few miles from here. If you want my help?" Kevin asks.

"Yes, for now," Bowen says.

"Come on, watchdog." Kevin ruffles my short hair like we're old friends, and then he strides out of the closet like he's the one in charge.

We scramble through the house for our possessions. I get

my backpack. Fo and Bowen get theirs. Jonah carries the beast-boy. Without asking, Kevin takes Jonah's massive backpack from the kitchen counter and eases it onto his shoulders, careful not to bump his injured arm.

"Don't you have any stuff of your own?" I ask him as we make our way toward the front door.

"Oh, I do all right. It's down there on the golf course, probably about to be intercepted by raiders."

"Well, that wasn't very smart."

He leans in close to me so our noses are almost touching, and I force myself not to take a step back. That would show weakness. "Here's the thing, Jack," he says. His breath smells like bubblegum. "I wasn't planning on getting stabbed tonight. If I knew you were going to turn on a flashlight and attack me when I tried to help you, I would have been sure to have my backpack *on*." Stepping away from me, he rolls his shoulders under the backpack's weight. "What's in this thing?"

"Water," Fo answers. "Lots of it."

"And you wouldn't spare any for me?" Kevin grumbles.

"No, sorry. And be careful with it!"

We step out the front door and as one, pause, looking toward the golf course. Everything is quiet and I wonder if Jonah was wrong about seeing something. Slowly, so slowly I don't realize I am hearing it at all for a moment, the night begins to pulse. The thump of feet grows steadily louder and becomes accompanied by the occasional clink of metal. I focus my eyes in the direction of the sound, and my knees knock together. The newly risen moon shines red against the eastern horizon and gleams against metal objects moving just beyond the edge of the property—weapons. I put my clammy hand over my gun.

"They're too close! We can't outrun them. Not with Jonah carrying the beast," Bowen whispers.

"I can outrun them," I blurt, and then realize what I've just volunteered to do—be the decoy.

"So can I," Kevin whispers.

Bowen's eyes go from me to Kevin and back to me again. Fo puts her hand on my arm. "Are you sure you're willing to do that for us?" she asks.

I stare at her, silent, because I'm *not* sure. Kevin's hand comes down on my shoulder. "We're sure," he says. "It's our—*your*—only chance for survival. Trust me."

Bowen nods. "Okay. Just don't lose Jonah's backpack! And meet us at Leyden Lake tomorrow at noon!"

"Leyden Lake, tomorrow at noon. Got it. You ready, feather-weight?" I grit my teeth and nod. Kevin grins and shoves me forward. "Oh no!" he yells. "Here they come! Run!"

My heart explodes in my chest, my feet dig into the drive-way, I put my head down, and I sprint.

CHAPTER 13

When I reach the road, I turn left and hope I really *can* outrun the raiders. I hope I can run to a safe place. But I don't know where any safe places are. I don't know if safety even exists. The darkness is pressing in on me, hiding things, obscuring danger, and I don't know what to do, except run and run and run. I have been programmed to run. Run from danger. Run for safety. Run to live.

But where?

My feet keep pounding the pavement and I feel small, insignificant, like if I'm not careful I'm going to run into oblivion. Run off the side of the world in my sprint for the ever-elusive safety I've been taught to hope for.

I hear feet pounding behind me and my muscles go taut. I'm fast. Too fast for Bowen or Fiona to keep up with. Too fast for Jonah. Too fast for Kevin with his injured arm and Jonah's massive backpack weighing him down. So that means one of the raiders must be faster than me, and I am about to get caught. Without thinking, I veer into the nearest yard, into a copse of stark aspen skeletons. Twigs cover the ground, cracking beneath my feet.

"Stop!" a voice hisses from behind. I don't stop. Instead, I try to run faster, veering between tree trunks, flinging my arms up against the branches whipping my face. A hand grabs my elbow and I try to yank away, but the grip tightens. I stop running and grab my gun, flipping around and pressing it against a chest.

"I've got nineteen bullets in here," I whisper. "But this close, it will only take one to kill you."

"Whoa, featherweight." It's Kevin, and he's gasping for air. "Don't point"—*gasp*—"that thing at me!" *Gasp.* Relieved, I lower the gun. I regret it instantly.

Kevin grabs me, throws me onto my back, and climbs on top of me, his hand pressed over my mouth. Compared to me he's huge. I can hardly breathe, can hardly move as I squirm between him and my bulky backpack in an effort to get away. I freeze with horror as he presses his cheek against mine, his lips brushing my ear.

"Hold still, Jack. They took the bait," he whispers, his breath cool on my sweaty neck. "The raiders."

I'm already frozen, so I stay that way, my ribs straining with every breath to lift Kevin's weight. Within seconds I can hear the sound of running feet over the noise of my pounding heart, over the swish of Kevin's breath in my ear. His body stiffens on top of mine, and he wraps an arm around my head and buries his face against my neck.

"Don't move," he whispers. I don't need the warning.

The pounding feet slow to a walk, scuffing the street. Noises carry to me, whispered questions, the sound of guns being cocked, of knives snapping open, of baseball bats smacking into open palms, and it is the scariest thing I have ever heard in my seventeen years of life. And then one sentence carries to me:

"Hastings should be here any minute with the dog."

Hastings. That's the name the cowboy said. Hastings is the leader of the raiders. And he's bringing a dog to sniff us out. I begin to tremble.

"Give me your knife," Kevin whispers. He eases off me and carefully slips his arms out of Jonah's pack, easing it silently onto the ground beside us. I slide the knife from my belt and hand it to him. Crouching, he darts out of the trees and into the moonlit night. I roll off of my lumpy backpack and onto my stomach to watch.

Men are everywhere, like an ant hill that someone has kicked. If ants still existed. They're on the road, darting into yards, going into houses. Kevin slinks to the side of the road and then gives me the biggest shock of my life. He stands tall and walks right into the middle of the raiders.

"Any sign of them yet?" he asks.

The closest raider turns and looks at Kevin and stops walking. "We know they came this way. Striker saw them go into one of these yards, but he was too far away to see exactly where. More than likely they're holed up in a house. They have a woman with them!"

"Yeah, I saw the flare. But you called this many guys out just for one woman?"

"Dire straits call for radical action, man. Flint shot a pink flare yesterday, but these runners didn't stick to his map. We lost them—until tonight. And since the women broke out of the compound last week—"

"They what?" Kevin blurts.

"Yeah. Eight days ago—every single one of them. They had help from the inside. That's why we need this new woman so bad. Hastings is on his way here now with a dog, so it's only a matter of time before we find her."

Kevin nods. "Good. I'll check this house while we wait." He turns toward my hiding place.

The raider grabs his shoulder, stopping him before he can step up onto the sidewalk. "What happened to your arm?" he asks.

Kevin pauses and glances at the dark-stained bandage tied over his biceps. "I got in a fight with Jack." My eyes grow round, and I press myself a little harder against the ground, hand clenching my gun.

The raider chuckles. "Jack's got a temper."

"Yeah, and he's surprisingly quick," Kevin says with a laugh.

"No he's not. You're just slow."

They step up onto the curb together and start walking toward my hiding place. The raider peers into the trees—my trees. His eyes gleam in his hairy face.

"Hey! Look!" Kevin whispers. The raider's gaze jerks away from me and follows Kevin's pointing finger to the house next door. "I think I saw something in that house. Let's go check it out."

He leaves with the raider. And I'm a sitting duck. And the dog is coming. And despite the fact that I've read an entire library of survival guides and karate guides and self-defense guides, I have no idea what to do. None of the guides covered being trapped in a copse of dead trees, surrounded by raiders. My head drops to the ground, my forehead in dirt, and I fight back panic.

Not even a minute later, I hear a dog bark and my stomach clenches, making me want to vomit. Another sound slowly oozes into my hearing, a sound that tugs at my memory, bringing me back to the world before bees died and before children turned into beasts: the low, steady rumble of an engine. I cautiously lift my head and look toward the sound.

Moonlight reflects off of a machine zooming up the street toward me. A four-wheeler. A dark shadow sits in the driver's seat, and another shadow lopes alongside the four-wheeler—a dog. A *big* dog. The raiders move out of the road to give the four-wheeler room to drive. One raider backs up until the heels of his steel-toed boots are within my arm's reach. I don't dare move, not even to put my head down. A sour smell wafts to me, burning my sinuses, and I realize it is coming from the man standing in front of me—a body-odor, dead-animal, unwashed-underwear smell. It might be the last thing I ever smell in my life.

My throat clenches. My eyes sting. If I die here tonight, my parents will never know what happened to me. Why did I want to find my brother? I want to go home. I never want to leave my house again. I am so dead.

CHAPTER 14

My dad told me once that if a man falls off a cliff, he has a terror-induced heart attack before he hits the ground. He's dead by the time he lands. As I lay here in the trees, my heart is on the verge of exploding in my chest. Maybe I will die before I am found. Death by terror. It's an appealing way to die from where I am right now.

The four-wheeler stops and the driver steps down. Even in the dark I can tell that he's a top-heavy guy, with a thick neck and thicker shoulders. He hooks a chain onto the dog's silver-spiked collar, and just in time. The dog turns toward my hiding place and yanks the chain taut. The animal's barking fills the night, and every single raider turns in my direction.

"Looks like we're close, Hastings," someone calls over the dog's barking. "Let's surround this house and—"

"I found something!" a man shouts. Everyone's attention is drawn from my direction and switched to the house next door. Kevin is leaning out of a broken upstairs window, my knife in his hand. The raiders swarm toward the house. The man with the dog yanks on its chain, forcing it to come with him, when all the dog really wants is the thing hiding in the aspen trees. The animal digs its feet into the dead grass and lurches toward me, but the raider holds the chain firm. He curses and kicks the dog squarely in the ribs. The dog yelps and skulks behind its master.

Within ten seconds, the yard is empty. Cautiously, I get onto my hands and knees and see Jonah's backpack—the extra water that Fo and Bowen are so touchy about. I try to lift it but barely move it two inches from the ground, so set it back down. I can't carry it, not when it will weigh me down. With a pang of regret, I jump to my feet and start sprinting toward the house in the opposite direction the raiders went.

Before I've stepped onto the next property, someone grabs me from behind, a rock-hard arm around my waist, and I start swinging my elbow into firm ribs. The person grunts and whispers, "Jack! It's me, Kevin! Let's take the four-wheeler and get out of here!"

I stop fighting. "What about Jonah's backpack? The water?"

"Forget the backpack! We'll get more water when we're not about to die!" We start sprinting toward the four-wheeler, my backpack thumping against my back. I jump onto the seat behind Kevin and throw my arms around his waist as he revs the engine. The machine lurches forward. I tighten my hold on him and watch in horror as the raiders pour out of the house, guns pointing at me—us. Kevin ducks. So do I. Bullets fly through the air around us, something tugs on the back of my neck like I'm being pinched, and then we turn onto another road and the sound of the four-wheeler overpowers the sound of fading gunfire.

Kevin sits up straight and I loosen my hold on him a bit. "Wahoo!" he hollers. And then he does that thing again. That *laughing*. I press my face against his back and cry. Wind tugs on my tackle vest and rushes through my short hair, and I can't stop crying.

We drive for maybe fifteen minutes, circling dark streets in every direction, and then Kevin stops the four-wheeler, turning it off.

"Will you drive me home?" I ask with a sniffle.

He climbs down and looks at me. "Are you crying?" His voice is soft and almost gentle. I dab my nose with the back of my hand and nod. Kevin leans toward me and wipes the tears from my cheeks. His fingertips are as rough as sandpaper.

"Come on, Jack. We need to ditch the ride." He helps me down, and it's a good thing because my legs are so weak I can hardly stand. Kevin fishes in his pocket and pulls out a small ball of something. He unwinds some of it, and I realize it is thread-thin wire. In less than two minutes, he's used the wire to anchor the four-wheeler's steering wheel so the tires are aimed north down a long, straight street. Next, he winds wire around the handlebar of the four-wheeler—the accelerator. "Hold the brake down with your hands," he says. "When I say let go, let go and jump out of the way." I nod and press the brake down with my hands. He cranks the keys and the four-wheeler roars to life. "Let go!" he shouts. I do and watch as the vehicle peels out and speeds down the road, the roar of the engine fading until it is eventually replaced by silence.

I look at Kevin, my jaw hanging open with shock. "Why did you do that? I could have driven that thing home and been there in an hour!"

He shakes his head. "The engine would have brought every raider within hearing distance. You never would have made it back to Denver alive." He tugs on my backpack and I let it slip off my weary shoulders without protest. His fingers find the back of my neck and touch a spot that's aching with tension. He pulls his hand away and sticks his fingers in his mouth. "Were you shot, Jack?"

"No," I say.

"Then whose blood is all over your neck?"

I touch the back of my neck. My skin is slick with sticky moisture. Bringing my fingers back into view, I gasp.

Kevin leans close and looks at my neck. "I don't think it's deep. Tell you what. If you doctor me, I'll doctor you. Deal?"

I start to nod but stop. The pain in my neck is growing stronger with each heartbeat. "Deal," I say, and sniffle one last time.

Careful not to bump his knife wound, Kevin puts his arms into my backpack's straps and loosens them so they're not straining against his chest. "We have to hurry," he whispers. "And be sure to keep your voice down. But I'd be willing to bet a packet of coagulant that the raiders are going to be following that four-wheeler for a while."

We start walking through a world aglow with eerie red moonlight. I look up at the sky. All but the brightest stars are hidden behind haze. "The moon looks like blood," I whisper.

"There's a fire burning somewhere," Kevin says. "The smoke makes the moon look red. So, where are you headed anyway?"

I firm my shoulders and cringe at the flare of pain in my neck, so let them slouch. "None of your business."

"Really?" His voice is full of mock surprise. "That's where I'm headed too." He starts walking west toward the massive shadow of the Rocky Mountains, and I follow a step behind, but he slows his pace until we walk side by side. He veers into the closest yard and starts walking on the dead grass, and it reminds me about what the vagabond said.

"We need to try to stay off the roads and sidewalks," I say.

"Agreed."

"You know . . ." I look at his profile. "It's pretty lucky the raiders left the keys in the four-wheeler."

Kevin laughs. "Yes, it is. I'm generally a pretty lucky guy." He takes a long look at me. "So, what's with the kid that big guy's been carrying around?"

"He's a beast," I whisper, peering into the windows of the house we're passing.

Kevin pauses and the moon highlights the planes of his face. "You're traveling with a tainted one? Is he still infected?"

"Tainted one?" I have never heard a beast called a *tainted* one. "Where are you from?"

He starts walking once more, and I stay a step behind, but he slows his pace so I am walking beside him again. "I'm from

here. I've been surviving here for about four years—ever since they branded the vaccinated kids."

"Are you a Siren?"

"Siren?" he asks without slowing his pace.

"They lead people away from the raiders."

"I think they're just a myth." He glances at me. "Why?"

"I'm trying to find my brother. I thought that maybe, if the Sirens were real, I could see if any of them met him. His name is Dean. Have you ever heard of him?"

"So, you're out here looking for your brother Dean," he says. "Is he from Denver too?"

The hair on the back of my neck bristles. "How do you know I'm from Denver?" I place my hand on my gun.

"Why is it the small guys always go for the guns? Look, I am only trying to help you out. I know the day you left *Denver* because the raiders shot off four flares. If you're worried about trusting me, think of this: we were standing in the middle of twenty raiders, and I saved you."

"Yeah, but you walked right into the middle of them like you're one of them." I fight the sudden urge to run. "They talked to you! They told you stuff like they knew you! Like you're a raider." I stop walking. "*Are* you a raider?"

"I already showed you my hands and arms. I'm clean."

"I didn't look," I whisper.

He sighs and walks up to the nearest house, onto the front porch. Stepping into the darkest recesses, he leans against the front door and folds his arms over his chest. "Come here," he whispers. I slowly walk onto the porch, wondering what in the world we're doing standing in the shadows beside broken flowerpots. "How many raiders do you think there are?"

"Thousands?" I shrug. "I have no clue."

"Neither do they. If you think about it, there have got to be guys coming and going all the time, right? So many men started coming and going from the raiders' camps that they had to mark themselves so they'd know who belonged where. That way they couldn't just walk into each other's headquarters and steal food or guns." He holds his hands out to me, palms up. "Feel."

I place my hands on top of his and gently trace his palms. His hands are wide and warm. Thick calluses coat the skin between the lines, but there are no brands—no raider marks.

"And here." He moves my hand to his forearm, the place where the southern raiders mark themselves with knife-slash scars. He leans over me, and all of a sudden I feel awkward touching him. I pull my hand away and take a step back.

"I promise I won't hurt you, Jack," he whispers. He steps toward me, takes my hand in his, and very slowly brings my fingers to the skin just below the bend in his arm. It is smooth beneath my fingertips, and warm. I trail my fingers down to his wrist. There are no markings. He sweeps my fingers over his other arm and it is the same. Clean. "Does that help?"

I nod and clear my throat and look at the ground, wondering if my heart is pounding from fear or from touching Kevin. Or both.

"Good. Now try to relax a little bit. You're so tense I'm getting a headache." He presses on his temples.

"How can I relax? I'm stuck out here with nowhere to go,

trying to find my brother!" I bite the side of my cheek and stare beyond the front porch.

"I already told you that I know a place where you and your friends can crash for a day or two—a safe place where the wolves won't get you, that the raiders don't know exists. You can plan where to go from there."

"Wolves? I thought they were in the mountains."

"They are, but that's where we're going. Come on." He steps out of the shadows and waits for me to fall into step beside him. "So, you left Denver yesterday. Did you leave family behind?"

My throat constricts with unshed tears. Unable to speak, I nod.

"Aren't you afraid they'll follow you?"

"I wrote them a note and said I'd be living inside the wall," I whisper. "They won't follow me there."

"How old are you Jack?"

"Twelve," I say, voice firm. When he doesn't say anything, I look at him.

"Twelve?" He shakes his head. "You've got to be the most capable twelve-year-old I have ever met. Bowen's lucky to have you along."

I stop dead in my tracks as a new realization sets in. "I don't know where the lake is that we're meeting them at tomorrow."

"But *I* do, and Bowen does. Trust me." He claps his hand on my shoulder. "I'll find them again."

CHAPTER 15

After what feels like hours of walking, we pass the last neighborhood and start going up into the foothills at the base of the mountains. I stop and let my exhausted body sag.

Kevin stops a few paces ahead of me. "Do you need a break?"

I shake my head. "No. I'm fine." It's a total lie. My bones feel like rubber trying to support lead muscles, but I'm not going to tell him that.

Kevin reaches into his pants pocket. "Here." He holds something out, and I lift my hand, palm up. He places a small round thing in my hand.

I squeeze and feel a hard lump wrapped in paper. "What is it?"

"Bubblegum."

I gasp and bring it to my nose, inhaling.

"Unwrap it first!"

I pull the two paper ends and the gum spins out of the wrapper. I pop it into my mouth and a surge of joy mixed with nostalgia fills me as I'm taken back to autumn nights trick-or-treating with my brothers. I love bubblegum. It is as hard as a rock, but after a minute of gnawing on it, the sugar bursts into my mouth and down my throat and seems to zoom into my body.

Reenergized, I take a step forward, and Kevin takes my hand. His hand swallows mine in warmth and he starts gently pulling me uphill. "What are you doing?" I ask, twisting my hand away from him.

"Helping you." He takes my hand again and pulls me. It feels awkward, having a guy hold my hand, and makes my heart beat a little bit faster than it already is. But I'm too tired to fight it. Our feet snap the twigs and branches that litter the ground—a constant reminder that everything is dead. After a while, the bubblegum loses its sweetness and turns tough in my mouth. I spit it out and keep pressing forward, letting Kevin help pull me uphill.

When the moon has moved over half the sky, Kevin squeezes my hand. "We're almost there."

I blink my grainy eyes and look around. I don't know where *there* is, but it doesn't look like we're almost anywhere. We're struggling up the side of a shrub- and tree-skeleton-covered slope. Well, I'm struggling. Kevin's not. Even though he's wearing my backpack *and* pulling on my hand, he acts like we're out on a happy little hike, about to have a picnic.

I stop walking and let my eyes close, and the world seems to spin around me. My jaw softens, my breathing slows, and my brain fills with dark cotton.

"Jack," Kevin whispers. I peel open my heavy eyelids. He's standing right in front of me, his face mere inches from mine. I jump and take a step back, pulling my hand from his. "I think you were asleep," he says. "We're almost there. I promise. Come on."

He takes my hand again and pulls me into a dense copse of some kind of dead bushes that scratch my arms and catch on my clothes. If I had long hair, the thorns would be catching in the tangles. No brittle branches snap beneath our feet, and it occurs to me that the ground has been cleared of loose tinder, whether for firewood or to make it silent, I can't say. But it makes me wonder about this Kevin person I'm blindly following. He's smart. He's a survivor. He's a fast runner. And he could take me down in two seconds, tired or not.

He leads me to a small shrub and bends, pulling it out of the ground. I blink and try to see more clearly what he is doing. No, he's not uprooting a dead shrub, he's lifted a perfect square of ground with a dead shrub attached to it, revealing a dark hole a little wider than a car tire. He steps into the hole and disappears, as if the darkness has gobbled him up. I peer into the sphere of black.

"What is this?" I whisper, eyeing the rungs of a ladder that lead into the darkness.

"A fortified structure," Kevin says, his voice coiling up from the darkness. "It's quite cozy. In fact, it's my home."

I look around. I'm more than halfway up the foothills, in a totally secluded area. What if he's leading me into a trap? What if there are ten men hiding below, waiting for me? What if Kevin's a murderer? I clasp my head in my hands and try to silence the what-ifs.

"Jack." His voice carries right up to me.

"What?"

"I know what you're thinking."

I doubt it.

"Have your gun out if that makes you feel better. I swear you're going to be safe down here."

Okay, so he does know what I'm thinking. I study the surrounding terrain again. Fresh sweat breaks out on the bridge of my nose and I feel like I might vomit. Not that there's anything in my stomach—the oysters are long digested. I don't know where to go. I don't know what to do. But what other choice do I have?

I take a deep breath, take my gun from my belt, and then step into darkness.

CHAPTER 16

The best hiding place is one that doesn't seem to exist. If I go down, I will never be found. I hope that is a good thing.

I pull the square piece of earth shut above me. With every step down, my muscles wind tighter, so by the time I reach the bottom of the ladder, I feel like a jack-in-the-box, ready to burst, and my palms are so damp I can hardly hold my gun.

My feet touch down on packed dirt, and cool air coats my face with sticky dampness. I turn and face a doorway spilling out orange light and step through onto a clean cement floor. My mouth falls open.

"Good thing there aren't any flies down here. You would be catching your dinner," Kevin says, followed by a laugh. He is standing beside the door—beside me. He puts his index finger under my chin and snaps my mouth shut. It falls back open.

With his uninjured arm, Kevin moves me a little deeper inside and then steps out the door and starts up the ladder.

"I shut the top," I say without taking my eyes from his home.

"I'm going to lock it." His feet thump on the ladder.

I am standing in a large room lit by two sputtering kerosene lamps. There's a worn brown tweed sofa against one wall, with two brown leather chairs facing it, and a coffee table between them. A red threadbare rug is laid out on the cement floor under the table. But the most shocking thing is the sculptures. Wire sculptures. A rabbit and a frog made of yards and yards of barbed wire perch on the coffee table, staring at each other. Wire cowboy boots and a wire saddle hang from the wall. And then there are hands, lots and lots of hands, in all positions—clenched into fists, fingers splayed, clasped in prayer, holding wire flowers.

On the far side of the room is a wooden chair with the chest and torso of a wire man sitting in it. Beside the chair is a box filled with tools—wire cutters, pliers, a blowtorch, a metal file. And next to that is a closed door.

"So, what do you think?"

With a jolt I realize I've let my guard down, and Kevin is standing right behind me with his hands in his pants pockets. Still holding my gun, I turn and study him by the light of the lamps. His hair is a couple of shades darker than copper and touches his shoulders, and his eyes are the color of the sky at sunrise. I tilt my head to the side. It is the first good look I've gotten of him, and I'm surprised to discover there's something familiar about him. Maybe it's because I've been in his presence for a few hours and, whether I've actually seen his face or not, I've sort of gotten to know him.

He takes his hands out of his pockets and gently pries my gun from my icy fingers. Without a word, he removes the magazine and then hands both pieces back to me. "I'm not going to hurt you, so you don't need to keep that loaded down here."

I nod and holster the gun, and tuck the magazine with nineteen bullets into my pants pocket. "Did you make all of these?"

His eyes light up. "Yeah. When I was a kid, my grandpa took me to a museum in Denver that had a woman and child sculpted out of barbed wire. I wanted to be a sculptor when I grew up. I get lonely down here sometimes and needed something to do to keep myself busy, so I figured I might as well learn how to sculpt with wire. One day I'll get brave and finish him." He nods at the torso. "Or try sculpting a face. If I live long enough." He grimaces and looks at his cut arm. "Now, if you don't mind, I need you to fix this." Skepticism plain in his furrowed brow, he looks at me. "You really do know how to suture, right?" I nod. "In that case, follow me."

He picks up my backpack and both kerosene lamps and leads me through the door at the far end of the room—beside the wire torso.

Another shock waits on the other side. I walk into a kitchen, complete with a small table and two chairs, two burners, a sink, a small stove, and a microwave. Metal cupboards line the walls on my left and my right, and I can't help myself. I walk up to a cupboard and open it. Shock number four: it is packed with giant labeled cans of food. *Flour. Beans. Red wheat. Dehydrated onions.*

Dehydrated eggs. Powdered butter. Buttermilk pancake mix. Baby formula. I reach for the pancake mix and practically weep. It is full!

Kevin clears his throat and I put the canister back. He's standing by the sink, a first-aid kit in his hands. "You have to pump the water in, but there's an endless supply, so use what you need. The waste water is pumped into an underground stream and flushed out."

I nod. "Take off your shirt." The words make my cheeks flame, so I turn to the sink and start pumping the water handle. Water flows from the faucet and I scrub my hands with a small cake of white soap. Next, I open the bottom right pocket on my tackle vest and remove a small plastic bag. Beside me, Kevin begins unbuttoning his shirt, once a shade of blue but now more of a tan. By the light of the lamps, everything about him is a faded shade of brown. He looks like a sepia photograph of the old West.

Easing his shirt off, he drops it into the empty sink, but when he tries to loosen the fabric bandage from his arm, sweat breaks out on his face and the air hisses between his teeth. I take a closer look at his wound and my stomach turns. I've seen a lot of wounds. I've doctored a lot of wounds under my father's supervision. I wish my father were here right now because the fabric bandage has gotten stuck in the coagulated blood.

I take my knife from my belt and flip out the blade. Kevin studies me with wary eyes but doesn't say anything as I slice the excess fabric from the bandage. "Maybe if we soak the fabric, it will come off more easily."

He nods and leans into the sink. I pump the water for him.

When he's thoroughly drenched the wound, he moves a chair from the small table to the side of the counter and sits. Very gently, I attempt to peel the dripping fabric from his flesh while he studies my face.

"So, how'd you learn to do this?" He talks to me like we're old friends.

"My dad's an oral surgeon. He's been teaching me how to do this type of thing since I was . . ." I close my mouth. Since I was about thirteen, which is a year older than I am pretending to be.

"Since you were what?"

I glance up at him and start to tuck my hair behind my ears . . . until I remember I don't have hair to tuck. Nervous habits are hard to break. "Old enough to learn how to do it," I say, and gently tug at the fabric.

Kevin groans. "You're killing me, Jack."

"Sorry."

"Hold on." He pinches the bandage between his finger and thumb. "You know the easiest way to remove a sticky Band-Aid?" In one swift yank he rips the fabric from his skin. His scream explodes into the room. I can picture the sound filling the other room, rushing up the ladder, and bursting out into the night like a beacon for every living thing within five miles. I clasp my hands over his mouth and hold the sound in. Tears stream down his cheeks and wash over my fingers, but he stops screaming and whimpers instead. Slowly, I let go.

"For the love of . . ." He wipes his eyes and sniffles. "These aren't tears. I am not crying," he gasps. "My eyes are just dripping from the shock of that."

My face does something that it hasn't done in days and days, maybe even months. The edges of my mouth quirk up. Just a little bit. Kevin notices and smiles back even though he's gone pale and tears are still dripping from his eyes. "Apparently the featherweight likes pain."

"As long as it's someone else's." Even my voice has a smile in it, and something tiny and warm flickers inside me for a moment, before fading back to darkness.

I clean his freshly bleeding wound, douse it with antiseptic from the first-aid kit, and then open the small packet I took from my vest—a curved suture needle with a long strand of thread attached. "This is really going to hurt without you being numbed."

"I figured," Kevin says, grimacing and leaning away from his wound. He grips the back of the chair with his right hand. "Ready."

I pinch the wound closed and ease the half-moon needle into his skin, looping it underneath the cut and through the skin on the other side. Kevin gasps and squeezes his eyes shut. There's a lot of fresh blood, so after each stitch I wipe the wound with the wet bandage. The cut is long, about two inches. It takes me several minutes to sew it together. Kevin doesn't say a thing, just groans through gritted teeth and keeps his face averted while I work. When I'm done, I tie off the thread and slather the wound with more antiseptic.

"All done," I say.

Kevin, face ashen and damp with sweat, takes a look at his swollen, bloody wound. "Not bad." He stands and puts his face in the sink. "How about you give me a little water."

I push the water lever and he lets the icy flow cover his face.

After a few seconds he stands up out of the water and looks at me. "Turn around and let me see your neck."

I do what he says. He leans in close and his breath brushes over the soft skin behind my ears. Gently, he folds down the collar of my tackle vest and I shiver at his touch. "I need you to take this thing off."

"No!" I turn to face him and wrap my arms over my chest. Heat scorches its way up my neck, over my ears, and sears my face. "It hardly even hurts. It can't be that bad," I blurt.

"You're right, it's not that bad, but the collar of your vest is rubbing it. I'm afraid it will get caught in the scab, and I can tell you from personal experience, removing it isn't fun." He puts a hand on my arm and turns my back to him once again. "At least let me put some of this on it." He gets the antiseptic and carefully slathers it over the back of my neck. Leaning even closer, he blows on my skin, drying the antiseptic. With feather-gentle fingers, he puts some butterfly bandages over the cut. "There. That should help." His fingers go back to my arm, and he lifts the sleeve of my T-shirt up a couple of inches. "So, what's this scar from? I could feel it through your shirt."

I look at the fresh scar. "I got shot by a raider two months ago. They were trying to catch Fo."

"Did it hurt?"

"Not at first. They shot me and I didn't even realize it. Getting it stitched shut hurt."

He sets the things back into the first-aid kit and closes it. His face is still pale and his left arm is swollen and bulging around the stitches. "Would you mind helping me clean up a little? I can't lift my arm right now, or I'd do it myself." There is dried blood on his ribs where his arm has rubbed against them. I take his wet shirt out of the sink, carefully lift his injured arm, and start wiping. As his skin comes clean, my hand pauses. There are two puckered, round scars on his right ribs. I touch them with my fingertips, and Kevin shudders.

"Are these bullet scars?" I ask.

"Yeah. I was shot by raiders about a year and a half ago."

"What were you doing when they shot you?"

"Running from them."

I keep washing the dried blood from his skin. He's got a nice chest, and nice, tight abs. I clench my jaw and wonder what in the world is wrong with me. This is really not a good time to be noticing stupid things like that. I shouldn't notice them at all.

"There's a bathroom through that door." I jump at his voice, like I've been caught ogling him. With his good arm he points to the opposite end of the kitchen, to a small accordion-looking folding door. "There's a shower, but the water is really cold, and you have to pump it the whole time. But help yourself. The door locks. I'll be in the other room, trying to get some sleep before I go find your friends." He takes the dirty shirt from me and puts it back in the sink, then picks up one of the lamps and leaves the kitchen, shutting the door behind him. Taking the other lamp, I go into the bathroom and lock the accordion door.

The bathroom is tiny, with a metal toilet, a narrow shower stall, and a metal sink. A toothbrush and small cup sit on the rim of the sink. Above the sink is a medicine cabinet with a mirror. I peer into the mirror. Black bags sag beneath my eyes, making them look more gray than blue, and a layer of dirt clings to my dark hairline. A smattering of freckles stands out on my nose, and my thin face has a healthy suntan. I look so *boy* that there is nothing pretty about me—a fact that should make me glad. Instead, I want to cry.

I step away from the mirror and press my ear to the accordion door. Convinced that Kevin is not in the kitchen, I take off my clothes. There's no soap in the shower. I open the medicine cabinet and blink. A box of tampons? Seriously? And they're open. There are other things—Tylenol, shaving cream, razors, powdered shampoo, cakes of soap wrapped in cellophane, several toothbrushes still in their packages, and toothpaste. I take out some shampoo and soap and get wonderfully, blessedly clean in the frigid water.

When I am done and shivering, I go into the main room. Kevin is lying on a cot that just happens to have been moved to block the door leading out of his home. His quiet, rhythmic breathing is accompanied by the nearly inaudible whisper of moving air. I look up at the ceiling and see a small vent. I hold my fingers up to it and cool air flows around them.

A pillow and sleeping bag have been laid out on the sofa. I pop a few calorie tablets before setting the kerosene lamp on the coffee table and then crawl into the sleeping bag.

I lie on my side and stare at Kevin, wondering if he can be trusted, wondering if I dare fall asleep with him in the same room. His face is a perfect blend of rugged and pretty, with slightly full lips, arched eyebrows, and a square jaw. I wonder how old he is, and if he has a girlfriend. Or a wife. Inside the wall, girls and boys marry as young as fifteen in an effort to rebuild the population.

My eyes move down his face, over his neck, and stop on his chest. The blanket has slipped down around his waist and he's not wearing a shirt. I notice things I didn't notice about him when I was washing the blood from his skin, like how wide his chest is and how his chest and shoulders are several shades whiter than his arms and neck and—he clears his throat and I look back at his face, meeting his intense eyes. For once, he's not smiling.

Fire fills my body, burning my face and making it hard to breathe. "G'night," I grunt, rolling onto my other side so my back is to him. I sound just like my brothers. Kevin douses the kerosene lamp and the room goes black.

"Good night . . . *Jack*," he says. Something in his voice makes me feel even hotter, and for a brief moment I worry he might know that I'm a girl. But there's no way. I look like a boy. I sound like a boy. I move like a boy. I pull the sleeping bag up until it's covering my entire head.

CHAPTER 17

The real me exists only in dreams now. The other me? The one that exists in the real world? That's the fake me.

Golden waffles drenched in maple syrup fill my dreams. They're on a plate, being held out to me by someone. I tuck my long, thick hair behind my ears and look up into Kevin's smiling face. He has nice teeth. Really nice, like he still flosses even though the world's gone all wrong. My dad would like his teeth. I lean toward him, but there's something in his eyes that sets off alarm bells. It is the way he watches me, like a boy watching a girl. He reaches out and twines his fingers through my hair. And then it hits me. My hair is too long. I have forgotten to be a boy. And now he knows.

I gasp and sit up, struggling to pull the sleeping bag from my face.

"You all right?" a deep voice asks.

I get the sleeping bag down and am face-to-face with Kevin. He's sitting on the coffee table beside a burning kerosene lamp and leaning toward me. I run my fingers over my buzzed hair and sag with relief. My hair isn't long and beautiful. It's short and ugly. I smooth my hair down at the crown—the spot that always stands up when I sleep—and Kevin smiles, flashing his pearly teeth. I can't help but look at them to see if they really are as nice as in my dream.

They are.

"I didn't mean to startle you awake. I said your name a few times before I shook your shoulder." He runs his tongue over his teeth. "And just for the record, I do floss."

My mouth falls open but no words come out.

He puts his callused finger beneath my chin and chuckles when my teeth snap shut. "You talk in your sleep, featherweight. There's floss in the cabinet above the bathroom sink—behind the spare toothbrushes—if you want some. You can use whatever you need while you're here. I get a few hours of accumulated solar power every day, so the stove and microwave will work for a hot meal or two."

He stands up and my eyes move over his hiking boots, jeans, and button-down shirt that probably used to be green plaid but is more like tan plaid now. There's a backpack on his back and a knife on his belt. And a gun—a Glock—the twin to my dad's gun, except his is fitted with a scratched and worn silencer. Silencers are used only when you want to kill someone without alerting others to your presence. A twinge of fear shudders through me.

Kevin takes a camouflage baseball cap from the table beside him and pulls it over his hair, which is in a ponytail at the nape of his neck. I jump from the sofa and let the sleeping bag slither down to my feet. "Are we leaving already?" I look at my watch. It's almost seven a.m. Stepping from the sleeping bag, I look around for my shoes and socks. They're where I left them, right beside the sofa.

"Jack."

"What?" I start pulling on my socks.

"*I'm* leaving. You are staying here."

I have put on both of my socks and shoved one of my feet into a shoe before his words sink in. Dropping my shoelaces, I look at him. "What did you say?"

"You can't come. I'm going alone."

"*What?*"

"To find your friends. I'm going alone. That"—he gestures toward the exit—"is no place for a . . ." He studies me for a long moment. "For a *twelve-year-old.*"

I glare at him and yank my shoelaces tight, then get my other shoe, pulling it onto my foot.

"I'll be back as soon as I can. Help yourself to whatever you want to eat," Kevin says, walking to the exit.

"I'm coming with you," I insist, tying my other shoe.

"Bye, Jack." His eyes meet mine for a brief second, and then he steps out the door, shutting it behind him. I stand and run into the kitchen for my backpack—there's no way I'm sitting here alone while he goes out looking for my friends. I'll follow him if I have to. I loop the backpack over one shoulder, sprint to the exit, twist the doorknob, and tug. My hand flies off of the handle and I stumble backward. I twist the knob again and realize it won't twist. Putting both my hands on the knob and bracing a foot on the doorframe, I pull as hard as I can. The door stays firmly shut.

"Kevin!" I scream. Balling my hands into fists, I pound on the door and scream his name again, but the door stays shut, and Kevin never answers.

I twist the metal key on the side of the kerosene lamp and the flame dies. Dim sunlight filters into the shelter, making it unnecessary to use the kerosene lamp during the day. The light comes from several round glass circles in the ceiling—skylights of some sort.

The lock on the exit is completely unpickable, though not for a lack of trying. I've read books on lock-picking and even learned how to pick the locks on my house. The shelter door won't unlock.

When I resign myself to the fact that I'm a prisoner, I give in to my Kevin-induced fury and start going through all of his stuff. Total revenge. I sort through a small chest of drawers in the main room. It's filled with a few pairs of boxer shorts, jeans, a couple of torn shirts, and ball caps. Boring.

Next I rummage through all his metal sculpting stuff. Tools. Tools. Leather gloves. Tools. Even more boring.

I take the cushions from the sofa and look under them, and I find some stale popcorn, a handful of pennies, a single bullet, and lots of lint. I examine the chairs, look under the rug for a nonexistent secret door, and rummage through the bathroom cabinet again (and borrow some floss for my teeth). Kevin says he lives here, but it's not like he *really* lives here. Aside from the wire sculptures and his underwear, there's nothing personal here, nothing that really tells me more about him.

My stomach rumbles, so I go to the kitchen and take out the buttermilk pancake mix and powdered eggs. While my breakfast is cooking, I mix a cup of powdered milk. In a matter of minutes I am sitting at the small round table nestled in the kitchen's corner, eating steaming pancakes and eggs. Dad always says hunger is the best spice. He's right. I have never tasted anything so delicious. After two pancakes, I get a container of powdered sugar and sprinkle it onto the remaining two pancakes. As the sugar melts onto my tongue, I melt against my chair.

When my food is eaten and my belly feels like it's on the verge of popping, I go to Kevin's dresser and get a pair of jeans with tears over both knees and a comfortably worn red hoodie with a torn shoulder and sleeves that completely cover my hands, and is bulky enough to hide any trace of curves. I swap my clothes for his and put mine—everything but the vest—into the sink, scrubbing them with the bar of soap and then laying them on the counter to air-dry. I get Kevin's bloody shirt from the day before and scrub it next, laying it on the counter beside my shirt.

While I wait for the clothes to dry, I start going through the kitchen cupboards one by one, already thinking about what I am going to eat for my next meal. If I have to be a prisoner, I suppose this is the way to do it. The cupboards over the sink and stove all contain food—dehydrated beef stew, dehydrated soy meat substitute, potato flakes, biscuit mix, chocolate pudding mix, freeze-dried bananas and strawberries. My mouth waters despite my full belly. Kevin has more food variety than I have seen in three years—since the pesticide destroyed everything that survived the honeybee decline. It makes me wonder about him again. Who is he and how in the world did he find this place?

The cupboards beneath the sink are loaded with supplies: candles, matches, lighters, batteries, bullets (though no guns), flashlights, flares, rope, needles and thread, sunblock, ponchos, all sorts of different sizes of random shoes—more things than I can remember.

The cupboards on the other side of the kitchen are filled with more supplies, like gallons and gallons of kerosene and extra blankets. I kneel down for a closer look. There's a box of diapers in there too.

I get to the farthest cupboard, nestled behind the table, and open it. This cupboard is different. It has a damp, musty smell. Shiny half-gallon cans of whole wheat flour with tan labels fill this cupboard from top to bottom. Visions of fresh-baked bread fill my imagination, and I wonder if I've overlooked any yeast. I take out a can of flour and pause. The musty smell has intensified.

I take out another can and find more cans of flour behind it. The flour is four cans deep, four cans wide, and three cans high. One by one, I take out all the cans of flour, stacking them onto the cement floor beside me, until the cupboard is empty and there are forty-eight cans of flour taking up most of the kitchen floor. With the cupboard empty, the musty smell is stronger, and the cupboard seems cooler than any other part of the shelter. I stick my head in for a closer look and my hands start to tremble.

Backing out, I go to a supply cupboard, get a flashlight and insert batteries, and shine it into the depths of the cupboard. At the back is a door handle. I crawl inside. Placing my hand on the doorknob, I twist and yelp with surprise when it turns. The back of the cupboard swings away from me, opening into pitch-blackness.

CHAPTER 18

Let Fear Outweigh Your Curiosity. Mom started sewing that one minutes after she finished stitching a knife wound on Josh's thigh. He was curious whether or not a Fec would actually cut him if he didn't give the Fec something to eat. There was still blood under Mom's fingernails as she jabbed the needle and floss into a stained linen napkin.

I stand in a narrow cement hallway that smells like soil and rock and moss. The beam of my flashlight illuminates about thirty feet of darkness in front of me before it is swallowed by black. The hall is utterly silent and I stand still, wondering if I should explore. Wondering if I *dare* explore. Fear and curiosity are waging a battle inside me.

Taking a deep breath, I grip the flashlight in one hand, pat the gun at my belt with the other, and then start walking. My mother would be furious.

My feet scrape on the cement floor, and the damp cement walls throw the sound back at me. In several places, water is seeping through cracks in the walls. I trail my fingers over one of these drippy cracks. The wall is slimy with a nearly invisible sheen of moss. I wipe my slimy-wet hand on Kevin's pants and smirk. "You totally deserve that, Kevin," I whisper.

As I continue along the narrow hall, my heart starts to pump harder. Every time my shoe scrapes cement, I whirl around and look back the way I've come, waiting for Kevin to appear out of the darkness and get me. But I don't stop walking because, for once, my curiosity outweighs my fear.

After a few minutes of walking, everything changes. The cement floor turns from a straight walkway to a twisting and turning path, and the cement walls are replaced with jagged rock. The ceiling disappears, and when I shine my flashlight up, it reflects off of rock high, high above.

I run my fingers over the jagged earth wall as I walk. There's a new sound here, a gurgling like boiling water. I take a step forward and icy water fills my shoe all the way to the crevasses between my toes and splashes up onto my borrowed pants. A narrow stream crosses the cement path before disappearing down a crack in the rock. I shine my flashlight at the source of the water and see a spring bubbling up out of the ground. Someone has built a small pool around the spring, trapping a decent amount of water, and there are pipes sticking into it.

"The source of Kevin's water?" My voice echoes and dances through the cave. I start walking along the cement path again—haven't taken three steps—when it begins to slant upward and the air loses a bit of its mustiness. I follow the sloped path for a few minutes and then *bam*. I am up against a wall.

I shine my flashlight around and discover I'm in front of a wooden door braced with rusty metal, making it look like a metal and wood checkerboard. I place my hand on the knob and turn. It doesn't move.

"No!" I glower at the door. "You have to open!" I try the handle again and find it is stuck fast. Shining my light on it, I see a lock, so turn it. The lock clicks, I twist the handle, and the door opens. A gust of warmer, drier, wood-scented air hits me. I step through the door and shine my light around. My jaw drops open.

I am in a massive warehouse-size room with cement pillars every ten or so feet. They look like immense tree trunks that reach up to the smooth cement ceiling. There are rows and rows of wooden shelves as far as I can see, loaded with half-gallon tin cans labeled with tan stickers. I shine my light on the cans and start walking. There has to be a decade's worth of food here. At least! *Dehydrated beef. Dehydrated chicken. Soy beans. Pinto beans. White beans. Chili. Beef bouillon. Dehydrated clam chowder.* The types of food seem limitless. I come to a section of shelves with brick-size vacuum-packed yeast and almost cry. I could make hundreds of loaves of bread with a brick of yeast and the forty-eight cans of flour spread all over the kitchen floor.

I keep walking to the other end of the room and find a metal door with bright-red words painted on it: *ENTERING COMPROMISED ZONE.* I unlock it and step into the next room. A blast of even warmer air wraps around me, leeching the dampness from my skin.

I've entered a room filled with empty wooden shelves and broken glass bottles. Fancy, stained paper still clings to some of the shattered bottles. I crouch down and read one of the labels—*Chardonnay*—and frown. I'm in some freaky, trashed wine cellar and the door I've just come through is covered with the same wooden shelves that line the rest of the walls. I never would have known there was a door here if I hadn't opened it from the other side.

I take a big chunk of broken wine bottle and prop open the door, then keep going.

I come to yet another door and open it. I flinch and throw my arm up over my eyes. Sunlight burns against my eyelids. Peering through my lashes, I see a stairway leading up. I'm on the surface of the world again, where everything is wrong. Fear makes my legs heavy, as if they're trying to keep me underground, trying to warn me. I pause, close my eyes, and listen for any type of human sounds. My heart and my breathing are all I hear. My hand moves to my belt, and I remove my gun. With my finger on the trigger, I go up.

CHAPTER 19

The light is so bright at the top of the stairs that I can't see anything at first. I press my palms over my watering eyes.

When my eyes adjust, I am shocked to be standing in a large room with an enormous intact window overlooking half-dead pine trees, and far below, the distant city. I am in a structure built on the side of the Rocky Mountains. The floors are rustic wood, the furniture is rustic wood and cracked leather. Dusty elk, moose, and deer heads are mounted on the walls, and the kitchen, to my left, has dusty granite countertops and stainless-steel appliances. The refrigerator still has scraps of paper stuck to it with magnets.

I walk to the fridge and pull a scrap of paper out from under a frog magnet. It's a grocery list scrawled in faded pencil. I put the list back under the magnet and open the fridge. It is empty,

as if someone cleaned it out before the food could rot in it. Same with the cupboards.

Leaving the kitchen, I find a flight of stairs that leads up. Framed photographs cover the stairwell walls, and I glance at them as I slowly ascend. They're school photos of a boy and a girl, from kindergarten on up until maybe middle school. And the boy has hair a few shades darker than copper, and eyes the color of the morning sky.

Upstairs, I find three bedrooms and two bathrooms. I pass the master suite and go into a small bedroom. It's a girl's room, with a pale pink quilt on a perfectly made bed, as if the girl who sleeps here is going to come home from school this afternoon, remove the three white throw pillows, and sleep in it. I step up to the bed and run my hand over the quilt, and my fingers leave stripes in the years' worth of dust that has settled on it.

The next room has a bed, a dresser, a closet, and a telescope pointing out a window that faces the city. A lacrosse stick hangs on the wall behind the bed's headboard, surrounded by first-place ribbons, medals, and plaques. I walk up to the wall and study a plaque—the name *Kevin Winston Emerson* is etched into the tarnished brass.

"Aha! So *here*'s the real you," I whisper, and read every single ribbon, medal, and plaque. They all have his name on them. Apparently he took first place a lot in lacrosse, and for some reason that tiny fact makes me feel like I know him a hundred times better. Like, just maybe, I can trust him. I run my fingers over his bed and pause. It isn't like the girl's bed. There is no dust on the faded red quilt.

I go to the closet and open the door. It's a deep walk-in closet with shelves on the left and bars with hangers on the right. The hangers hold filthy clothes that desperately need a washing. I run my fingers over a threadbare trench coat that has so much dried mud on it that it is stiff to the touch. Little granules of dirt fall off and sprinkle over the dusty wood floor. On a shelf above the clothes are other things—scarves, hats, and beanies, and grass and twigs from mouse nests.

I leave the closet and go to the chest of drawers and start going through them, through boys' socks, through boxer shorts that look way too small for Kevin but have his name written on the waistband in permanent marker. The next drawer holds lacrosse stuff, like cleats, a mouth guard, a jock strap, and grass-stained padding. They still smell faintly of grass and sweat. The bottom drawer isn't filled with clothes but with newspaper clippings, yellow and faded. I kneel on the hardwood floor and take one out. The headline says:

Oldest Man to Scale Everest
Charles Winston Emerson of Denver, Colorado

I get two more clipped articles:

Crazy or Genius?
Charles Winston Emerson's Views on the Future

And:

Entrepreneur and Adventurer Charles Winston Emerson to Adopt Grandchildren in Aftermath of Son's Death

The article has a picture with the text. The boy has auburn hair, bright eyes, and a wide smile. Kevin. The girl has the same hair and eyes but looks several years younger.

I put the clipped articles back into the drawer and go to the telescope. It isn't pointed at the sky, the obvious place, but slightly north of the city. I put my eye to the lens, careful not to change its position, and take a look.

My heart leaps into my throat, and I force myself not to flinch. What I am looking at is miles away, but it still makes me want to run home and hide under my bed. I am staring at raiders. Lots and lots of raiders. They're gathered in a Walmart parking lot, wearing guns and camouflage, standing around five four-wheelers. Several are holding chains attached to big dogs, as if they're about to go hunting. But hunting for what?

I take an unsteady step away from the telescope. I know exactly what they're going to hunt. Me. And Fo, Bowen, Jonah, Kevin, and the beast-child. We need to get away before they find us, which means right now.

"Where are you, Fo?" I whisper, glancing at my watch. It is half past three. Kevin has been gone for nearly eight hours. I press my eye back against the telescope and slowly start moving it toward the foothills, toward what I think is the direction of the underground shelter. Slowly, methodically, I move it back and forth, scanning the area. A flash of movement catches my eye and I jump back from the shock of it. Pressing my eye once more to the scope, I brace myself and take a look.

My muscles relax as Kevin's camouflage ball cap and face bob into view, followed by Fo and the others. They're close, and they're fine. I sigh with relief. And then it hits me. I'm supposed to be imprisoned down in the shelter, not rummaging through Kevin's underwear drawer and newspaper clippings. I turn from the scope and quietly hustle through the house, down two flights of stairs, and into the wine cellar. I pass from the wine cellar into the dark, musty food storage room, turn on my flashlight, and close and lock the wine room door behind me.

Digging my toes into the cement floor, I start running.

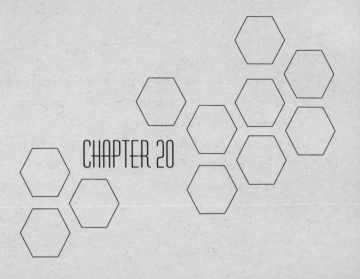

CHAPTER 20

I sprint to the end of the underground room and lock the door behind me.

The cave is cold and clammy, and the air rushing past my face coats it with cool moisture. When I get to the spring, I leap over it and keep going. At the long cement hall, I increase my pace, pumping my arms, measuring each breath like I'm at home on the treadmill again. It feels just like running in place. Distance loses meaning as nothing around me changes, and I might as well *be* on a treadmill.

The end of the cement hall comes abruptly into view and I dig my shoes into the ground and skid, putting my arms up to absorb the impact with the wall. I crawl through the cupboard and into the shelter's kitchen. Without bothering to stand, I begin shoving cans of flour into the cupboard, one at a time. I've put sixteen cans away when I hear the muffled sound of voices. My hands start to tremble. I stack the flour faster. When I hear the *thunk-thunk* of feet on a ladder, there are nine cans left. I cram them into the cupboard. The door in the other room opens as I slam the cupboard shut.

"Jack? Hello?"

I slide the table and chairs back into place and then lean against the counter with my arms folded over my chest. Kevin, brow furrowed, peers through the kitchen door at me.

"Hi there," I say, and pretend to stifle a yawn. I am trying not to pant despite the fact that my body wants me to gasp for air. His face softens and a smile dances in his eyes. And then he looks me up and down, his gaze lingering on my pants—his pants. "I'm drying my clothes. I hope you don't mind that I borrowed something to wear," I explain. I swipe a hand over my hot, sweaty forehead and wipe it on his pants.

"I don't mind." He pulls his hat off and takes another thorough look at me. "What have you been doing? You look hot and sweaty."

"What have I been doing?" My gaze wanders to the dirty pancake batter bowl. "Cooking. I've . . . been cooking," I stammer.

"Cooking."

I nod.

"All right. Working up a sweat in the kitchen." He ducks out the door and something happens to my face. The muscles around my eyes and mouth twitch and pull until I'm . . . smiling. I walk to the door, smile still plastered to my face, and stare at Kevin's back, watching the way he moves when he walks. He glances at me over his shoulder, and I suck my lips against my teeth so he doesn't know that he has made me smile.

Kevin pulls the entry door wide and Jonah comes into the shelter, followed by a black-haired kid—the beast. The boy is awake, though he looks only semiconscious as he's guided into the room by Kevin. His slanted eyes don't seem to *see* anything. I study the kid, searching for signs that he's about to attack someone, but he doesn't even look at anyone.

"Here you go, little man, sit right here," Kevin says, taking the kid's elbow. The boy wobbles and throws his hands up for balance, and I jump. Kevin lifts the kid and sets him on the sofa and then wraps a blanket around him, tucking it beneath the boy's chin. "Jack, do you think you can cook something for them?"

I shake my head. "No. We need to get going. The raiders . . . they *might* be out searching for us. We should get as far away as possible before their dogs pick up our scent."

Walking over to me, Kevin whispers, "Your friends need to rest." He looks right into my eyes, and the breath seems to get stuck in my throat. "They stand a better chance of surviving if they're well rested and fed."

"But the raiders are *probably* going to start looking for us. Like, right away."

Bowen comes into the room, followed by Fo.

Kevin leans closer to me and whispers, "They haven't slept at all. They've been too worried about you, Jack. The least you could do is let them eat a decent meal and get some sleep."

Bowen's and Fo's faces look stretched too thin, with dark bags beneath their bloodshot eyes. Guilt floods me and I look back at Kevin. A pale ring of gold circles his pupil, slowly fading to soft blue. I don't mean to notice—now is definitely not the time to marvel over his eyes—but I can't help it. I blink and look away. "Are we safe here, even if the raiders have dogs?"

"Yes." There is no doubt in his voice.

"Okay. I'll cook." I look back at his face, at his eyes, and he smiles.

"Jack says he'll cook you guys something to eat," he announces, clapping me on the shoulder.

Fiona crosses the room and throws her arms around me. "Jack. When you guys didn't show up at the lake on time, we thought for sure the raiders caught you." She sniffles. Tears fill her eyes and stream down her exhausted face, rinsing dirt from her cheeks. "I am so glad you're okay!"

Bowen comes over and wraps his arms around both of us. "Good to see you, Flapjack. When Kevin came to the lake alone, I thought something must have happened to you."

"I wanted to come but he wouldn't let me. He *locked* me down here," I explain.

Bowen nods. "I know. He told us you were safer here. I just didn't *believe* him at first." He drops his voice to a barely audible whisper and says, "I thought maybe he realized a certain truth about you and sold you." He hugs me again. "Now, go cook something for us before we die from starvation. Weren't you a 4-H cooking champion in sixth grade?"

I push away from Bowen and glare at him, and then glance at Kevin to see if he's heard, but he's standing at the chest of

drawers, helping Jonah find something for the boy-beast to wear—something besides my tighty-whities.

"How is the kid?" I ask. Bowen and Fiona release me, but keep their arms around each other.

"He woke up this morning before sunrise. He isn't attacking us anymore, but he's still got a long way to go," Fo explains. "The first sign that the cure is working is the change from violent attack mode to nonviolent and dazed. After that, the cure takes weeks to fully take effect. It is almost like the beasts have to relearn everything except the skills they retained while being beasts—like walking and eating." Fo sighs and rests her head on Bowen's shoulder. Bowen puts his face against her hair and inhales, and a wave of jealousy hits me. I want that closeness. "He just stares into oblivion," Fo continues. "Sometimes he cries. Jonah says he probably remembers everything he did as a beast and is traumatized by it. Maybe a hot meal will help him feel more human."

"Then I'll see what I can whip up."

I go to the kitchen and take out dehydrated ground beef sub-stitute, cumin, garlic salt, and powdered tomato paste. The thought of taco meat makes my stomach clench in anticipation. I put the ingredients into an iron skillet with some water and set it aside. Next I take cornmeal, sugar, salt, powdered milk, pow-dered butter, and baking soda from the cupboards and make a pan of corn bread batter. I put it into the oven and set the timer for thirty minutes, and then I fill the sink with cold, soapy water and start washing the dirty dishes.

I don't know what it is about having my hands in the water

and running a washcloth over measuring cups, but the knots in my shoulders ease and I start humming.

Behind me, someone clears his throat. I turn and find Kevin leaning against the door frame, staring at me. "I've gotten everyone settled and was wondering if you could help me out for a few minutes."

"Sure. What can I do?" I set a freshly washed measuring cup on the counter to air-dry and wipe my dripping hands on my— Kevin's—pants.

He holds up his right hand. I walk over to him and take his hand in mine, examining it. Thick brown splinters of wood are embedded in his bruised palm. I gently run my finger over his skin and he exhales.

I look up at his face. "Sorry. Did that hurt?"

"Yeah, like heaven." He smiles, which makes me blush.

"Sit down at the table," I blurt, too embarrassed to keep looking at him. I get my Leatherman from my vest and open the small attached tweezers, then sit across from him with my back to the kitchen door. Taking his right hand in my left, I hold his fingers back and begin tweezing the splinters out of his palm. His skin is warm and streaked with dirt. I like how his hand feels in mine, how it is totally limp, completely trusting. But I don't trust him.

"What would have happened to me if you died?" I ask. When he doesn't answer, I look up.

He tilts his head to the side. "What do you mean?"

"You *locked* me down here and left. No one knew where I was. What would have happened to me if you died?"

"You're smart. You're capable. You would have found a way out." He says it like it's a fact—like he is absolutely certain. And he's right.

"So, how old are you?" I ask, fitting the edge of the tweezers under a splinter and pulling it out.

"Eighteen. I would be starting my first year of college any day now if things were normal. Instead I'm . . ."

"What?"

"Sitting in a bomb shelter, getting splinters gouged out of my hand by a kid named Jack."

A smile flickers across my face. "Do you have any family?"

He pauses for a long time before saying, "A sister and a grandpa."

I look at him. "Are they alive?"

"As far as I know."

I work in silence for a few minutes before asking, "What's with the tattoo on your hand? I've never seen a mark without lines in it."

"When the vaccine passed the FDA and was in such short supply that only the gifted and talented kids got it, I applied for it and qualified."

I remember those days. When the vaccine passed, mobs of people stormed the health clinics and tried to take it by force. But there was a vaccine shortage, so the government decided that only "the hope for our future" would get it until they could mass-produce more. No adult got the vaccine. No child got the vaccine without first passing the government's requirements. Fo got it because she was a piano prodigy. Jonah got it for his science brain. I didn't qualify. I wasn't smart enough, and sewing and baking really good bread weren't considered important enough talents to qualify me.

"Apparently," Kevin continues, brow furrowed, "I have a higher-than-average IQ. I'm really good at math and spatial reasoning." *Spatial reasoning.* I think of the wire sculptures he's made, and my fingers tighten on his. I am holding the hand of an artist.

Kevin clears his throat. "My little sister, on the other hand, has a higher-than-average compassion for others, a quality I believe is more important than understanding numbers and space. Unfortunately, the government and I didn't see eye to eye on that. So I went in and filled out all the paperwork for the vaccine—in her name." His hand goes rigid in mine. "She went in monthly and got my dose."

I stop pulling splinters and gape at him. His eyes have lost their sparkle. "Did she turn into a beast?"

He nods. "She got nine months of the poison shot into her blood. She's a Level Nine, just like the boy Jonah found."

"Is she alive?"

"I hope so," he whispers. "I haven't had any contact with my grandfather for a while."

"Where is your grandfather?"

"As soon as he realized the government was *branding*—by force—all the children who got vaccinated, he took my sister and ran."

"And you didn't go with them?"

He shakes his head.

"Why?"

"Because I was being retained by the government for questioning."

I sit up a little taller and stare at him, enthralled. "What kind of questioning?"

"The government came to my house and took me by force to get branded, thinking I was the one who got the vaccine. They gave me the circle." He holds up his right hand for me to see the black oval on the back of it. "But when they did the bloodwork, they realized I didn't have a trace of the vaccine in me, so they didn't give me any marks. But they kept me for questioning."

"Did you get in trouble?"

"Sort of. They had me locked up for a few weeks. But then they decided I was the least of their problems and let me go."

"Where did your grandpa and sister go?"

He shrugs.

"I'm so sorry," I whisper.

"I'm not. My sister's safe. That's all that matters."

I lean over his hand and get back to work. "How old is your sister?"

"Probably about your age."

I think of the newspaper picture of Kevin and his sister. She looked a couple of years younger than Kevin. That would make her somewhere around sixteen. "Wait, your sister is twelve?"

"No. She's sixteen."

The tweezers freeze against his skin, and I don't dare to look at him. "We're not close to the same age. I'm twelve," I say. He doesn't reply. I've been pulling splinters in silence for a few minutes when I realize Kevin is staring at me. I look up, startled to find his face only a few inches from mine. "What?" I ask.

He shakes his head, dismissing my question. I lean over his hand again, more aware of him than I've ever been of anyone before. I can feel the air stir every time he breathes out. From the corner of my eye I see the way his chest expands when he inhales. Under the table his knee bumps mine and stays there, making a hot spot that seeps through my pants and into my skin. And I know if I look up, he will be staring at me.

"How is your cut arm feeling?" I ask, searching for a distraction.

"Like someone slashed it with a knife and then sewed it back together again without painkillers. Thanks for asking."

I can't help but smile as I ease another splinter out of his skin. "And how did you get splinters in your hand?"

"By wrenching a club out of some guy's hand before he could smash my head in."

I stop tweezing and look at him. There's no smile on his face. "You're serious."

He nods. "And all I could think about when it happened is what I would regret not doing if he killed me."

The look in his eyes makes my breath come a little faster. I quickly look back at his hand and pull a thick chunk of wood out of his skin. "What *would* you regret?" A drop of blood oozes out of the hole the splinter left. Using my knuckles, I wipe the blood away. Kevin leans to the side and I look at him. He is staring over my shoulder, out the kitchen door.

I whip around and follow his gaze. There's nothing

there—everything is quiet in the other room. "What are you looking for?" I whisper, still staring out the door.

"Jack, I know you're not twelve, and I know you're . . ."

I turn and face him, and my heart starts pounding. Kevin's eyes are intense, his pupils huge. He intertwines his fingers with mine and then leans in so close that our lips touch. I freeze, unable to move, to breathe, and stare at his bright eyes. His mouth smiles against mine, and then his eyes close and his lips part the slightest bit. His hand leaves mine, moving to cradle the back of my head. I lay my trembling hands flat on the table, close my eyes, and let my lips soften.

It is like eating fire, having Kevin's lips on mine. My entire body ignites. I almost expect flames to shoot from my nose when I breathe out. Kevin's free hand finds mine and lifts it, setting it on his uninjured shoulder. He takes my other hand and places it on his cheek. I press my palm against his warm, stubbly skin, slide it to the back of his head, and weave my fingers in his hair.

"That's better, Jack," he whispers against my lips.

My stomach sinks, as if I've swallowed a brick of ice, and I jerk away from Kevin.

He stares at me, eyes wide. After a moment, he blinks and lifts his hand, touching his lips with his fingertips. "Sorry?" He says it like he's asking a question, and then clears his throat.

My face starts to burn. Humiliation claws at me, making my stomach turn. I grab the tweezers and stare at the wood grain of the table, waiting for him to give me his injured hand so I can hurry up and get the rest of the splinters out of it. He doesn't. We just sit in awkward silence, and I can feel him staring at me.

"Jack," he whispers after a few minutes. "I'm sorry. I thought I saw something in your eyes—thought you might let me kiss you."

I still stare at the table.

"At first you seemed like you didn't mind," he says. "In fact, you seemed like you *liked* it."

I clench my teeth. All I want is for him to shut up. Every word he says adds fuel to my humiliation. I close my eyes and am hit with a memory.

CHAPTER 21

The Crow family was the last family left in the neighborhood besides ours. They had a daughter Dean's age and a son a few months younger than me. Gabe. He had blond hair, green eyes, and crooked teeth, and we went to school together before the schools closed down.

Once or twice a week he came over and sat on my roof with me when it was my turn to keep roof watch. We looked like two boys with guns and slingshots, trying to kill the occasional rat that skittered across the street, or trying to hit the random Fec that wandered out from the sewers. If beasts came down our street, Gabe and I were hustled to the basement to wait while my dad, uncle, and brothers tried to scare them off. We didn't kill beasts if we could help it.

Sometimes we got to stay on the roof and watch the sun set before Dad made me come inside. On those nights, Dad and one of my older brothers would escort Gabe home even though he lived only two houses down. Nighttime was dangerous. Nighttime was when the raiders came out. Nighttime meant shoot-to-kill and ask questions later. I never kept watch after sundown.

One evening, Gabe cleared his throat and looked into my eyes. Sunlight glowed against the freckles on his cheeks, reflected from the rifle in my hands, and framed the mountains with pink and orange. It was the end of April, and the evening air held a chill, so we sat close to share body heat. The sides of our legs were pressed against each other's, and our shoulders were touching.

"So, how does it feel to be sixteen?" His eyes traveled over me as if searching for visible changes.

"The same as being fifteen, except my dad delved into our food storage and gave me a can of warm Coke. I just wish we had ice." I tried to smile but it didn't reach my eyes. This was my first birthday without Dean sneaking out to find me a really amazing gift. When I turned fourteen, he brought me an iPod he'd found in an abandoned house. When my mom turned the generator on for me to run on the treadmill, he secretly charged the battery. I listened to a song a night until it ran out of juice. I didn't even care that it was loaded with country music and show tunes. Beggars can't be choosers. When I turned fifteen, he raided the library and brought home a backpack full of books.

"And a homeless guy gave me sunglasses," I added, touching the glasses balanced on top of my head.

Gabe looked west at the form huddled in a doorway across the street. "That creepy guy over there?" He fit a small rock to his slingshot and aimed.

I scowled and pushed his hand down. It's not like he'd actually hit the guy—Gabe was a terrible shot—but it bugged me that he'd even consider shooting the vagabond. "He's been coming around my house for a month. My dad says he's harmless, so leave him alone."

Tucking the rock back into his pocket, Gabe frowned and looked at me again. "Have you ever wondered if you and I are the only two uninfected, unrelated teenagers living on the wrong side of the wall?" He rolled his shoulders and leaned a little closer to me.

"Yeah, I think about it all the time." I hadn't seen an unmarked teenager, besides Gabe and my older brothers, in more than a year.

"Have you ever wondered if you're going to . . ." When he didn't finish his thought, I looked at him. He blushed and his gaze moved from my eyes to my mouth and stopped. Taking a deep breath, he leaned toward me and put his chapped lips against mine. I didn't pull away, but I had to force myself not to. I liked Gabe. He was nice. He was my only friend. And even though I'd never thought of him as more than a friend, his lips against mine made my breath catch in my throat. So I closed my eyes and kissed him back. My first kiss. And on my sixteenth birthday.

His lips were rigid and damp. When he put his tongue in my mouth, he drooled on my chin and I almost gagged. One of his clammy hands touched the side of my face, then moved to the back of my head, into my freshly buzzed hair. Gabe shuddered and jerked away from me like he'd been shocked, then wiped his mouth on the back of his arm.

"Are you all right?" I asked, wrapping my arms around my knees and studying him.

He grimaced. "My dad told me to try kissing you to see if there were any sparks. But . . ." He wiped his mouth again and stood. "When I kiss you, it feels like kissing a guy. No offense! You're really cool, but you don't seem like a girl anymore. Even a little bit."

I stopped breathing and stared at him as his words battered against my minuscule self-esteem.

"I've got to get going. We're leaving tomorrow."

"Leaving?" I asked, my voice a dull monotone.

"Yeah. We're going to make the trip to Wyoming. My dad said if I wanted to, I could ask you . . . now, never mind." He looked at the sunset. "I probably won't see you again, Jack, unless your family decides to come to Wyoming. Good luck with everything." I stood and made myself smile at him. He squeezed my shoulders, and I returned the hug.

"Be careful out there," I whispered.

He patted my back twice and let me go. "I will be."

I didn't watch him climb down the ladder because movement on the road below my house caught my attention. I stared down at the shadowed street, at the man standing in the middle of the road, hands braced behind his upturned head, watching me. I reached for my rifle, but when I saw it was only the vagabond, I took my hand from the gun. He waved at me and lumbered down the street.

When Dad came for me two minutes later, I hid my face from him. Because boys don't cry.

"Jack, look at me," Kevin whispers.

I blink and remind myself that I am sitting in a kitchen, in a bomb shelter, and I've just been kissed. I take a deep breath and look at him—look at his frowning lips before staring at his eyes.

"What happened? Why did you pull away from me like that?" he asks.

I focus on the table again and wonder if I can tell him. Wonder if I *can't* tell him. So I say, "You know I'm not twelve."

"Of course I know you're not twelve! Do you think I'd be kissing you if I thought you were a kid?"

I press my hand to my forehead and close my eyes. "Do you know—" I can hardly breathe.

"What? Do I know what?" he asks.

"—that I'm not really a boy?" The words squeak out, as if affirming what I've just said.

There's a long silence that makes my face burn with shame, and tears threaten to fill my eyes. And then Kevin starts laughing. Laughing! My body goes rigid. His laughter stops dead, and he leans in close to me again, staring into my eyes. "Yes, Jacqui. I do realize you're female. I've known since the first time I saw you."

It takes a minute for his words to sink in. My mouth falls open but no words come out. Kevin puts his finger under my chin and gently closes my mouth.

"Can we try again?" he asks. When I don't say anything, he stands and takes my hands in his, pulling me to my feet in front of him. One at a time, he places my hands against his chest, palms over his heart. His trembling hands frame my face, warm against my skin, and tilt my head back.

"Why are your hands shaking?" I whisper.

He looks right into my eyes. "Because I'm scared to kiss you." We stay that way for half a minute, just looking at each other, and then slowly, he leans toward me until his lips come down on mine. They're warm and firm, like he's been practicing this very thing for years. I've hardly had any practice, but it doesn't matter. It is as if my lips know what to do, turning soft and supple and moving like they've been programmed to respond to his.

I press my palms against his chest and feel his beating heart, feel it accelerate. Fire floods me again and makes me bold. I stand on tiptoes and press my mouth more firmly against his. Kevin sighs and one of his hands leaves my face to rest against the small of my back, holding me steady. His other hand moves from my cheek and circles around to the back of my head, his fingers sweeping over my short hair and sending shivers down my entire body. And then I hear birds singing and smell food cooking and feel sunshine warming me from the inside out.

Kevin's lips pause against mine and he releases me, but the birds don't stop singing.

"What is that?" I ask, self-conscious that my voice sounds so breathless.

"The food."

"What food?"

Kevin smiles, and my knees nearly buckle. "The timer is beeping for the food you put into the oven. Corn bread, I think."

"Oh!" I peer inside the oven. The corn bread is golden on the edges but pale in the middle. Stepping to the stove, I turn on a burner and put the skillet with the meat mixture onto it. "This should just take a few minutes," I say, and start stirring the meat with a wooden spoon. Taking a deep breath, I close my eyes and lick my lips. I press a hand to my heart and shudder with the aftermath of the kiss. Wow. Just wow.

Kevin leaves the kitchen, and I hear the quiet rumble of voices in the other room. A minute later he comes back in, followed by Bowen and Fo. My eyes meet Kevin's, and my heart skips a beat. Fo looks at me with sleep-blurred eyes, then looks at Kevin. She rubs her eyes and looks at me again. I can't help but blush.

"Hungry?" I ask, studiously avoiding Kevin's gaze.

"Yeah. Famished." Bowen puts his hand over his stomach. "But where's Jonah's backpack? Kevin says you were the last one with it."

"You mean the water? I left it in a neighborhood somewhere."

All the color drains from Fiona's face. Bowen presses the balls of his hands against his eyes. "Please say you're joking." He slides his hands down his stricken face and looks at me.

I glare at him. "That backpack weighs as much as me! I was alone, surrounded by raiders, and they had a dog. A dog! I'm lucky to have gotten out of there alive! And besides, we can get more water here. Kevin has an endless supply."

Bowen's eyes turn nearly black. He strides to the door leading into the main room of the shelter and quietly closes it, and then starts cursing. His entire body begins to tremble, and he leans against the counter, gripping the edge of it so tightly that his knuckles turn white. "Bowen. It's okay." Fo steps up beside him and puts her hand on his back. His nostrils flare and his jaw muscles pulse. He closes his eyes and starts taking fast, deep breaths. "Bowen. We're both alive. That's the most important thing." She wraps her arms around him and holds him close. After a minute, his breathing slows and he lets go of the counter. Turning to Fo, he takes her face in his hands, rests his forehead against hers, and closes his eyes.

"I love you, and we're both alive," he whispers. He starts kissing her—*really* kissing her—and I scratch the back of my head and look at the floor.

After a minute, Bowen and Fo pull apart to walk to the table. Bowen sits in a chair and Fo sits on his lap.

"What is wrong with you, Bowen?" I ask, looking up from the floor. "We can get more water here."

Bowen growls and leans his face into Fo's back. "It wasn't *water*, Jack."

As if nothing out of the ordinary is happening, Kevin puts on red plaid oven mitts, takes the corn bread out of the oven, and moves the pan of meat from the burner.

"Then what was it?" I ask, sitting in the chair across from them.

"The cure. Hundreds of doses of it. And the chemical equations to reproduce it," Fo explains.

Bowen leans back and glares at me. "Why else do you think Fiona and I would leave the walled city minutes after we were married? That's the only thing that made it worth it!"

"What?" Kevin and I say at the same time. Kevin scoots me onto half of the chair and sits on the other half, draping his arm over the backrest.

"You're *married*?" I say, just as Kevin blurts, "You had the *cure* with you?"

Fo looks at me, Bowen looks at Kevin, and at the exact same time they both say, "Yes."

I gnaw on the side of my cheek and glower at them. "Gee. Thanks for the vote of trust. You're married, and you had the cure with you, but you didn't mention either of those things to me!" I shake my head in frustration. "If you had told me that we were carrying the cure, I would have risked everything to keep it safe."

"There's only one thing to do," Kevin says. "We have to get the cure back."

"Are you crazy?" I ask, looking at his profile.

A warm hand comes down on the back of my head—Kevin's hand—and he looks at me. "I'd be crazy *not* to try and get it. If I could get some to my sister . . ." His face is so close to mine that our noses almost touch. I swallow and look away.

Bowen narrows his eyes. "Do you think we can find it? Do you think the raiders have it?"

"Of course the raiders have it. It was left in the middle of a group of them, and they *did* have a dog. Their MO is to sweep for dropped possessions after they catch people—or don't catch them. I don't know if we can get it back, but we need to try." He presses his lips to my temple and sighs, and it is like someone has set off fireworks beneath my skin.

Fo's eyes grow round. Bowen looks between me and Kevin. His gaze lingers on Kevin's lips, still pressed against my temple. Kevin leans away and clears his throat and moves his hand to my knee. "So, what's up with you two?" Fo asks, her voice nonchalant.

My throat constricts and I stare at her, unable to utter anything. Because what would I say? I have no idea what's up with Kevin and me.

"I've got a major crush on Jacqui," Kevin says, squeezing my knee. I jump and Kevin laughs.

Bowen scowls at me, his gaze so sharp it could draw blood. "Kevin, would you mind giving us a moment alone?"

Kevin gives my knee another squeeze before he stands and walks into the other room, shutting the door behind him.

The moment the door latches, Bowen snaps, "Are you crazy? Why did you tell him that you're a girl?"

"*Me?* Stop blaming me for everything! I didn't tell him!" I rub my knee, which is still tingling from Kevin's touch. "*You're* the one who told him my real name."

"I didn't tell him your real name."

"Then Fo or Jonah must have when you guys were walking to the shelter today."

Fo shakes her head. "We were only around Kevin for a couple of hours, and so tired we didn't talk unless we had to."

"And none of us *had* to say your name except to ask if you were dead or alive," Bowen adds. We stare at each other for a long, silent moment. Finally Bowen shrugs. "One of us must have slipped up and said it, I guess. There's nothing we can do now except hope he's a decent guy. Do you realize how much you're worth if he decides to sell you to the raiders?"

I shake my head. "No, actually. My mom and dad didn't tell me stuff like that."

"A beautiful young woman could buy him several *years'* worth of food."

I rub my hand over my buzzed head. "Then I guess it's a good thing I don't fit into the beautiful category." And it's not like he needs food—not with a warehouse-size room filled with it. He wouldn't be easy to bribe.

Bowen takes a good, long look at me. "Have you actually looked in a mirror lately? You're hot. This whole female Rambo look suits you. I'm sure Kevin would agree."

"Or maybe I just happen to be the last woman on the face of

the earth who isn't *married* or a beast!" I retort. "Why didn't you tell me you guys got married? And on the day I found you. So this"—I wave my hand around—"is your honeymoon?"

Fo won't look at me. Bowen laughs a cynical laugh. "No, this is definitely not our honeymoon. And at this point, I don't know if we'll live long enough to have one." He pulls her gently against him and kisses her hair.

I stand and make a heaping plate of food, setting it on the table in front of them. "Well, eat up. At least you won't starve to death."

I go into the bathroom. Just enough light filters through the skylight to show me my reflection in the mirror. The way I am standing, with my arms folded over my chest and my chin thrust forward, screams boy. I drop my arms, throw my shoulders back, and try to smile. It helps a little bit. But I still look like a boy.

I roll my eyes and leave.

CHAPTER 22

I sleep in one of the chairs, wrapped in a wool blanket, with my feet propped up on the coffee table beside the wire frog and rabbit. I am the first to wake up and smile when I think about taking a shower, even if the water is cold. A cold shower is a lot better than hauling bucket after bucket of well water from the backyard to the bathtub.

My clothes, still laid out in the kitchen, are slightly damp, but I take them into the bathroom with me. With icy water, I scrub myself clean and then put on my damp clothes. Using supplies from the bathroom cabinet, I brush and floss my teeth. I could get used to living here. I could live here the rest of my life. With Kevin. That thought makes me warm despite the cold shower and the damp clothes that are leeching my body heat. I put Kevin's red hoodie on over my shirt and tackle vest, and pull the hood over my cold, wet hair. Taking the jeans I'd been bor-rowing, I go into the kitchen and rummage through supply cup-boards until I find needle and thread and scissors and some fabric scraps that used to be a shirt.

Sitting at the kitchen table, I cut the fabric scraps to the right size and start sewing them over the tears in the knees of Kevin's pants. When the holes are patched, I wash the jeans in the sink, wring them out as best I can, and drape them over the counter to dry.

My stomach grumbles. With way more anticipation than making breakfast should bring, I open the cupboard above the sink and take out three cans: biscuit mix, powdered eggs, and powdered gravy. And then I start to cook.

"Good morning, Little Red Riding Hood." Kevin is standing in the kitchen doorway, watching me with a smile on his face. I forget to breathe. He goes into the bathroom and shuts the door, and I hear the water running. And then he starts to sing. A few minutes later he steps out of the bathroom. His hair is wet and combed back, his face is smooth and clean, and he smells like a man—like shaving cream, soap, and aftershave. He smiles, and it feels so normal, standing in the kitchen with him just out of the shower while I make breakfast. The empty space in my heart gets a little fuller.

I measure powdered biscuit mix and water into a stainless-steel bowl. "How did you find this place?" I ask.

"Luck."

"Was all the food here when you found it?"

He stares at me for a long minute, brow furrowed, before

answering, "I scavenged abandoned neighborhoods for food after everyone left. Or died."

I start to stir the biscuits. "I wish you had yeast. I love fresh bread." Kevin takes a can of something from the cupboard to the left of the sink. He opens it, takes a measuring cup from the counter, and scoops pale yellow powder out. Without asking, he drops the powder into the biscuit dough. "What was that?" I already followed the directions on the can of biscuit dough, which amounted to adding water to the premade mix. It didn't say to add anything else. I turn and lean the small of my back against the counter while I stir.

Kevin leans against the counter beside me and folds his arms over his chest. "Powdered butter. It makes everything taste better. A trick to living on dehydrated food." He watches me stir. I can feel the heat from his arm against my shoulder. It makes me feel too light, his closeness, like I might float away.

I clear my throat and stir faster. "You don't think that might ruin it? I mean, good food's so rare. I would hate to ruin these." My words are rushed and I wonder if he knows how flustered I get when he stands close to me.

He turns his body so it is facing mine, and I stop stirring. Slowly, he unfolds his arms and puts one finger under my chin, turning my face up so I am looking right into his eyes. They're so bright, so focused. He pulls the sweatshirt hood off my head. And then he angles his head to the side, leans in, and our lips touch. I almost drop the bowl of dough.

His lips move slowly on top of mine, and mine respond, like they're dancing with his. We stay that way for a long time, with both of us holding perfectly still except for our lips. And my heart. It is beating like it wants to break out of my chest.

I hear voices in the other room so I pull away from Kevin and start stirring furiously. Kevin's hand comes down on mine. I look at the dough. It's smooth. Biscuit dough is supposed to be lumpy and have chunks of powder in it. If you stir it too much, the biscuits turn out tough.

"Jack." That's all he says, but he says it like it is the most important word that will ever come out of his mouth. I look into his eyes and brace myself for his lips on mine again. Instead of kissing me, he says, "If I knew you were going to grace my home with your presence, I would have been sure to have yeast."

The room seems to darken. He's lying. He *does* have yeast. Lots and lots of it in the food storage room at the end of the cave. I turn away from him and scoop twelve even portions of biscuit dough onto a greased cookie sheet.

"Too bad you didn't know I was coming," I say, forcing my voice to sound light and happy when I'm reeling with mistrust on the inside.

He steps up behind me, so close that the front of his body is touching the back of mine, and puts his hands on my shoulders. "I'm just glad you're here. And safe." I fight the urge to squirm away and tell him I know he's lying about the yeast, but I stand rigid.

He steps back, and from the corner of my eye I warily watch him rummage through one of the supply cupboards. He takes out a messy tangle of wire about as thick as paperclip wire, and a pair of needle-nose pliers. Sitting at the table, he starts working, bending and twisting the wire, forming and shaping. The smell of baking biscuits fills the kitchen, and my mouth starts to water. I make the eggs and gravy while Kevin works at the table, but I'm more focused on what he's doing than on the food. After five minutes, he holds something in the palm of his hand and looks at me. "What do you think?"

He stands and hands it to me. I study the sculpture, a silver wire car with curlicue wheels. "Wow. It's amazing."

"Do you think the little boy will like it?"

The suspicion I felt a few minutes earlier is whisked away, and my heart warms up. "I don't know. Maybe."

He smiles and takes the car out of my hand, letting his fingers linger on mine for half a second before going into the other room.

When breakfast is ready, I dish eggs, gravy, and biscuits onto four plates (all of the plates Kevin owns), and carry three of them into the main room, setting them on the coffee table. Bowen and Fo are still asleep on the sofa, tangled in each other's arms. Jonah is in one of the chairs, watching Kevin—down on his hands and knees—drive the wire car across the cement floor in front of the child.

"Here. You try," Kevin says, holding it out. When the boy doesn't take it, Kevin physically puts it into the child's hand. The child's eyebrows pull together, and he looks at the car, but only for a moment. The car clatters out of his hand, he turns his face up, sniffs the air, and whips his head in my direction. In one leap, the kid is on top of me. I scream and put my hand on my belt, but there's no gun—I forgot to put it back on when I woke up.

"Jack! Don't hurt him," Jonah says, jumping to his feet. "He's just hungry."

The boy crawls off me, picks up a handful of eggs and gravy, and crams it into his mouth. He licks gravy from between his fingers, off the nine-legged tattoo on the back of his hand, and I feel a sharp, strange kinship with him. I know just how he feels. If Kevin hadn't been in the kitchen with me while I cooked everything, I would have done just the same thing. Starvation is funny like that.

Fo and Bowen wake, as if they are one collective mind, and untangle from each other. Bowen sits up and takes a plate of food, handing it to Fo. "Thanks, Flapjack." He smiles a groggy smile at me.

"Jack, you're the best," Fo says.

I go back into the kitchen and Kevin follows me. My stomach is growling to hurry up and eat. I put the remaining plate of food in the middle of the table and sit. Kevin sits across from me and puts his hands behind his head, leaning against them and watching me.

"Aren't you hungry?" I pick up a biscuit and eat half of it in one bite. It isn't tough. In fact, it is the best biscuit I've ever tasted, as if kissing Kevin while holding the bowl of batter added something magical to it. He watches me load my fork like it is a shovel and smiles. "Well, what are you waiting for?" I ask.

"When you eat, your face softens, you sigh, and it's like you're transported to heaven for a minute. You look so happy. I eat alone down here most of the time, so when I actually have company, it's better than food."

My fork comes to a screeching halt an inch before it reaches my mouth. "Most of the time? You eat alone most of the time, but not all of the time?"

He nods, still leaning against his hands like they're a headrest.

"Who do you eat with when you're not eating alone?" I've searched this entire place. There aren't signs of anyone else staying down here. . . . Except . . . I set my overloaded fork down and my eyes go wide. There are tampons in the bathroom. And the box has been *opened*.

He's still staring at me.

I'm not the only girl he's had down here before. Am I the only one he's kissed? I look at his lips. Based on the way he kisses, like he's done it a thousand times, I'd say he's probably kissed a lot of girls. Probably every girl who's been down here.

"What are you thinking?" His question makes me realize I'm staring at his mouth and scowling. I look at the plate, take my fork, and shove the food into my mouth. And then I shake my head.

"You look kind of worried." He takes his hands from behind his head and rests them on the table, leaning toward me. His knee bumps mine and stays pressed against it. I move my leg away and shake my head again.

He sighs. "If you're wondering if I bring women down here and mess around with them, the answer is no. Sometimes I help strangers out, and some of them are women. But I never have time to get to know any of them. They just come and go."

"It's not like you know me either, though," I point out.

He opens his mouth to say something, pauses, and then

picks up his biscuit and takes a bite. He swallows and says, "But I feel like I know you. I feel like I've known you for months." He leans toward me and whispers, "When I kiss you, I want to get to know you a lot better."

"Me too. A *lot* better," I say without thinking. My face starts to burn, and I press my fingers against my lips before any more accidental confessions jump out, like, *I could live down here with you forever!* Or, *I have such a massive crush on you that I forget to breathe when you walk into the room!*

Kevin takes my hands in his and opens his mouth to say something, but Jonah picks that moment to walk into the kitchen, holding an empty plate. He doesn't look at us, just loads the plate with the remaining food and turns to leave. He pauses and asks, "Is it okay if the child and I finish off the rest of this?"

"Go ahead," Kevin says, releasing my hands. He clears his throat and picks up his fork. "If you're still hungry when that's gone, let me know. I can whip up some more."

After everyone's eaten, Kevin and I wash the dishes while Fo sits at the table, sipping powdered milk from a tin mug. "Do you remember when we were ten and our families met at the park on the Fourth of July, and your mom made an American-flag sheet cake that I accidentally sat on?" she asks. "I had a frosting flag plastered to my shorts all night."

I smile at the memory. "And my brother Dean had a huge crush on your sister, Lissa, even though she was three years older than him and two inches taller. And Jonah did some experiment and combined the gunpowder from two fireworks and caught his shirt on fire."

Fo laughs, but her eyes are sad.

When the dishes are washed and put away, Kevin goes into the other room, and I sit at the table with Fo. "So, you're married to Dreyden Bowen," I say, glancing at her empty ring finger. "I never, in my wildest dreams, would have put you two together."

A smile lights up Fo's face, making the sadness leave her eyes, making her eyes sparkle—the same look she used to get as a kid when she talked about playing the piano. "I'm so lucky," she says. "If it wasn't for him, I wouldn't have much to live for. If it wasn't for him, I wouldn't be alive." She glances at her crooked pinky finger and scowls. "So what's up with you and Kevin?"

"I don't know. It's sort of hard to think about the future when you're not sure if you'll actually have one." I glance into the other room. Bowen, Jonah, and Kevin are standing together, their heads close, talking about something. "I really like him," I whisper. "Which is weird, because I've been resigned to the fact that I'd have to pretend to be a boy for the rest of my life, and never allow myself to be attracted to anyone. But now he's here, and it makes me realize how much I'm missing."

Bowen walks into the kitchen, carrying one of the leather chairs from the other room. He sets it down at the table and then stands behind Fo, resting his hands on her shoulders. "What are you guys taking about?" he asks.

"Girl stuff." Fo grins up at him, and he lifts his eyebrows.

"Would you mind taking your girl stuff into the other room? We've got to plan how to get the cure back." He sets a pad of paper and a short, stubby pencil on the table.

Jonah comes in and sits down in the leather chair. Without

a word, he takes Fo's cup and swallows the last of her milk. She gasps and smacks his arm, and the sides of Jonah's mouth quiver and then turn up the tiniest bit. "Sorry, Sis." He stands and rinses the cup, and then fills it with water and powdered milk, stirring it before setting it down in front of Fo. "I guess some habits never die," he says in a quiet voice. Fo stands and throws her arms around Jonah.

"I love you," she whispers. She kisses his cheek and then leaves the room, forgetting her milk.

Kevin comes in carrying a rolled-up map. He sits in Fo's empty chair and sets the map down on the table and unrolls it, using Fo's mug as a paperweight. Bowen gives me a look, and I fold my arms over my chest. "I want to help," I say.

"Help us plan, or help us get the cure back?" Bowen asks, eyes guarded.

"Both! I'm the one who accidentally lost it, so I will help you get it back."

Bowen shakes his head. "You can help us plan but you can't come. I need you to stay with Fo. I need you to protect her while I'm gone."

"She'll be fine here. I want to help."

"I agree with Bowen," Kevin says. "You need to stay here. It's way, *way* too dangerous for you out there."

His words nearly knock the wind out of me. I tremble with the effort it takes to keep from yelling and very calmly say, "Too dangerous for me? I have been living *out there* for years, and doing just fine! Let me help! I don't think I could stand being stuck down here while I worry about you guys!"

Bowen runs his hands through his hair and keeps them there, gripping the roots. "Yes, you have been surviving out there," he says. "And yes, you are part of the reason we're in this mess in the first place—and so am I. I should have told you we had the cure. But you've been *sheltered* out there. And you're . . . you're a woman, Jack. It would be too risky bringing you. You absolutely cannot come!"

I open my mouth to fight for the right to come, but my throat is too tight to talk. A warm hand grabs mine. "I need to talk to you for a minute," Kevin says, pulling me into the other room, past Fo and the child, and to the shelter's exit. He opens the door and we step out, so we're both crammed into the small space with the ladder. He shuts the door halfway, so there's just enough light to see by, and lets go of my hand.

"I want to go with you to get the cure," I whisper.

His brows pull together, and he looks like he's in pain. "Jack, no. It's too dangerous."

I fold my arms over my chest and glare at him.

"Okay, you're not understanding what I am trying to say. That"—he points up—"is no place for a woman!"

I bite the side of my cheek and fight off tears of frustration. "*I hate being a woman.*" My words are filled with bitterness. "It is the worst thing a person can be in this world." I stare at him, daring him to contradict me.

"You don't know what you're saying. You are a *woman*! You're like an endangered species! Bad men kill to have you as their property. Good men will do everything they can to protect you—even die for you."

"I don't want to be protected! I'll pretend to be a boy. I just don't want to be left behind again." Tears fill my eyes. I try to blink them away, but they spill down my cheeks. "Everyone I care about leaves me behind, and then they never come back."

A hint of sorrow touches his eyes. "That's because they care about *you*. Don't you get it, Jack?"

"Get what?"

He takes one of my hands in his. "Out there, you are just a commodity. You're something to be bartered with, then used up and discarded. But in here"—he puts my hand on his chest, right above his heart—"you are more precious than the sun, than air, than water, or bees. You are pure life. If I take you out there, *you* are what I will die to keep safe. Not the cure. If you come with me, I will be useless to Bowen because everything I do will be for you. You are more important than the cure, and so I have to know you're safe."

I close my eyes and drop my forehead against his chest. His arms come around me and hold me close. "Please let me keep you safe," he whispers. "Please stay here."

I turn my head to the side and press my ear against his chest, listening to the slow, quiet rhythm of his heart. "All right," I whisper, and wrap my arms around him.

CHAPTER 23

Someone shakes me long before my body wants to wake up. A
blanket is draped over my shoulders, and a warm hand frames my
cheek. "Jacqui." My name, spoken with his voice, makes me smile
and wonder at the same time how he knows my real name.

I open my eyes. Kevin is crouching on the floor beside the
kitchen table, holding a lit lantern.

"Did I fall asleep?" I rub my eyes and lean my elbows on
the table and try to remember the last thing we were talking
about—how Jonah, Bowen, and Kevin were going to get into the
raiders' headquarters in the first place. "Did you guys figure out
how to get inside?" I ask, stretching.

Kevin nods. "We got it all worked out. Thanks for your
help," he whispers. A tiny smile touches his mouth, but his eyes
are sad. He sits in the leather chair that used to be in the family

room and I ask him the question that's been on my mind for a while.

"Who told you my name?" I ask.

He blinks at me, his face unreadable. "Does it matter?"

"Yes. It means one of us wasn't careful enough."

"I'll tell you after we get the cure back from the raiders. Right now there's something more important for us to talk about."

My skin prickles with apprehension. Kevin pulls something out of his pocket. He takes my hand and places a paper into it—a neatly folded rectangle.

"What is this?" I start to open it, but Kevin's hand comes down on mine.

"That is something that could potentially get hundreds of people killed." I drop the paper onto the table. Kevin laughs and picks it up again, closing my fingers around it. He keeps his hand on mine. "It's what is written on it that is the danger," he explains. "If the raiders ever read it, I will be dead, and a lot of people will be in danger."

"You mean dead as in metaphorically speaking, right?"

He releases my hand and leans back in the chair. "No. Literally dead. As in *dead*."

I start unfolding the paper but Kevin's hand comes down on mine yet again. "What? I can't read it?"

"Not yet. It's for in case . . ." His voice fades away, and he closes his eyes, still leaning back as if he's asleep. He stays that way for a long time, breath moving evenly in and out of him. I stare at his face, studying the way his shoulder-length hair frames it.

"It's sort of like a last resort—plan Z." He opens his eyes. They're heavy and dark. Defeated. "If things get to the point that you don't know what to do, read it."

"Wait. If things get to *what* point?"

"If you get there, you'll know. If you have to read the paper, memorize every single line of it. And then burn it or eat it or tear it into a thousand pieces and bury it under a boulder. But don't lose it, and don't let the raiders get it! Can you promise me that?"

All of a sudden I feel sick. What he's *not* saying is there's a chance he won't be coming back. The paper seems to squirm against my skin, so I curl my fingers over it. "I promise," I say, and unzip one of the pockets on my vest and tuck it in, right beside the spare suture packets.

Kevin stands and pulls me to my feet. "Come here." He wraps his arms around me and sits back down in the chair, cradling me against his chest. I nestle my head into the space where his shoulder and neck join, pressing my cheek against his warm skin. Kevin props his feet up on one of the kitchen chairs, and his arms slowly grow heavy around me, settling over me like a blanket. The rise and fall of his chest gently rocks me, and his body heat fuses with mine, making me feel warm and soft and safe.

"Jack, are you asleep?" he asks after a long while.

"No." I don't want to sleep. I want to be aware of every minute of my life right now, enjoy every second just in case. . . .

"You're an intense runner," Kevin whispers. "And you're brave." His right hand moves to his left arm, touching the spot where I cut him. "You know how to heal. You can cook." He sighs. "And you're beautiful." He puts his warm, callused hand on my cheek and tilts my face toward his. "You're like this perfect package all mixed up into one small, stunning person."

My nerves seem to come alive, pulsing with an electric current that warms my skin and quickens my heart. My gaze drifts from his eyes to his mouth, and I pull his head down until our lips meet. I will savor this moment and remember it until the day I die.

My dreams aren't about food. They're about Kevin. I need to get his attention because something dark is trying to consume him. I scream his name, and he finally notices me. And that's when I realize the truth. The darkness isn't trying to consume him. He *is* the darkness. And he's consuming *me*.

Something clutches my shoulder and I jerk away.

"Jacqui."

I open my eyes, peel my cheek off Kevin's shoulder, and then sit up.

Kevin is staring at me, his eyes so serious they look gray instead of blue. "I need to get ready to leave now."

"Already? I thought you were leaving at sunrise." I rub my eyes and glance at my watch. It's six o'clock. "Oh. It is sunrise." I stumble to my feet and try to look like the thought of him leaving isn't tearing me up on the inside. I hug the blanket around me and go into the other room.

Bowen and Fo are standing in the corner, wrapped in an embrace. Jonah, wearing a massive backpack, is waiting by the exit with the hood of his sweatshirt pulled up over his head. At his side stands the beast-boy. The boy looks at me. His slanted eyes are huge in his gaunt face. Jonah crouches by the boy. "That's Jack," he says. "She's going to keep you safe until I come back." Jonah gently wraps his arms around the boy and pats his back a few times.

"Flapjack." Bowen walks up to me and gives me a quick hug. "Keep her safe." I nod. With one more look at Fo, he strides out the door.

Fo crosses the room and wraps her arms around Jonah. "Be safe," she says. "And take care of Bowen."

He tries to smile at her. "I don't think Bowen needs me to take care of him, but I'll do my best." He lets her go and nods at me, his blind eye looking in the wrong direction. "Be brave, Jack," he says, and goes out the door.

Kevin comes out of the kitchen with his hair pulled back in a ponytail, wearing his camouflage hat. He lifts a big backpack off the floor and puts it on, careful not to bump his left arm. Then he takes my hand and pulls me out the door and into the narrow space where the ladder is. I look up just as Jonah reaches the top and blink at the dawn sky. Kevin shuts the shelter door, closing us into the tiny space. Because of his backpack, there's no extra room. I have to stand pressed between him and the wall. His closeness steals my breath, and I look at his face.

Before I know what's happening, he kisses me like he's starved for my lips. My knees buckle, but he's pinning me against the wall.

He pulls his mouth away. "Lock the door, and don't let

anyone in unless you know it is me or Jonah or Bowen. Don't come up for anything!"

I nod. "I'm going to miss you. Please come back." The words barely come out.

Kevin smiles and trails his fingers over my cheek. "You are so beautiful," he whispers. "I'm glad you finally got to meet the real me." And with that, he opens the door, gently shoves me back into the shelter, and slams the door shut. The hollow thud of his feet on the ladder resonate in the shelter.

"Wait," I whisper, staring at the door. "Wait!" This time I yell it. "What do you mean I finally got to meet the *real* you?"

Voice muted by the door, he yells, "Hopefully you'll find out!"

CHAPTER 24

Kevin's words echo in my head. *"I'm glad you finally got to meet the real me."* As opposed to the *fake* him? Does he know that I found a way out of the shelter, and found his warehouse full of food? And that I searched his bedroom? For a minute I am so confused, I forget to be sad. And then I remember that I might never get to see Kevin again. My heart crashes, my stomach drops into my hips, and I want to scream. It feels just like the day Dean left.

The air seems to thicken around me, squeezing me, making my head throb, making it hard to breathe. I bite the inside of my cheek and force myself to breathe the dense shelter air.

Something touches my hand, a feathery warmth that wraps around three of my fingers. I look down into a pair of dark eyes. The beast-boy's eyes. They have the same hopeful expression my little brother's eyes get right before he starts begging me for something. But the beast-boy stays silent. His lower lip quivers.

Without a thought, I crouch down in front of him and throw my arms around his narrow shoulders. It feels just like hugging my eight-year-old brother, which intensifies the emotions already swirling through me as I start to cry. Sob. And this little boy stands perfectly still and lets me hold him—lets my tears drip down onto him until the shoulder of his oversize T-shirt is soaked.

"Sorry," I whisper, sniffling and leaning away from him. "Do you have a name?"

His black eyebrows furrow and he studies me.

"How old are you?"

The kid doesn't say a thing—just stares at me with haunted eyes.

"We'll call you Vince. That's my little brother's middle name. He's eight. Are you hungry?"

Haunted eyes. Staring.

"Come on. I'll make you some breakfast."

Like a lost little puppy, he follows me into the kitchen. As I measure powdered pancake mix out of a can and dump it into a bowl, Vince stares at me. I add the water and hold the bowl out to him. "Wanna stir?"

He stares.

"*Parli italiano?*" I ask. *Do you speak Italian?* He blinks at me and scratches his head. "I didn't think so, but it was worth a try."

When I put a plate piled high with steaming golden flapjacks onto the table, Vince doesn't bother to sit or use a fork. He grabs the stack of pancakes and shoves as much into his mouth as he can.

Fo comes out of the bathroom, hair wet and brushed away from her face, eyes red and swollen. A lump forms in my throat, nearly choking me. Today might be the first day of the rest of her life as a widow.

"Here." I put a second plate of pancakes on the table.

"Thanks, Jacqui," she whispers, sitting.

I walk to the stove and lift the frying pan from the burner. "Watch, Vince," I say, forcing myself to sound happy. I flip the pancake up into the air. Vince, mouth still full, watches it soar up almost to the ceiling. It slaps back down into the pan and he focuses on his food again. "Huh. That one always makes my brother laugh."

A minute later I take the hot pancake from the pan and slide it onto Vince's plate. He's already eaten five. At least *someone* has an appetite. My stomach hurts too much to eat. Fo stares at her plate but doesn't even pick up a fork.

"They'll come back," I say, but it sounds weak.

"How can you believe that when your own brother never came back?" She whispers this, but it hits me in the gut like she's punched me. I turn and brace my hands on the counter, staring into the stainless-steel sink. She's right. Nothing works out the way it should.

"I just wish there was a way to stay in contact with them. Why doesn't Kevin have walkie-talkies? He freaking has everything else in his little shelter," Fo says, voice full of anger.

Slowly, I turn around and stare at her.

"Why are you looking at me like that, Jacqui?" She stands up from the table, her eyes begging for a scrap of good news.

I whisk Vince's plate out from under him, midbite, and drop it into the sink. Fo's plate goes in next, stack of pancakes and all. Wasting food is a sin . . . unless it is for a really, *really* good reason. That's definitely an embroidery-worthy phrase.

"Move!" I grab Fo's hand and pull her away from the table, then scoot the chair and table to the middle of the kitchen and open the flour cupboard. One by one, I start yanking out cans.

"What are you doing?" Fo asks.

I peer over my shoulder at her. She's staring at me like I've gone nuts. "There's a door in here."

"Wow. I think you've lost it. The door is that way." She points in the other direction.

"No—a secret way out that leads to a place where we can see how they're doing. We can watch them."

Without another word, she's at my side, helping me get the last of the flour out of the cupboard. When we've gotten all forty-eight cans out, I grab two flashlights, insert batteries into both of them, and hand her one. We both glance at Vince. He is still eating—taking the pancakes out of the sink—and staring at us. I hold out my hand to him. "Come on, buddy. You're coming with me." He stares at my hand, so I take his hand in mine. His fingernails are all different lengths and filthy. I wrap my fingers around his hand so they're covering his tattoo.

"Is it safe? Do you really think we should let him come?" Fo asks.

"Do you really think we should leave him here alone? What if something happens to us? He could die down here without someone to take care of him." I duck into the cupboard, pulling Vince with me, and climb out on the other side.

"How do you know about this door? Did Kevin tell you?" Fo asks, crawling out of the cupboard and shining her flashlight down the cement hall.

"I found it when Kevin locked me in the shelter to go and get you guys."

"So he didn't tell you about it?" She sounds disappointed.

"No. Why?"

"Jonah thinks Kevin is an undercover raider. He thinks Kevin may be leading them into a trap, because if Jonah and Bowen are gone, then you and I are easier to capture. And with a secret passage down here, we're not as safe as I thought. He could send men in to get us without us ever unlocking the door."

"That doesn't make sense," I argue. "He could have already handed me over to the raiders."

"Jonah thinks the only reason Kevin didn't hand you over to them already is because he would lose his chance to hand me over too."

"No way. Kevin's not a raider." Anger makes my voice too loud and I wonder at this strong attachment I've grown to him.

"I didn't say I agreed. That's just what Jonah thinks. *I* think he's a Siren."

That theory actually makes sense. Almost. "But if he's a Siren, what does he gain? What is a Siren's ultimate goal?"

Fo shrugs. "That's the question."

We start walking and I keep hold of Vince's hand.

The walk through the cement hall seems to take forever,

with Vince slowing us down to touch every crack in the wall. When we get to the cave, the going is even slower. Vince pulls against my grasp on him and stares at everything, touches everything, has to jump in the stream that flows over the pathway until his pants—Kevin's oversize pants that are rolled up about ten times—are completely soaked. When he's done splashing, he crouches and lets the water run over his fingers, staring at it like he's never seen water before.

"Come on, Vince." I gently pull him away from the water. We continue through the cave without talking and then arrive at the food-storage room. Fo's mouth falls open as she looks at the rows and rows of food.

"I know," I say. "There's enough food in here to feed everyone in the city."

"Or to last Kevin a lifetime. Where did he get all of this food?"

"He said the food came from scavenging abandoned houses after the bee flu epidemic and pesticide wiped everything out."

"That's impossible. There's too much food. No one would have been able to gather this much."

I think of the meager rations my family lives on, despite searching abandoned houses and buildings for food on a semi-regular basis. Fo's right. There has to be another explanation.

Finally, we arrive at the wine cellar. Sunlight floods the cellar stairs, warming the air.

"Come on. We've got to go upstairs." I lead the way to the bedroom with the telescope. Without wasting a moment, I press my eye to the lens.

Morning sun is streaming through the window, warming my skin. I move the telescope, scanning the hillside. The motion makes my stomach turn, because moving the telescope one inch is like watching the world zoom by at one hundred miles per hour. Finally, when I'm queasy with motion sickness, I see a flash of movement. Three heads are bobbing down the foothills at an alarming rate, and they're almost at the bottom. I scream and look at Fo. "Found them!"

Fo takes my place at the telescope. I sit on the edge of the bed beside Vince and tap my toes. "Do you see them?" I ask.

"Yes. They're almost at the bottom of the foothills."

Vince leans his head against my shoulder, so I turn and look at him. He's holding something, turning it over and over in his hands. I take a closer look because I recognize it. "Can I see that?" He doesn't seem to understand, so I take the thing from his hand. It is an empty single-serving applesauce container with the foil lid still attached on one edge and fingernail marks gouged along the edges. "Fo, where did Vince get this?"

She takes her eye from the telescope, looks at the applesauce container, and points to a small bedside table that has a shallow drawer. I stand and open the drawer. There are other things in it—an empty tube of watermelon lip balm, a peanut-butter cracker snack-pack wrapper, and the letters *AB* made out of wire. My heart starts pounding, and I lift the wire letters.

Before anyone came into view, the dogs started barking, their noonday shadows blunt on the snow beneath them. I was on watch, so when I saw who it was, I told the dogs to be quiet and waved my dad back inside. "It's nothing," I said.

He was back, the homeless guy who seemed to find his way to my house a couple of times every month. Today he wore calf-high leather snow boots and layers of rags to keep the cold at bay. Dry mud was matted into his clothes, his eyebrows, even his beard, and there were enough twigs in his shoulder-length hair to make it look more like a bird's nest than hair. I couldn't even tell what color it was. Where did he find mud and twigs? Everything had been buried beneath eighteen inches of snow for more than two weeks.

"Hello, Jack." A smile lit his face. He looked worse than normal—the skin visible on his face was chapped, his lips were cracked and peeling—so I did what any human being would do. I reached into one of my vest pockets and took out a tube of watermelon lip balm. Since it made my lips slightly pink I wasn't allowed to wear it. The only reason I'd held on to it this long was because I loved the smell.

I held the lip balm out to him. He glanced at my hand and then up at my face, and his eyes filled with wonder. "Go on. Take it," I said. He reached for the lip balm. Fingerless wool gloves covered his hands, and when our bare fingers touched, he held on and looked right into my eyes. I forced myself not to yank away from his skin. When he let go, I covertly wiped my fingers against my pants.

"Thank you," he said, eyes still locked on mine. He tucked the lip balm into a fold of his ragged sweater. "I need to speak to your father."

He almost always wanted to speak to Dad, and Dad never turned him away and never told me why. He'd just brush off the vagabond's sporadic visits like they were a normal occurrence. And they were after a while.

"Why do you want to talk to him?" I asked, folding my arms over my chest.

His cracked lips curved up just a bit, giving me a glimpse of fuzzy teeth. "Just tell him I'm here. Please. I'll wait."

"Who should I tell him is here?" I asked. It had been nine months since he'd started showing up, and every time I asked him his name, he gave me the same reply:

"Names aren't important. Just tell him the vagabond is here." A smile twinkled in his eyes and pulled his lips away from his green, crooked teeth.

Not daring to take my eyes from the man, I walked backward to the front porch and opened the door. "Dad, the vagabond is here again."

Dad came to the door. When his gaze settled on the filthy man, Dad smiled. "Wait here, Jack," he said, and strode across the yard to meet him, holding out his hand. The bum took Dad's hand in his, and they shook like old friends. They spoke a few quiet words to each other, leaning close so their voices didn't carry, and then Dad turned and walked back into the house.

I stood on the porch and stared at the vagabond. He stared back, gaze riveted on me, hint of a smile on his mouth. "It's been cold," he called, kicking at the crusty snow.

The snow was everywhere, blanketing the whole visible world since no snowplows scraped the streets, and no one was around to shovel their driveways or sidewalks. It covered the trash and filth that littered my neighborhood—the broken-down cars, useless garbage cans, broken mailboxes—and made everything appear fresh and innocent.

"Are you guys staying warm?" His breath puffed out like white mist when he spoke.

"More or less." I shivered despite my goose-down coat and walked across the yard. I stopped beside Dean's dog, Bosco, and rested my hand on his head. "We have a big supply of useless furniture to burn, and when we run out, we just go into one of these houses for more." I nod toward the nearest house, a brick rambler that used to belong to the Johnsons. The bee flu killed them all.

The vagabond nods and takes a step toward me. I could reach out and touch him if I wanted to. I don't. Bosco's fur bristles and he growls, but the stranger doesn't look at the dog. He's too intent on me.

"The snow makes your eyes look like they are flecked with silver." His voice is quiet. My eyes grow round and I shrink away from him. Warning bells gong inside my head, and I put my hand on my gun. The vagabond lifts his hands up in the air and takes a step back. "Sorry. I didn't mean anything by it. It was just a random observation."

I take my hand off the gun and put it back on Bosco's warm head.

"Thank you, Jack." He lowers his hands and stares at me. And stares at me. And stares. There's something in his eyes, something I know well. Hunger. I can take a hint. I dig in my coat pocket and pull out a small piece of flatbread, flicking little pieces of lint from it, and then hand it to him.

He seems startled by the offering, but takes it and puts it in his mouth, and while he's chewing, he searches through his clothing and pulls out a thumb-size letter J made from wire, holding it up for me to see. It's beautiful—the wire is bent and weaved so it looks like the J is made out of a silver vine.

"There's a loop on top of it so you can put it on a necklace or keychain," he says.

I take the J and step back into my yard. The vagabond takes one more long look at me. "Good-bye, Jack."

"See ya," I say, and watch him walk down the snowy street, until he turns a corner and is gone from view. Then I unzip the top pocket on my vest—the pocket where I keep my most treasured things, like the lip balm I just gave away—and tuck the J safely inside.

I pick up the wire word *AB*, which is woven to look like it is made from silver vines. Lifting Kevin's sweatshirt halfway up my chest,

I unzip the top pocket on my vest, take out the *J* I was given nine months ago, and hold it to the *AB*. It fits perfectly—the wires lining up so exactly that the three letters had to have been woven at the same time and then had the *J* snipped off later.

A shiver runs down my spine. *JAB.* Those are my initials—Jacqui Aislynn Bloom. I put all three letters into the top pocket of my vest and walk in a daze to the closet. I already know what is in there, and it makes perfect sense. But the perfect sense is too weird to wrap my brain around.

The bars on the right side of the closet are full of hanging clothes, filthy oversize clothes, covered with dirt and dried grass—clothes no one would want to wear, not to mention hang up in a closet. On a shelf above the clothes are wigs, scarves, hats, and beards—all caked with dried mud and twigs and grass. Kevin's words echo in my head again. *I'm glad you finally got to meet the real me.* As opposed to the nasty, filthy, homeless version of him that I've sort of known for a year and a half. He is the vagabond. I shudder at the thought of kissing that homeless man. And then blush when I think of Kevin's lips on mine.

I lean against the closet door frame as opposites battle inside me. Trust versus mistrust. Attraction versus repulsion. Truth versus lies.

But the biggest thought running through my head is: *why in the world has Kevin, dressed as a filthy bum, been coming to my house for all these months?* Because it obviously wasn't for the minuscule tidbits of food I gave him.

"Oh no," Fo mutters. I grab the door frame and hold my breath, waiting for bad news. "Jack! You need to see this!"

CHAPTER 25

Vince is still sitting on the bed, driving the applesauce container, like it is a truck, over the faded quilt. Framed by the window, Fo is standing beside the telescope and watching me, her eyes wide with fear.

"What happened to the guys?" I ask, as if I've known all along something bad *would* happen. As I walk to the window, images of all the different ways Kevin, Bowen, and Jonah might die assault me—I've seen enough death to imagine some pretty gruesome things.

Fo shakes her head. "They're fine." But the look on her face, like she's in pain, belies her words. "At least for the moment."

"Then what is it?" I don't dare to look through the telescope. She doesn't answer, just tucks her long bangs behind her ears and stares at me with her big brown eyes. And then she starts to hum something sinister, like my life now has its own personal theme music.

"What are you humming?" I snap.

"Sarabande."

I stare at her.

"By Handel? Sorry. Morose, I know. I'll be quiet." She gestures to the telescope.

Bracing for something bad, I hold my breath and stare out the window. The morning sun has painted the world a hopeful shade of bright, but long shadows bleed out beneath everything. The distant interstate looks like a faded, tattered gray ribbon laid out in a long straight line over the brown landscape. Taking a deep breath, I put my eye against the telescope eyepiece. It's still warm from Fo. The distant world zips into view, and as if on cue, Fo starts humming again.

I am looking at a neighborhood at the base of the foothills. A group of men is walking along the road. I start counting them, an almost unconscious reaction. But when you're facing an enemy, the first thing you need to know is how many there are. As I count the last head, I have never been happier to be out of the city. Even my family would be hard-pressed to make a stand against fifteen big, stout, armed men.

"Looks like the raiders are out," I say.

Fo stops humming and says, "Keep looking. Move the telescope west."

I do what she says, and my blood runs cold and my ears start to ring. I back away from the telescope, clear to the other side of the room, until the wall collides with my back and I can't go any farther. "No. Please, no."

Fiona is staring at me. *Vince* is staring at me, as if finally, for the first time since he's woken, he understands something is wrong. He reaches out and grasps Fo's long fingers.

"They're about to get caught, aren't they," Fo says. She's not asking, just affirming what she already knows. She walks to my side. Vince, still holding her hand, trails a step behind. "Is getting caught part of the plan?"

"No. The plan is to sneak into raider headquarters and get the cure." I unzip the top pocket on my vest and take out a folded square of paper. I hold it out to Fo.

"What is this?" She takes it from my trembling fingers.

"Plan Z, for if all else fails," I whisper. I hug her and my gun grinds against my hip. "Take care of Vince." In a daze, I turn and stride out of the room.

"Wait!" Fo comes after me. "Where are you going?"

I take a deep breath and fight the urge to vomit. "To warn them."

"You can't go out there! You'll get caught or you'll die!"

I wipe the tears from my eyes. "Then I'll die trying, because I am *sick* of sitting around while everyone else fights!"

"Just hold on for one second. You have to do this right!" She pulls me back into the room, to the telescope, and puts her eye to it, slowly moving it back and forth. "Look." She takes a step away and gestures to it. I look.

The guys have stopped running down the foothills. They're in a copse of dead scrub, huddled together. Kevin is talking, occasionally pointing toward the city.

"Do you see that water tower?" Fo asks. Not far below the guys, just at the base of the foothills, sits a massive tan water tank.

"I see it."

"That's your landmark to help you find them." She hugs me so hard I can't breathe. And then she bursts into tears. "Run fast."

"I will."

Drenched with sweat, I approach the bottom of the foothills and don't slow down, not even to remove Kevin's red sweatshirt. There's no time to waste on frivolous things like that. And I am doing what I do best. Only, for the first time ever, I am running *toward* danger, not away from it.

My gun is in my hand, catching sunlight. My muscles ache, my breath is ragged, and the metal letters in my top vest pocket clink together with every step I take. Fo's hummed music, Sarabande, is playing and replaying in my brain—constant theme music that keeps beat with my pounding feet.

I get to the bottom of the foothills and jolt to a stop. I have reached my destination—the massive water tank, which looked tan from the telescope but up close is grainy with rust and dotted with patches of flaking paint. There is no sign of the guys.

I lean against the water tank and hug my arms over my chest. I am now in raider territory and have no idea what to do. Spread before me is a neighborhood of silent midsize houses that once had nicely landscaped yards. Now, dead bushes and bleached weeds choke the rock-lined flower beds.

I step away from the water tank, roll my tense shoulders a

couple of times, and creep into the backyard of the closest house. My shadow huddles beneath my feet. The sun heats my dark, damp hair like it is trying to sooth me with its warmth. It doesn't work. I'm feeling less and less confident with every step I take.

I am walking between two houses when someone whispers my name. *"Jacqui."*

My gun is up, my arm ready to absorb the impact of a shot, and I circle around, searching for the source of the voice.

CHAPTER 26

"Jack!" Kevin, eyes shadowed by his camo baseball cap, waves at me from the doorway of the house to my right.

Relief makes me want to melt—somehow, with the appearance of Kevin, I know everything is going to be okay. I put the gun away and sprint to the house, throwing myself at him and wrapping my arms around his neck. He stumbles backward through the doorway and pushes me arm's length away. His eyes flash and his fingers dig into my shoulders. "What are you doing here? You shouldn't be here, Jack."

"The raiders. They're in this neighborhood. Lots of them," I explain, knowing that as soon as he hears why I'm here, he'll agree I've done the right thing. "I came to warn you guys."

Kevin stares at me for a long moment, eyes burning with fury, and then he sighs and sags, as if he's been completely deflated. His hands drop from my shoulders, and he presses his fingers to his temples. "This isn't what we planned. You shouldn't have come!"

"We didn't plan for you to get caught by raiders either!" I say. His brow furrows, and he strides over to an east-facing window, peering out of it.

We're in a dining room that has no table and no chairs—just a dusty copper chandelier hanging from the ceiling in the middle of the room and a china cabinet against one wall. The dishes inside are untouched, their gold trim gleaming.

"Where's the note I gave you?" Kevin asks.

"I gave it to Fo. In case she needs a plan Z."

"So, you read it." He turns from the window and looks at me, disappointed.

I shake my head. "No. I said I wouldn't, and I didn't."

"Then how do you know there are raiders in this neighborhood?" His gaze moves slowly over me, searching every inch of my body, as if it will give him the answers to his questions.

"The day you locked me in the shelter so you could meet my friends at the lake, I found the tunnel and followed it to your house. Fo and I were watching you through the telescope." I unzip the top pocket of my vest and take out the wire initials, placing them in my palm and holding them out for him to see. "Why did you dress up as a vagabond and come to my house?"

Kevin stands perfectly still and stares at the letters. Then his eyes locked on mine. "Jacqui Bloom," he whispers. He steps away from the window, strides up to me, and puts his hands on my shoulders. "I went to your house to see you." He speaks fast, so fast I almost can't understand him.

"Me?"

He nods. "Every time you gave me food, I could see how big of a sacrifice it was for you to part with it. It made me want to know more about you. The day you gave me applesauce, and then started crying because you didn't want to give it away? That's the moment I started to fall in love with you. Every time I saw you after that, I fell in love with you more, until it felt like I was living for the days when I got to see you, and the rest of my life was just spent waiting for those days." His words are still rushed, so rushed I wonder if I've heard him right. I don't have time to ponder what he said because he blurts, "And now, I need to kiss you one last time."

He takes off his hat and leans toward me until our foreheads are touching, staring into my eyes like he's seeing all the way to my soul, and I can't stand it. I grab his face in my hands and kiss him. He tastes like salt, and all I can think is how glad I am that the raiders didn't catch him, how glad I am that he is right here with me, safe. How glad I am that I made it down the mountain in time to warn him.

His hand moves to the back of my neck and squeezes, hurting my scabbed bullet wound. I pull away from him. For a moment, he studies my face, but then his eyes focus on a point above my head, and he takes a deep breath of air that fills his lungs until the buttons on his shirt start to strain.

I turn and look behind me, trying to see what he's staring at, but there's nothing. "Kevin?" He won't look at me. My skin starts to crawl. "What's wrong?" I whisper.

He puts his hands on my shoulders and gently turns me around so that my back is to him, and then he pulls his hat onto my head, tugging the bill low over my eyes. His hands trail across my shoulders and down my arms. I close my eyes and try to shake the feeling of wrongness growing in me. When he gets to my wrists, his hands stop. He tugs my arms behind my back.

"I'm sorry," he whispers, his lips against my ear, and then something rough and scratchy circles my wrists, cinching them together so tightly my skin chafes. I jerk away but he's holding me tight. He takes the gun from my belt, and then my knife, and just like that, I am disarmed and restrained.

CHAPTER 27

I whirl around to face him. "Why in the world are you tying me up?"

He tucks my gun into the waistband of his pants and slips my knife into his pocket. Taking my shoulders, he turns my back to him again and grips my arms. "I'm a raider, Jack."

His words jolt me. "But you don't have any raider markings."

"The better to catch unsuspecting prey." His hands tighten on my biceps. "I'm the 'wolf' that Flint warned you about."

Survival mode kicks in. I ram my head backward and feel a crunch on the back of my skull. Next, I stomp on Kevin's foot. When I try to run, he digs his fingers into my skin until I yelp.

"For future reference," he says, "don't try to headbutt someone who is eight inches taller than you."

I twist in his arms and lunge, head bowed, ramming him in

the stomach. He loses his footing and falls backward. His head crashes into the copper chandelier, and then somehow he grabs me and *I* am the one falling. My head crunches against the hardwood floor and my vision blurs.

He's straddling me with my bound arms pinned over my head. I can hardly lift his weight to breathe, so I lie there, stunned, staring at the swinging chandelier. The throb of a deep voice floats into the house through a broken window and my heart soars with hope. "Bowen? Jonah?" I yell.

Kevin shakes his head. "It's the raiders. Pretend you don't know me." He grips my upper arm and climbs to his feet, pulling me up with him. And then his entire face changes. The muscles under his skin seem to harden and turn to cement, and the corners of his mouth turn down.

The front door opens. "Yo, Kev," someone calls.

"Over here." Kevin's hand tightens on my arm.

Three men and a dog file into the dining room, crowding it.

"So, did Lil' Red Riding Hood get caught by the big bad wolf?" one of the men asks. He's the youngest of the group, probably a few years older than me, with a shaved head and a black goatee that's braided halfway down his chest.

"Yep." Kevin's hand tightens on my arm to the point of painful, and I can't help but think about the food in his shelter. What was it Bowen said? The raiders pay several years' worth of food for a female like me? I wonder how many women Kevin has sold in exchange for his enormous food supply. I want to barf. I *ate* some of that food.

The dog, a German shepherd, starts barking and lunges at me, snapping its chain taut before it gets close enough to sink its teeth into my flesh. The man holding the dog's chain pulls it until the dog is restrained at his side.

"That was fast," the goateed man says, holding his raider-marked hand out to Kevin for a high five. "How'd you catch him? We thought you might need backup."

Kevin slaps the guy's hand. "Stupid boy walked right up to me."

Goatee Man looks me over and sneers. "We thought he might be tough like those other two."

Those other two? He's turned Jonah and Bowen over to the raiders. Hot, violent anger scalds my insides. I thrash against Kevin's hold on my arm, kicking him in the shins, trying to knee him in the crotch. He grimaces and holds me at arm's length but doesn't loosen his hold.

Goatee Man laughs. "He looks kind of on the scrawny side. And young. Do you think it's worth it for us to take him to headquarters? I'll put him in the crosshairs right now and save us the trouble." The raider lifts a rifle that's strapped to his back and points it at me. I stop thrashing and stare down the barrel.

"He's tougher than he looks," Kevin says. "But you're right. He is young. Maybe we should let him go. Unless he wants to join us?" Kevin shakes my arm. "You want to join us, kid, and be a raider?"

I spit on Kevin for an answer, though like in all things currently happening in my life, my spit falls way short of what I intended. It hits the edge of his sleeve.

Kevin frowns at my spit. "He doesn't want to join. Just let him go and save ourselves some trouble."

Goatee Man grins. "Let him go? Let him *go*? Let's set him loose in the foothills and use him for target practice!"

I whimper. The dog growls, its lips curling up to expose yellow teeth. Goatee Man's eyes light up, and he rubs his hands together. "Better yet, let's bring him to the compound and use him for throat-tearing practice."

"Oh, man, Striker, now you're thinking," the raider holding the dog says. The third raider, a grizzly man with a long gray beard, glares at me and leaves the house.

"What's throat-tearing practice?" Kevin asks.

"That's right. You haven't been around the compound for a while," Goatee Man—Striker—says. "Have you met that new guy, Soneschen?"

I clench my teeth. That is a name I will never forget.

"Soneschen? Is he at the compound?" Kevin asks.

Striker nods.

"You mean the guy who used to be the governor of the walled city?"

"Yep," Striker says, beaming with pride.

"What does Hastings think about that?" Kevin asks.

"Hastings hasn't killed the guy, so that's something. Believe it or not, Hastings has been less violent since the women got away. He's only beat one guy to death this week."

I shudder.

"In fact, Hastings and Soneschen have been working together. You know Hastings's little science experiments?"

Kevin nods.

"Soneschen figures it's time we started training them for

better things. He also says we need something to take our minds off the missing women. This kid is just perfect." Striker grabs the scruff of my neck and yanks me out of Kevin's hands. "We left your supplies on the porch. Catch ya next week, Kev-man, if we don't see you sooner."

I am being herded out of the house. Striker is squeezing the back of my neck like he's trying to make my head pop off. The dog growls at me and snaps when I walk by, but the leash-wielding raider yanks it away.

Striker opens the front door and a gust of wind whips Kevin's sweatshirt against my chest, making all the bulky pockets of my vest bulge against it. *Please don't take my vest!* I think. Because for now these guys think I am a boy. I duck my head, letting the brim of Kevin's hat hide my face even more, and walk down a cracked and crumbling cement driveway.

Earlier, when I got to the water tank, I thought I didn't know what to do. I was wrong. Then, I had choices. *Now* I don't know what to do. I am completely defeated.

"Wait," Kevin's calls. A burst of hope fills me. In my mind's eye I can see what he's about to do—pull my gun from his belt, knock off the raiders and their dog with four perfect shots, run to me and untie my hands, and then tell me he did all of this because it was the only way he knew to save my life. I turn and watch him, his head held high, his hand on my gun as he strides out of the house. The wind blows loose strands of his dark-copper hair across his face so he whips his head to the side. He opens his mouth to speak, and I tense for the boom of gunfire.

"I'm coming with you guys. I want to see what neck-tearing practice is."

My hope shatters, leaving me filled with so much despair I can hardly lift my feet, but somehow I do. I make my feet walk in a straight line down the middle of the street. The wind lashes dust and sand against the side of my face, so I turn my head away. Something hard crashes into my cheek, forcing my face back into the wind.

"Eyes forward." Striker lowers his rifle.

Kevin steps up beside me. "Listen to him," he says, voice rock hard. But I don't want to. And I *really* don't want to listen to Kevin. I grit my teeth and taste blood and kick the side of Kevin's knee as hard as I can, sending him sprawling.

The ground leaps at me. I am on my stomach and someone is smashing my face against pavement, grinding loose gravel into my cheek. "First rule of the raiders: you never lay a finger on one of us," Striker says. "You touch one of us again and I will shoot you in the leg and leave you to die." He pushes my face harder and then drags me to my feet. I blink sand from my eyelashes, stare straight forward, and walk.

We come to a fork in the road and turn left, but instead of continuing forward, we turn left again, onto a driveway that is covered with the dark shadow of tire marks.

I peer up at a two-story house covered with fractured tan stucco. Armed men are staring down at me from second-story windows, so I look away. The dead grass in the yard has trails worn into it, and, where it isn't covered with dog crap, is filled with shallow holes. The man with the dog goes into the yard and hooks the dog's chain to a spike in the ground.

"Yo! Open up!" Striker bangs the butt of his rifle on the garage door. A motor hums and the door rises, exposing two four-wheelers and a side-by-side in front of a wall lined with red plastic gas cans. We walk between two of the vehicles and up some steps that lead into a small mudroom.

The first thing I notice are the glaring electrical lights. Next, I notice the purr of a generator. And then the smell hits me— man smell—and not a good soap/cologne/aftershave type of man smell. Something more along the lines of sweaty armpits, greasy hair, athlete's foot, dirty butt, and teeth that haven't seen a toothbrush in years.

I am shoved through a doorway, into the next room, and I forget about the smell. I have stepped into raider central.

CHAPTER 28

Raiders are everywhere, packed into the house like sardines—eating, cleaning weapons, sleeping on the filthy carpet, standing at windows with binoculars. I want to run and never look back. I want to faint. I want to pee my pants.

In a corner of the room, beside a cold, ash-filled fireplace, sit Bowen and Jonah, their hands tied behind their backs. Jonah's face is bleeding, his blind eye swollen shut. Bowen's eyes meet mine, and I can hear him curse clear across the room. The raiders, all greasy and burly and armed, turn and look at me and the room goes silent.

Someone starts laughing. "Is that scrawny-assed kid the person Morrison saw running down the foothills?" Other raiders laugh. "Why don't we set him loose and use him for target practice?"

Striker puts his hot, damp palm on my shoulder and towers over me like he owns me. "I have a better idea." He cups my chin in his hand and slowly tips my head back. I'm too scared to protest, to fight back. And I hope and pray they can't tell that I'm female. His fingers caress my neck and I squeeze my eyes shut. "Let's bring him back to the compound and volunteer him for neck-tearing practice."

The raiders explode with conversation, ignoring me so completely I might as well have just died. Their eyes gloss over as they start betting food, clothing, and weapons on how long I'll last.

One man steps up to me and puts his beefy hands around my neck. I flinch and wait for him to tear it, but all he does is measure it, and then hold his fingers up in a small circle. He frowns. "I don't see how he's even worth betting over. Look how tiny his neck is!"

I think I'm going to be sick, barfing up all the food I ate at Kevin's house over the past two days—not that I wouldn't mind getting it out of my body.

An icy hand clamps my elbow and Kevin is at my side, yanking me a little too roughly toward the corner where Jonah and Bowen sit. I glance at Kevin. He's pale, even his lips, and a thin sheen of sweat covers his face. A couple of feet from the fireplace, Kevin shoves me. I trip and slam into Jonah. He feels like a pile of bricks.

Bowen leans forward and glares at me, his green eyes like daggers. "Of all the *stupid* things you'll ever do in your life, this one will top them all! Why are you here?" he asks through gritted teeth.

"Give Jack a break." Jonah shifts his body so my head is against a slightly softer spot on his chest, and I'm so limp with terror, I can't help but press all my weight against him. "Are you all right?" he asks.

I nod and sniffle.

"Don't cry!" Bowen whispers, which makes me want to cry even more. His face softens a tiny bit, and he looks right into my eyes. "Calm down, okay? We've got time to think of a way to get you out of here."

I take a deep, shaky breath and nod.

"Good boy. Now, tell me why you're here. Is Fo all right?" Fear darkens his eyes when he says Fo's name.

It takes me a minute to compose myself enough to speak without bursting into tears. "Fo is fine. I came to warn you that you were about to intercept the raiders." I wipe my nose on my shoulder. "I was too late. I didn't know you'd been caught!"

Bowen hangs his head forward and groans. I want to scream. I want to fight. So many emotions are pent up inside me, I want to explode and take everyone in the house with me.

"It's going to be okay, Jack." Jonah's voice is a gentle rumble barely audible above the sound of the raiders. And even though I don't believe him, I relax a bit and look around.

Aside from a dining table and eight mismatched chairs, the house is empty of furniture. A glance through the window shows why—all of the furniture has been chucked into the backyard and chopped into a pile of firewood. In the kitchen, the gray-bearded man who came when Kevin captured me is pouring cans of something into a massive cast-iron pot. As if he can feel my stare, he glances over his shoulder and our eyes lock.

"Why does he keep looking at you?" Bowen whispers. "All of the other raiders seem to have forgotten us. Except him."

He's right. It is as if the raiders are so confident in their invincibility, they've forgotten we are here. Even Kevin is standing with his shoulder against a wall, spitting on a whetstone and dragging a knife across it—my knife. He doesn't so much as glance in our direction.

"I can't believe he did this to us!" I whisper, trying to kill him with my glare.

"Who?" Bowen follows my gaze. "Kevin? What are you talking about?"

"Turning us over to the raiders! That's got to be where he got all of his food."

Bowen and Jonah share a meaningful glance. "Don't be too hard on him," Jonah says. "He probably wouldn't have let them take you if he had a choice, but a raider spotted you running down the foothills. They sent him to intercept you. I don't think he could have done anything differently."

As if he can hear us, Kevin glances in our direction. I squeeze my eyes shut. I don't want to look at him. If I never see him again, it will be too soon.

"Grub!"

The lone word has the power of a vortex, sucking every single raider into the kitchen—eighteen in all. They're each given a bowl of food—chili by the smell of it. Most of the raiders don't bother with spoons, instead opting to scoop the chili into their mouths with their filthy fingers. Within less than three minutes, the food has been devoured and the raiders are throwing their dirty dishes into the sink and wiping their hands on their clothes or the walls. Except Kevin. He's still standing with his shoulder against the wall, dragging the knife across the whetstone. I suppose, since he's a raider, he needs a *really* sharp knife. I stare at his profile, the way his nose leads to his lips, and my blood speeds up a bit—which makes me want to slap him, and then slap myself twice as hard. *He betrayed you,* I tell my body. *Stop liking him!*

Striker lifts both his hands above his head, and the raiders fall silent. "Anyone not stationed here, let's get back to the compound!" He struts over to us and kicks at me until, with Jonah's help, I stand. "Go." He nods toward the garage and I go.

The door leading into the garage is open, and the exterior garage door is still up. Wind stirs the air, gusting into the garage and erasing the man smell. I gulp clean air into my lungs, then something hits the back of my knees hard enough to send me toppling down the garage stairs. At the bottom, I smack my head on the cement floor and the world goes fuzzy. Someone laughs, but only for a second. Even in my dazed, hurting state I recognize the sound of fists contacting flesh. I can't help but wonder if Kevin is standing up for me, so I look up.

Striker is punching someone in the face, over and over. I can't tell who the other person is because his face is already covered with blood. "Don't hurt the kid!" Striker yells as he punches. "He's my contribution to the neck-tearing pool!" No one moves to stop Striker—not even the guy who's being punched to a pulp. When the guy falls to his knees, Striker stops and wipes his bloody knuckles on the battered man's shirt. "Let's go." He steps past me without a backward glance.

Cold, clammy hands ease my head up off the floor, and I am staring into eyes the color of the morning sky. Kevin's fingers probe my skull for a brief moment, and then he lifts me to my feet, drags me to the closest four-wheeler, and takes my—his— hat off of me. He pulls a black wool beanie onto my head and down over my face, and the world goes dark. I'm hoisted up onto the back of a four-wheeler and strapped down. More people climb on, making the vehicle sink and bounce. The engine revs and we speed away.

Direction is meaningless. The belt strapping me to the four-wheeler digs into my hips as the driver of the vehicle takes turns too fast. With each turn my stomach becomes more and more unsettled. Finally, after what feels like hours, the driver slams on the brakes and the four-wheeler skids to a stop.

"Hastings is in charge of the animals. Bring the dog treat to him," someone says.

Still blinded by the beanie, I feel the strap holding me to the four-wheeler—the only reason I stayed on it—being removed from my hips.

Hands wrap around my waist and I'm thrown over someone's shoulder, my head the lowest point on my body. My throbbing head and motion-sick body can't handle the shoulder pressing into my stomach. Vomit shoots out of me with enough force to make my entire body recoil, and then it gets trapped in my beanie and I can't breathe. My entire body goes taut as I try to lurch away from the beanie, try to spit vomit out of my mouth and blow it out of my nostrils, so that I can suck air into my lungs before I suffocate.

The shoulder no longer presses into my stomach. For half a second I seem to be floating, and then something hard collides with my head, making an audible crunch. Whatever hit my head slams into my body, and I am conscious just long enough to realize I've been dropped.

CHAPTER 29

Sounds come first. Muffled voices, a barking dog, my pulse slowly throbbing in my ears. Pain comes next. My brain is trying to burst out of my skull, pushing my eyeballs against their sockets so hard they feel like they are going to pop. And then emotions—betrayal, sorrow, fear—but I can't remember why I am feeling any of them. And finally sight.

Darkness. A square window slotted with bars shows me the silhouette of a charcoal sky. A bolt of lightning flashes outside the window, giving me a glimpse of pale rectangles covering the floor of my room—mattresses with barely enough space between them to walk. I squeeze my eyes shut and see the jagged slash of light that has been seared into my vision.

And then I wonder where I am.

Memories slam into me, memories that correspond with my

emotions. Betrayal caused by Kevin. Sorrow caused by Kevin. Fear caused by Kevin . . . and the raiders. I have been caught.

My eyes pop open, and my hand goes to my belt, but I have no weapons. I jolt up from the mattress I've been sleeping on, groan, and cradle my head. The pain is so bad that I want to vomit again, but my stomach is empty. I take a deep breath and wobble across the room, my feet unstable on the mattresses, and peer out of the window.

Droplets of water speckle the glass, making the world outside a blur. Everything is dark, even the sky. Lightning flashes again, turning the sky pale gray and illuminating a large expanse of dead grass with a giant tree skeleton in the middle, enclosed on all sides by a brick wall.

Stumbling through the dark, I go to the other side of the room, to a door with a window barely bigger than my hand, and peer out. The room on the other side of the window is even darker than my room. Wrapping my hand around the doorknob, I twist, but the door is locked.

I go back to the window showing the tree and dead grass. Lightning flashes again, illuminating a window latch. I undo the latch and slide the window up, and wrap my hand around rain-wet prison bars. Pressing my face between two bars, I take a deep breath. The world smells clean and fresh. It is neither of those things.

Cool air seeps into the room and down to my feet. I wiggle my toes and a wave of panic hits me. *Where are my shoes?*

Another flash of lightning lights up my clothes. Kevin's red hoodie is gone. I am wearing my vest—a really good thing—but the shirt underneath it is an oversize black T-shirt, not my regular dingy white T-shirt. Someone took my shirt off of me. My knees tremble and I fall onto my butt, bouncing on a mattress. The jolt sends a shock of pain through my head and a surge of nausea into my empty stomach.

Another rush of memory assails me—vomit being held tight against my face by a black beanie. I gasp a breath of rain-scented air. My hands go to my clean face, to my clean hair. Someone washed my hair. Someone changed my shirt but left my sports bra on, then put my vest back on me. I pat the pockets. They're full. Even fuller than normal. I unzip the bottom pocket—the biggest—and something crackles.

Lightning flashes again, revealing the whole room, and I scream the very second it goes back to dark. Seared into my eyes is the pattern of the lightning broken by the shape of a huge man walking toward me.

I turn to run and trip on a mattress, falling to my hands and knees. Pressure zings my head and I groan, letting my neck wobble so my head dangles between my shoulders. A big hand grabs my shoulder and pulls me up to sitting. I curl my fingers into claws and start lashing out at the shadow. My short nails scrape against metal.

"Jack, it's me, Jonah."

My hands drop to my sides, and I stare at the massive shadow crouched beside me. And then I throw my arms around him. I don't think I have ever been happier to see someone in my life. He doesn't hug me back, not with his hands restrained in front of him with metal cuffs that go from his wrists to his elbows. "How's your head?" he asks.

I let go of him and groan. "It hurts. I can hardly stand it."

"I think there's something in your vest that might help with that."

I reach into the pocket I unzipped before Jonah scared me almost to death and pull out a plastic-wrapped rectangle. I open the wrapper and the smell of oats and cinnamon hit me like a burst of optimism. My stomach jumps and flips and tries to sail away with joy. I bite the granola bar and *almost* forget my pounding head. At least until I chew, because every time my teeth crunch, my head throbs.

"Give me a piece," Jonah says. I break a big chunk off and hand it to him. He holds it to his mouth and then gives it back to me.

"You don't like granola bars?" I mumble through my half-chewed food.

"I'm not hungry," he says.

"Suit yourself." I swallow and put the piece I handed to him into my mouth, chew twice, and stop. There's something wet and warm on top of it. "Wat did you put on dis," I mumble, mouth full.

"Something that will make your head feel better."

"Medicine?"

"Yes. Chew and swallow, Jack. Chew and swallow."

I fight the urge to gag and chew as fast as I can, then gulp it down. "What kind of medicine was that? It was warm and thick like . . ."

"Spit?"

I shudder. "Yes."

"My spit has the ability to help you heal faster. Hasn't Fo

told you about the time when she shot Bowen?" His voice is quiet, almost emotionless.

"She *what*?"

"Blew a hole clean through him. He would have died, but her saliva had the leftover effects of being a beast, and she happened to be kissing him a lot at the time. Because he ingested her saliva, his body healed faster. You know that the government modified the bees to withstand all pesticides and predators, right?"

"Of course. Everyone knows that."

"It gave the bees incredible physical strength and the ability to heal more quickly. Lucky me. I was given a vaccine that had traces of the chemicals they gave the bees. It altered my genetics, just like it altered the bees'. I'm freakishly strong and heal more quickly, too." His voice is toxic. "How is your head feeling now?"

I slowly move my head from side to side. It feels like my brain has doubled in size and is going to squirt out of my ears at any second. "A little better, maybe," I lie.

"Do you want some more spit?"

"No! Unless you can find a less disgusting way to give it to me."

Silence settles over us. I look at Jonah and realize he's looking at me. The window lights up and the room is flooded with a split second of light, just enough for me to see the way he's staring at me—like I've got explosives strapped to my chest—before everything goes dark and thunder rumbles.

"I would never make you kiss me," he whispers. "I see the repulsion in your eyes when you look at me. I'm not the kind of guy you should be thinking about kissing anyway, especially when you've got a decent guy trying to win your heart."

The double meaning behind my words sinks in, and I lean away from him. "Okay, I did not just ask you to kiss me. And my eyes aren't filled with repulsion when I look at you." My voice is filled with repulsion. A wave of guilt makes me want to shrink and disappear. "Wow. That sounded really bad. I'm so sorry, Jonah. I guess I have a talent for doing really stupid stuff."

He drops his head and laughs a hoarse, whispered laugh, possibly the first laughter that has come out of him in four years. "I know I'm hideously ugly. You don't have to pretend I'm not."

My heart aches at his words. I know how it feels to look at yourself and see nothing beautiful there. And then I think about how Jonah held the beast-child for hours while we waited for the cure to start working, and how he spoke so gently to me when the raiders caught me and Bowen was furious. He is good and kind and meek. *That* is real beauty.

"Jonah," I whisper. I kneel in front of him, take his face in my hands, and lean forward until my lips are on his. They're cool beneath mine and so much softer than the rest of him. He kisses me back, soft and so gentle that tears spring to my eyes. He shouldn't be here. He's too good for this place. I pull back but don't let go of his face. "Real beauty can't be seen." My voice trembles with the truth behind the statement.

He's quiet for a long moment, and I don't let go of his face. Finally, he says, "Thanks, Jacqui."

I sit down on the mattress and wrap my hands around my knees. "And I hate Kevin, if he's the *decent guy* you're talking about."

"Don't hate him. Not until you can make a fair judgment about him." Jonah lies down on the mattress beside mine. "Life's too short to let little things bring you down."

My nostrils flare and I grit my teeth. "You call Kevin's handing me over to a gang of raiders a little thing?"

"Yes. Trust me. There are worse things that could happen."

"There are?" I don't understand how he can say this when I am living my worst nightmare. "Like what?"

He lies absolutely still and silent. When he doesn't answer, I take the rest of the granola bar out of the wrapper and eat it. It's not until I swallow the last bite that I realize my head didn't hurt when I chewed. I blink and my eyes don't feel like they're going to burst out of their sockets. Maybe there *is* something beneficial about eating beast spit.

I lie down on my mattress, rest my hands over my stomach, and stare into darkness.

"Being tortured by a group of raiders because they want you to tell them where your new bride is. That's probably worse."

I sit up too fast and my head feels like it's going to snap off. Pressing my hands against my temples, I ask, "Are you talking about Bowen?"

"Yes." He shifts, and the mattress he's on squeaks beneath him. "Or, having your free will stripped from you, and then being struck with the overpowering desire to kill and eat anything that moves. And then remembering it every waking and sleeping second of your life. That's worse than being handed over to a gang of raiders."

I barely hear his whispered words over the drone of rain falling on the roof. But I *do* hear them. I think of the empty look in his eyes, his long silences, and my heart aches.

"I don't want to find my mom," he whispers.

I gasp. "Why not?"

"I killed my dad. I remember it. It was in the music room. My hands . . ." He takes a deep, trembling breath. "My mom will never be able to forgive me."

I reach out and touch Jonah, resting my hand on his shoulder. Kevin's betrayal is dwindling down to insignificance. My problems seem small now, relatively speaking.

"He's the Siren," Jonah says.

I frown in confusion. "What?"

"Kevin. He's the Siren."

I blink twice before answering. "Are you serious?"

"He denied it when I asked him, but I still think he is." Jonah shifts on his mattress and the cuffs on his arms reflect the dim light seeping through the window.

"No way. He's a raider."

"No, I'm pretty sure he's the Siren. Think about it, Jack. The cowboy warned us to keep away from the Sirens because, in the cowboy's opinion, Sirens are bad. But the cowboy is a raider. That means the raiders don't like the Sirens. That means the Sirens are probably good. Do you see what I mean?"

"Maybe," I say.

"If I'm right, Kevin is playing both sides—raider and Siren. The raiders didn't brand him because more innocent people trust him that way. It was our *plan* to have him hand Bowen and me over to the raiders so we could get into this building without getting shot."

"We didn't plan that," I blurt.

"*You* didn't help us plan that part, but that's what we planned. Kevin didn't want you to know he was working with the raiders."

I bristle with frustration. "Why wouldn't Kevin tell me something so important?"

"To protect himself and you. The fewer people who know what he really is, the more likely he is to live. The raiders think he is one of them, so they trust him. He can go where they are, and know what they have planned. That's how he saved us when we were at the golf course—by knowing how the raiders work—and how he saved you when you guys were surrounded by them later that night. Today, he didn't tell them that you're a girl, which drastically increases your chances of surviving."

He pauses for a long moment and then adds, "I believe he's the one who freed the raiders' women."

I think of the things I saw in his shelter—the tampons, the baby formula, the diapers. "Did they have babies? The raiders' women?"

"I don't know."

It almost makes sense. Except for the fact that he handed me over to them. Especially if he broke all the women out in the first place.

"But he *gave* me to—"

"He had no choice," Jonah retorts. "You were wearing a bright red sweatshirt! They *saw* you coming. If Kevin let you go, the raiders would have known he's the Siren, and his cover would have been blown. Can you imagine what they would do to him if they suspected he was the one who broke all of those women out? He'd be *lucky* if they killed him."

I think of how I treated Kevin when he handed me over to

the raiders. If Jonah is right, I owe Kevin a huge apology. "So, why didn't they put me in wrist cuffs?" I ask.

Jonah laughs under his breath. "You're just a little thing—not a big enough threat. They cuffed me and were going to put me in with the beasts. . . . Electromagnetic cuffs are only necessary for beasts and Fecs. They'll shock me with them if I get out of line, and they are held together with five hundred pounds of force."

"They have beasts here?"

"About ten."

"Why?"

"Something about the 'new guy' wanting them. I don't know if Fo told you, but drinking beast blood is a lot like eating beast spit. It makes you stronger and makes you heal faster."

I shudder.

A light flickers, something more yellow than the stark, pale blue of lightning. An icy hand grabs mine, squeezing. "They're coming," Jonah whispers. "Be tough, don't say anything stupid, and act twelve!"

The light flickers again, illuminating the square window in the door. A shadowed face appears in the window, and the slow arc of a flashlight sweeps across the room before stopping on Jonah and me. The door rattles and then is opened, and a black mass is dropped inside. The door slams shut and a lock clicks into place. Before I have time to wonder what just happened, Jonah is on his feet and across the room, grappling with the dark mass. It takes me a moment to realize what it is—a person.

CHAPTER 30

"Jack, come here!" Jonah maneuvers the person onto a mattress.

I scramble over to Jonah's side and jump when a light flashes on. Jonah shines a small flashlight onto the person and I can't tell who it is because his face is swollen and bleeding. But then the mouth moves. "Jack?" And the voice gives it away.

"Bowen?"

He groans and one of his eyes opens just a tiny bit, too swollen to do more. "I was hoping you would have escaped by now." His eye flickers to Jonah. "Have you been feeding her spit?"

"A little. She won't eat it."

"Jack, you've got to eat the spit! If you don't get out of here, they're going to give you to—" He tries to sit up but Jonah pushes him back down.

"Who? They're going to give me to who?" I ask. There's something urgent in his voice. He doesn't answer. Jonah squeezes

Bowen's cheeks so his lips open and then spits into his mouth. I don't mean to, but my mouth puckers and I shudder.

A horrible gagging sound comes from Bowen's throat and then he swallows. His less-swollen eye cracks open again. "Wow. That's so much more pleasant when it comes from your sister."

"Well, get used to it," Jonah says. "You're going to need a lot more."

Something bubbles up in me and spills out. Giggles. I press my hand over my mouth and hold them in.

Jonah and I clean up Bowen as best we can and then make him comfortable on one of the mattresses. By the time we're done, my head is hurting like I have an average, ordinary stress headache—a miraculous improvement. I lie down on a mattress with Jonah's mattress on the left, and Bowen's mattress on the right, and close my eyes. They haven't been closed that long before Bowen and Jonah both start to snore. I lie still and open my eyes, listening to Jonah's thrashing and mumbling. The sound mingles with the occasional rumble of thunder, the barking of dogs, and the deep hum of rain. I worry about my family, and Fo and Vince. But mostly I worry about me.

And then I hear a scratching, like a mouse scratching for food. I hold my breath and listen. The scratching changes to a tiny clicking sound, coming from the direction of the door. I prop myself up on my elbows and look at the door's dark window just as it swings open and someone comes inside. Whoever it is eases the door shut before creeping toward me.

I grab Jonah's shoulder and shake him. He gasps and sits up. "What?" he whispers, voice heavy with sleep.

"There's someone else in here!"

"Who's there?" Jonah asks.

"It's me," the shadow whispers.

Jonah claps me on the back. "Good luck, Jack. Hopefully I'll see you soon." He lies back down and rolls onto his side and I want to scream. The raiders are here for me and that's all he can say? *"Good luck, Jack? Hopefully I'll see you soon?"*

I hug my knees to my chest. The shadow kneels down on the mattress beside me and throws his arms around my shoulders. "I am so mad at you right now I could almost kill you!" he says. He squeezes me until my ribs creak against his.

"Kevin?"

He lets me go and then I am being kissed—warm, soft lips on my own. I shove him away hard, and he sighs. "You have *no right* to kiss me without my permission," I whisper, voice bitter. "Oh. I forgot. That's what raiders do, isn't it?"

"Ouch," Kevin says. Pulling me to my feet, he drags me toward the door. I dig my bare feet into the floor, but he's way stronger than me. "We've got less than an hour to get you out of here, so will you please cooperate? Once the sun is up, the raiders will be able to see us!" The door swings open like a slice of darkness, and Kevin pushes me through. I grab the door frame and hold tight, and Kevin walks into me.

"Jack, what are you doing?"

"What are *you* doing?"

"I'm breaking you out of here!" he whispers. "Hurry up! Let's go!"

"And leave Jonah and Bowen?"

"Yes! They still need to get the cure, and they're not about to die."

His words hit me like a slap in the face. "*They*'re not about to die . . . but I am?"

He pries my fingers from the door frame and pushes me into the dark hall. "Not if I can help it."

"Wait . . . I'm really about to die?"

He shuts the door, and we stand in the black hallway. "Yes. They're giving you to their dogs this morning for practice."

My brows furrow. "Practice? What kind of practice?"

"They've infected three of their dogs with the bee flu vaccine and taught them to hunt humans."

I stare at the black wall as everything slowly makes sense. When a dog catches an animal, it always goes for the neck, either snapping it or tearing into it with its teeth.

I am neck-tearing practice.

For the raiders' dogs.

Which have been turned into dog-beasts.

The ground seems to drop out from under my feet, and I claw at the wall to keep from falling. Arms come around me, warm and gentle, and strong, and hold me upright. I press my face against Kevin's chest and inhale. He smells faintly of vomit.

"We need to go, Jack. I'm so sorry you ever had to come here in the first place."

"You're sorry? You're the one who gave me to them!"

"Because I had no other choice. And now I am getting you away from them." His hand trails down my arm and clasps mine. My life is spinning out of control, and the only thing grounding me is his hand. I clasp our intertwined fingers with my free hand and hold on like my entire existence depends on it.

Together, we walk down the long, dark hall. The only light

is from the square windows on the doors that line it—one shade lighter than pitch-black. We turn a corner and pause. The distinct *tap-tap* of hard-soled shoes walking on a hard floor fills the hall, and the golden glow of a flashlight dances off a wall not far ahead of us. Kevin yanks me back into the hallway we just left, opens a door, and shoves me into a room that is so dark I could be walking off a cliff and not know it. He shuts the door and puts a cold hand over my mouth.

The sound of tapping shoes gets closer. And closer. I stare wide-eyed at black nothing, stop breathing, and listen as the shoes get closer and then stop. The small space beneath the door lights up like a thin line of gold. My muscles come alive, ready to run or fight. Indistinct voices rumble on the other side of the door, and then the light beneath it pales to dark and the shoes start tapping again, fading, fading, until I cannot hear them anymore. Kevin sucks in a deep breath of air and puts his hands on my shoulders. They are trembling.

My heart swells with an emotion I don't understand, that I've never felt before, and I think of how terrible I was to him. "I'm sorry I kicked you," I whisper. "When you handed me over to them. I didn't know what was really going on."

His hands tighten on my shoulders. "It's okay."

I take a deep breath and smell a trace of vomit again. "Are you the one who cleaned me up? After I got sick?"

"Yeah."

I put my hand on his arm. "Thank you."

Slowly he moves his hands from my shoulders, down to my hips, and leaves them there. "Jack."

"What?"

"Can I kiss you? Please?"

For an answer I put my palms on his chest and lean the front of my body against the front of his. His thumbs slip under my T-shirt and touch the soft skin above my waistband and I shiver. The darkness completely hides him from me, so when his lips brush my forehead, I jump. He traces his lips across my forehead, over my temple, and then our noses bump as his lips find mine. His hands squeeze my hips, and fire burns behind my closed eyes. I grab his face and pull his mouth harder against mine and kiss him like I'm going to die. I kiss him *because* I am going to die if he can't get me out of here.

He pushes me back and it takes a minute for him to catch his breath. "I hope we both make it out of here alive. I want more time with you," he whispers. He opens the door and I follow him out.

The hallway is lighter than the room we've just left and I can almost see. We turn the corner we turned earlier, pause for a minute, and then Kevin starts walking fast, pulling me behind him. I have to trot to match his pace. At the end of the hall looms a big gray rectangle. As we approach it, I realize what it is—glass doors leading outside—and my heart starts pounding with anticipation.

We reach the doors and Kevin doesn't pause, just pushes them open and walks out into the pale-gray predawn world.

We are in a parking lot with four-wheelers parked on top of faded parking-space lines. The cracked pavement hurts my bare feet. Kevin pulls me behind one of the vehicles, and we crouch. His eyes lock on mine, and I want to cry at the fear that is making his pupils huge and his mouth a hard line. "There's this place," he whispers, "where uninfected bees are alive. Where people are growing a new way of living." A dog howls, and Kevin jumps and looks over his shoulder.

I'm too shocked to move. "Where?" I ask.

"In the Rockies—there are high-pressure pockets in the high elevations where the pesticide didn't reach. Ward, Colorado, is one of them. People are there, hoping for a cure. Waiting for a cure. My sister—" Kevin jumps again and looks over his shoulder.

"You're the Siren. You lead people to this place, don't you? You get them away from the raiders and help them find these places."

He nods.

"Did you ever meet a man named Dean Bloom? Did you take him to this place?"

Kevin nods and then looks down.

"Is he still there? That's my brother! That's who I'm looking for out here!"

"He brought an older woman up there to live—Abigail Tarsis—but he didn't stay."

"Why didn't Dean stay? Where did he go?"

Kevin focuses on my face. "He said he needed to get back to Denver."

All the hope I have been clinging to since the day my brother left fades away. Dean never made it back to Denver. He's probably dead.

I think back to what Jonah said. "If you're the Siren, did *you* free the raiders' women?"

"Yes, but I had help." He presses his palm to the side of my face. "You have to go now. Find Fo. She has the map I made for you. When you get to Ward, tell them I sent you, and tell them a cure has been found. Tell them I'll try to bring it to them." His hand drops to his side.

Every part of me freezes except my mouth, which drops open.

"Go!" Kevin grabs my shoulder and gives me a small shove.

"But—" I grab his shirt and pull him so close our noses touch. "Aren't you coming with me?"

"No! Go! You only have . . ." He looks at his watch. "You only have four minutes before they switch out the watch. You have to go now!" He stands and pulls me to my feet. "Run!"

Slowly, I take a step away from him, staring at him so hard I might absorb him into my mind forever. And then I turn. I put one foot in front of the other. And I run.

CHAPTER 31

"Weight," Mom said, setting the scale on the floor by the treadmill. I climbed on, peered between my feet, and watched the dial spin almost straight up.

Mom clicked her tongue. "One hundred and forty-four pounds." She smiled, making dimples appear in her soft cheeks. "Now, onto the treadmill."

I tried to tuck my hair behind my ears before I remembered it had been shaved off a week earlier. I stared at the machine. My brothers had brought it home, piece by piece, a few days before. They'd found it in the Sanchezes' basement—something they had left in their house when they fled the city to get away from the approaching gangs.

"I'm fourteen. That's too young to start exercising," I whined.

"And I'm too old," Mom snapped. "But that doesn't matter. We need to be strong, Jack. And we're not. So toughen up. If I can do it, you can do it."

Mom set the treadmill at four miles per hour and told me I couldn't slow it down until I'd run for ninety seconds. I gritted my teeth, balled my fists, and then tried to make my pudgy legs run. I could barely lift them. My thighs rubbed together. My body bounced with each step. Everything started to hurt. When I hit the sixty-second mark, I slammed my hand on the emergency stop button and clutched the sidebars, wheezing.

"Maybe you should dangle a doughnut in front of her," Dean said, coming down into the basement.

"Do we have any doughnuts?" I asked, standing a little taller. Dean laughed. Mom swatted him and frowned.

Dean walked over to the treadmill and started it again, slowly increasing the speed until I was walking at three miles per hour. "The key to gaining endurance is starting slow and going long," he said.

"Says who?" I gasped, forcing my legs to march forward.

"Coach Winward used to tell that to the guys on the team. Tell you what. If you can do that for twenty minutes, I'll find you something sweet the next time I go scavenging. Deal?"

I looked at the timer on the treadmill. I had eighteen minutes and thirty-seven seconds to go to reach that goal.

"It will be a good treat," Dean coaxed.

I turned my nose up.

"I'll find you two treats, Jack. I know you can do it."

"Oh, all right." I thrust my chin forward and started swinging my arms as I walked. But I did it—twenty minutes.

After that day, I got on the treadmill three days a week, and each time I got on, I could run a little bit longer. Sixty seconds turned into one hundred. And then two hundred. And it hurt. Every single time, it hurt.

But after a month, not only could I run a whole mile in just under fifteen minutes, but my thighs didn't rub together quite as much. After two months, I could run two miles in twenty-five minutes, and my body didn't *jiggle when I ran. After three months, I could run five miles in an hour. None of my brother's old clothes fit because they were too big in the waist. Even his belt was too big. I sewed all the waistbands of his clothes to fit and gave the belt to a Fec. The fourth month, I started running six days a week, five miles a day minimum. Right before I fled from my house, I could run twenty-six miles in under four hours and thirty minutes. I had turned into a running machine.*

I run away from Kevin, run toward the black mass of the Rocky Mountains, and it is like I'm the chubby fourteen-year-old again who could hardly lift her legs. My body feels like lead. My ribs feel too tight to breathe. My heart hurts so badly that I hardly notice the rocks and gravel bruising the soles of my bare feet. Tears start streaming down my face, turning the gray world into a colorless blur.

I've only been running a minute when I hear feet pounding the ground behind me. I glance over my shoulder. A man is chasing me. He's thick and hefty, wearing big boots. There's no way he can catch me, even *with* my bare feet. I veer toward a parked car and something collides with my chest, knocking my feet out from under me. I fall backward and slam into the ground.

My head seems to triple in size as it explodes with pain. Stars flash before my eyes and I can't breathe. I cough and gasp for air. Slowly, the stars fade. Standing above me, framed by the morning sky, is a man with a baseball bat.

"Looks like Soneschen was right to switch up the patrols," a gruff voice says. I blink at the man.

"What you got?" someone answers from farther away.

"I just caught the dog bait running toward the hills," the man with the baseball bat says. He turns and starts walking away. "Take him back to the compound," he calls over his shoulder.

Boots scuff the ground by my head. I am yanked to my feet and stare into the bearded face of a stranger. My gaze travels down his face and stops on his dingy shirt. Sweat stains have turned the red fabric nearly black under his armpits. The man flips me around, grabs the scruff of my neck, and starts marching in the direction I've just come from. My muscles barely respond, and I am too dazed to fight. In less than two minutes, a wide one-story brick building comes into view. Words are painted on the side of it. I can just make them out in the pre-dawn light: *Newhaven Psychiatric Hospital*.

I scan the parking lot for Kevin, but he's gone.

We walk to the building and enter the same glass doors I just left through. Instead of going straight down the hall toward the room where Jonah and Bowen are, we turn left and stop in front of the first door on the right. My captor lifts his hand to knock, but he hesitates. His grimy fist falls to the door handle and he twists.

The door swings open on squeaky hinges, and dozens of candles flicker from the draft. A man is in the room, wearing an unbuttoned white dress shirt and sitting in front of a polished mirror, sipping something from a mug. "You're supposed to knock," the man says, never taking his eyes from the mirror.

Without a word, the bearded man pulls the door shut again. As soon as the latch clicks, he grumbles under his breath, "That son of a . . . Who does he think he is? When Flint was in charge . . . " And then he balls his beefy hand and pounds so hard I expect the door to break in two.

"Come back later." The words are muffled. "I'm busy getting ready for the morning's planned event."

The raider's hand tightens on my neck and he curses. He knocks again, but before the man on the other side can reply, my captor blurts out, "I caught the bait running!"

In two seconds, the door whooshes open and the candles in the room sputter. The man in the unbuttoned white dress shirt looks at me. His hair is neatly combed to the side, and his face is freshly shaved.

"Where did you find him?" the man asks. I wrinkle my nose at the strange smell of his breath.

"He was running toward the mountains, Mr. Soneschen, just like you guessed."

I take a closer look at the man standing in front of me, at his smooth skin, clean fingernails, and sharp eyes, which look left, then right, and then settle back on me. I feel fourteen again, standing at the wall, with a plate of scones in my pudgy hands. Heat floods my face—anger, not embarrassment. This is the man who wouldn't let us live inside the wall.

"Who set him free, Bob?" Soneschen asks, putting his clean hands on his hips. His dress shirt falls open, giving me a glimpse of sculpted abs and tight pectorals, and a perfectly round scar over his pasty white ribs.

I feel the man behind me shrug, and a cloud of body odor hits me. Soneschen scowls and fans the air in front of his face. "You don't know who set him free?"

"He was alone. Maybe he got out on his own."

Soneschen eyes me from my bare feet up to my buzzed hair and shakes his head. "No. This kid isn't smart enough or strong enough or brave enough to get out on his own." He looks right into my eyes. "Who helped you, Jack?"

I swallow hard and clench my teeth together. He glares into my eyes, and it feels like he is going to steal the soul out of my body. I shrink and look away.

"Coward," Soneschen whispers, as if proving his statement of a moment before.

"What do you want me to do with him?" Bob asks.

"Have you ever heard of Solomon?" When Bob doesn't reply, Soneschen adds, "from the Bible."

"I've never read the Bible."

"Jack? Have you heard of Solomon?"

I glower at the floor and nod. "He was a king."

"Not *just* a king," Soneschen corrects. "He was the most brilliant king in the history of the world. When two women came to him claiming they were both the mother of a baby, what did Solomon do, Jack?"

"Threaten to cut the baby in half and give each woman half of the baby." My voice comes out a shaky whisper.

"Correct. And what happened?"

I have no idea what this has to do with anything, but I answer, "The real mother offered to give the baby to the other woman."

"That's right. And why did she do that?"

I look at him. "Because the mother loved her baby so much

that she was willing to give it up forever as long as it wasn't hurt." I think of my mother, that day at the wall, willing to live outside the wall as long as her precious children were protected. I ball my hands into fists and fight the nearly overwhelming urge to punch Soneschen in the face.

A smile splits Soneschen's lips, showing slightly crooked white teeth tinged with pink. "Very good, Jack." I breathe in his copper-smelling breath and shudder—I am smelling blood. He has blood on his teeth. He looks above my shoulder, at Bob. "Go tie him to the tree in the courtyard. We're about to find out who loves Jack."

Eyes the color of the morning sky flood my thoughts and all the air seems to whoosh out of the hallway. I can't breathe. Soneschen slams the door in my face. Bob squeezes my neck and starts herding me down the hall.

I force my ribs to expand and contract. And then I duck and twist, wrenching myself out of Bob's grasp, and sprint toward the glass doors. There's no way he'll be able to catch me. After five steps, when I am so close to the door that I lift my hand to open it, something flicks against my back, like a grasshopper jumping on me, and my whole body seizes up. My muscles contract as if they are trying to compress my bones into dust. I fall to the floor and slide to a stop beside the exit. My body lurches uncontrollably from the electricity sizzling through it.

Bob puts a Taser back into a little black leather pocket on his belt and then walks over and stops beside me. Pain consumes me, and I stare at the threadbare hem of his jeans and listen to the sound of my teeth rattling in my skull.

When I stop convulsing and sag against the floor, Bob grabs my left ankle and drags my trembling body down the hall. Too weak to move, I stare at grimy white tile as it passes below my cheek. We stop at a glass door and he opens it, pulling me outside.

I'm dragged over cement, then onto thin, brown, rain-soaked grass. The sky blazes pale blue overhead, and I blink up at the brightness of it, wondering how it can be so blue when the world is so vile.

Bob lifts me to my feet and props me up against the rough, splintery trunk of a tree. I close my eyes and smell the deep, rich scent of damp wood as a rope is wrapped around my wrists and cinched tight. Bob grunts and groans as he hoists me up until I am dangling by my bound wrists from a tree branch, with my toes barely able to touch the ground and spasms of electricity still twitching in my muscles.

For a moment Bob studies me, and then he pulls a gun from his belt, from right beside his Taser. My stomach drops and I wonder if I am about to die. Without looking at me, Bob points the gun to the sky and fires. The sound hurts my ears and eats the morning's silence. Dogs howl, and the gunshot echoes off the mountains and back, like rolling thunder. Bob turns and walks away, and I am alone, dangling in a slow circle. The branch I am tied to creaks under my weight.

And then the morning is filled with human sounds as raiders start massing onto the roof of the building surrounding me. I am in the courtyard I saw from my barred window.

CHAPTER 32

Two men walk into the courtyard, and I dig the tips of my toes into the ground, making the rope I'm attached to turn in the other direction so that I can see them. One is ex-governor Soneschen, his white shirt buttoned and tucked into a pair of fancy black pants. His eyes are riveted on me. The other man is a raider with a thick black beard and shoulder-length black hair. He's wearing torn jeans and a dingy tank top that exaggerates his heavily muscled, scarred shoulders.

"If you guys will shut up, I'll start," the raider yells, eyes scanning the men on the roof. The hair on the back of my neck prickles. I know that voice. "I said shut up!" he says, even louder.

I squint against the morning sun, trying to get a better look at him, but the rope binding me twists and slowly spins me around so my back is to him. Aside from the muted barking of a dog, the morning goes quiet. I peer up at the roof, at the gathered men, and momentarily forget the raider in the courtyard. There have got to be more than a hundred men up there. And right in front stands Kevin, staring down at me like he couldn't care less what happens to me.

The rope keeps slowly spinning, turning me away from Kevin, back to the two men in the courtyard. When I'm facing them, I dig my toes into the ground again and stare.

The raider is watching me now. His fierce blue eyes lock on mine. If the rope wasn't holding me erect, my legs would give out and I'd be on the ground.

"Chest, head, chest," I told my baby brother. "That way, if you miss twice, you've still got a third chance to kill your target."

I helped Chris lift the rifle to his shoulder. He wobbled under the weight. "It's too heavy," he whined. "I can't do it yet. And I'm cold."

"That's all right. You're only six. I don't think you'll actually need to learn to shoot for a few more years." He nodded and stumbled through the thin layer of snow on the ground and into the house with the rifle.

I rested my rifle on my shoulder and peered down the street, looking for the Fec who came to trade ammunition for food on a semiregular basis. I don't know why he still came. We stopped trading with him when he slashed Josh's leg. And even though I was always armed with a rifle, and the Fec had only a knife, he scared me. He moved like a shadow in broad daylight, and he'd attacked me more than once for the scraps of food I carried in my pockets.

Dean had seen the Fec sneaking around right before sunrise, so I knew he was close by. I'd emptied my vest pockets before I started my watch. I wasn't going to take any chances.

I pulled my wool beanie down over my ears and stared into the shadowed windows and doorways of the abandoned houses lining the opposite side of the street, but nothing moved. The dogs lay huddled together on the dead grass, completely unconcerned.

Around lunchtime my nerves finally settled down enough that I actually felt hungry. I glanced at my watch, calculating the minutes before Steve came out and took over the front yard long enough for me to eat something. When I looked back up, the Fec was standing in the middle of the road, a smile gracing his filthy face.

My gun was up and aimed before I had time to draw breath, before the dogs even started barking. The Fec didn't care. He smiled even bigger and swung his greasy hair out of his eyes.

"What do you want?" I asked, loud enough that my voice would carry over the sound of the dogs.

"I brought you something," he called. He lifted his thumb to his mouth and started nibbling the skin around his brown fingernail. The dogs stopped barking, but their chains were pulled taut, and they were all staring at the Fec as if they wanted to eat him for lunch.

"We don't want anything you have," I said, not lowering my gun. "Get out of here."

The Fec shrugged. "Fine. Be that way. You might not want her, but she wants you guys." He turned and started slinking down the road, feet utterly silent.

"Wait!" I whipped around at the sound of Dad's voice. He stood framed in the doorway, pajamas wrinkled, white hair mussed.

"Who do you have, Arris?" Dad asked, coming to stand beside me.

His eyes slowly moved over every inch of the Fec, calculating, like when he was trying to determine whether to give someone a root canal. And then he took the rifle from my hands and aimed it at the Fec.

Arris turned his back to us and cupped his hands around his mouth. "Come on out!" His yell echoed down the street, and in less than two seconds all three of my older brothers were standing in the yard with Dad and me, guns ready.

Five houses down, someone stepped out of a front door. A man, not a woman. He put his hand above his eyes, blocking the noon sun, and looked at us. Behind him, another person came out the door. Her tan pants were filthy from the knees down, like she'd been wading in something brown, but her shirt was still mostly white, like her hair. The man put the woman's hand on his arm and the two of them started walking toward us.

"Lower your guns," Dad said. My brothers obeyed without a word.

The man and woman skirted around the Millers' abandoned truck, stepped over snow-covered trash and tumbleweeds in the road, and stopped beside the Fec. My skin crawled. They obviously didn't know their lives were in danger by merely being in the same vicinity as the Fec. And then I saw the Taser in the man's hand, pointed at the Fec. Maybe he did know.

I looked at his face, at his dark hair and blue eyes, and frowned. I knew this man. He was from the walled city. He was the doctor who tried to get my dad to live inside the wall.

"Jefferson Bloom? Is that you?" the woman asked. She hugged her arms over her chest and started rubbing them for warmth.

I stared at her. It had been a long time since I had seen a woman other than my own mother. I forgot how soft women were, how small and gentle their hands looked, how their bodies formed subtle curves instead of hard angles. I had forgotten how long hair hung in waves when it was clean. Hers wasn't as white as I first thought. It was dark blond, streaked with white.

"Abigail Tarsis." The words came out of Dad's mouth on a breath of air. I knew that name. This woman was Fiona and Jonah Tarsis's mother, one of my mother's best friends from before. She'd been living inside the wall.

Eyes wide with disbelief, Dad handed Dean his gun and then strode out of the yard and stopped in front of the woman. The Fec crouched on the balls of his feet like he was about to pounce and stared at my dad. Dean lifted his gun and pointed it at the boy.

Dad put his arm around the woman's shoulders and held his free hand out to the doctor. "Doctor Grayson, how are you?" he asked.

The doctor shook Dad's hand and gave him a tight smile. "I'm well enough."

Dad nodded and looked both ways down the road. "Let's get you two inside," he said, and then ushered them into the yard, past the dogs, and to the house.

"I need payment," the Fec yelled after him.

"Jack, give Arris a plate of beans," Dad called. "Josh and Steve, stay in the yard."

Josh and Steve put their guns on their shoulders and simultaneously aimed them at the Fec. "Don't come any closer," Steve warned.

Dean walked into the house with me and stood at my side as I opened the pot of warm beans and began scooping some onto a plate, but he wasn't paying any attention to me. His attention was riveted on Abigail Tarsis.

Dad, Doctor Grayson, and Mrs. Tarsis were sitting at the kitchen table. Mom joined them. Tears started streaming down her hollow cheeks, and she reached across the table and took Mrs. Tarsis's soft hands in her hard ones. "Abigail, it is so good to see you, but what are you doing here?" Mom asked.

"I turned fifty-five last week," said Mrs. Tarsis. Her eyes lost focus. "When I refused to be euthanized, the Inner Guard forced me out of the walled city, and Lissa's husband . . ." Her words caught in her throat.

"I'm married to her daughter. I couldn't leave her on her own out here," the doctor explained. "I asked the militia at the north gate to help us find somewhere safe for Abigail, but none of them would even look at us. The boy who brought us here was hiding outside the militia's camp. In exchange for food, he led us belowground. He said you might be willing to help her."

Dad's mouth formed a hard line. "You're her son-in-law. Why can't you continue to help her?"

"I wish I could, but I am on the brink of finding a cure for the beasts! If I leave now, all my work will be cast aside, and no one will help the infected kids." His eyes were wide with desperation.

"And I would rather die out here on my own," Mrs. Tarsis said, "than risk losing any chance of curing those children. My daughter is in the lab waiting for the day the cure is perfected."

"I'm sorry, but we can't help," Dad said. Mom started crying harder. "And I can't let you stay here because you'd be putting my family at risk. As far as the raiders know, only men and boys live here. If they knew I had a woman staying here, they'd kill all of us to get to you."

Mrs. Tarsis's eyes grew round and she glanced at me, then back at

Dad. "I'm sorry. I wouldn't have come if I'd known. I would never have knowingly put your children in danger."

"Thank you," Mom said, sniffling.

"What I can *do*," Dad said, "is give you some food, a water purifier, and have one of my boys escort you to the edge of the city."

The doctor hung his head in his hands. Mrs. Tarsis stared at Dad. After a moment, a sob escaped her. She put her hands over her mouth and started weeping giant tears that poured down her face and over her slender hands, over a gold wedding ring with three diamonds. The doctor put his arm around her shoulders and started crying with her.

"Dad." Dean's voice made me jump. I forgot that he was standing beside me, forgot that I was supposed to be getting beans for the Fec. I looked into the pot and stirred it, then dipped the ladle deep, where the beans and rice had settled. I lifted the ladle from the pot and waited for it to stop dripping.

"I'll take her," said Dean.

"Thank you, son." Dad smiled at Dean, but it wasn't the kind of smile that touched his eyes. It was the smile he did when he resigned himself to bad news. Really bad news. "You'd better get going as soon as possible if you're going to get back here before dark."

I turned the ladle upside down over a bowl, and the beans and rice slopped into it.

"No. You don't understand me," Dean said. Mrs. Tarsis sniffled and looked at him. The doctor sat up tall and locked his bright, hopeful gaze on my brother. "That's Lissa's mom. I don't think I can walk to the edge of town with her and then leave her to fend for herself. I'll take her somewhere safe. And then I'll come home."

Dad stood up. "You don't know what you're saying," he whispered, walking to Dean's side. "We don't know anyone who has survived out there and lived to tell about it. The raiders rule! It's suicide!"

"That's my point. I can't let her walk into that! She will not survive alone!"

"But what if you both *die*?" Dad argued.

Dean pounded his fist on the counter. "I don't care! I am so sick of sitting here, doing nothing but surviving while all around, people are being massacred by the raiders! I am sick of standing by when I might be able to make a difference—sick of being part of the disease when I could be part of the cure. I'm strong! I'm healthy! What if I save just one life? That would be worth it to me! I would rather die knowing I did something right, than live knowing I am such a coward that I have to hide in my house for the rest of my life! That is no way to live."

The house fell utterly silent. The doctor wiped his damp cheeks and leaned back in his chair. I looked from Dean to Dad to my mom, still sitting at the table. She had stopped crying. A tiny smile curved up the edges of her mouth, and her eyes shone with something I hadn't seen for a long time. They used to get that look in them when Dean made a good play in football or when I won first place at a 4-H competition. I hadn't seen my mother beam with pride in so long that I'd almost forgotten what it looked like.

She stood from the table, walked around the counter, and threw her arms around her son. "Thank you," she whispered in his ear. "I knew I raised you right."

One hour later, I stood in the front yard and watched Dean walk away from my house for the last time. He turned back once, right before he and Mrs. Tarsis came to the bend in the road, and raised his hand in farewell. A smile danced on his face despite the fact that he might be walking to

*his death, but that smile warmed me from the inside out. I raised my hand
back at him and held it high until he was gone from view.*

I am staring at a face I have known since the day I was born.
But I don't know it anymore, with its hard, cold expression and
emotionless eyes. Who I am looking at is not my missing
brother, Dean, but the man he has become. My throat tightens.
I guess I've finally found out what happened to him. And now,
more than ever, I wish I had never tried to find him.

CHAPTER 33

"What's going on, Hastings?" someone yells.

My brother looks away from me, up to the roof. "I'm about to tell you," he calls, his voice so familiar it stabs at my heart. "It seems there has been a small change in our scheduled event." Men groan.

Perched in perfect stillness, I stare at my brother and wait for him to continue. Wait for him to say the change in the schedule is that he's going to set me free.

Dean's eyes lock on mine again, and he lifts his arm and points at me. "Someone helped this boy escape today." His face hardens, and he takes a step closer. I can't help but wonder if he doesn't recognize me. Have I changed so much since he left? Does he not realize that it is his little *sister* hanging from a tree out here?

Slowly, eyes boring into me, he walks forward, black boots making small squelching noises in the wet grass. *Please recognize me,* I silently beg. If he recognizes me, he will find a way to let me go. I know that without a doubt. I know it deep down in my heart.

He walks to the middle of the courtyard. Stripes of light and shadow cover his face where the sun shines through the bare tree branches. He stops in front of me and I open my mouth to speak, but don't know what to say—he is staring at me like he has never seen me before, like I am a stranger.

"Dean," I whisper. "Help m—"

"Shut up!" He yells it so loud my ears start to ring.

"But Dean—"

His shoulder muscles bulge beneath scarred skin and his hand flies into my face, crunching against my mouth before I can finish speaking. I spin in a fast circle, the rope biting into my wrists, my shoulders straining.

As I come full circle, I stare at Dean's retreating back, the way his shoulders roll with every step. Even his walk is familiar. Tears fill my eyes and I bite my tongue, trying to keep the tears from falling. Boys don't cry.

"This boy," Dean yells, stopping just beyond the tree's broken shadow, "will not be fed to the dogs today."

My head falls forward and I sigh with relief. I knew it. I knew he wouldn't let them kill me.

The raiders start screaming their protest and I look up, waiting to see what my brother does. Dean pulls a gun from his belt and shoots the sky, and the raiders quiet down. "We are postponing the fight and spreading the word to all our brothers to come and see the event. Even our illustrious former leader is going to come," Dean explains.

Wait. *Postpone?* I don't understand.

A name is spoken in quiet voices, but whether the raiders speak it in reverence or fear, I can't tell. The name makes my skin crawl. *Flint.*

"Flint will be here tomorrow, so we will postpone the feeding of this boy to the dogs until then. Unless . . ."

The raiders lean closer to Dean, their eyes intent on him. I hold my breath. "Unless what," someone calls.

Dean looks at me and grins, but it isn't the same grin that used to light up his face. His mouth turns up at the corners, but his eyes darken and close to mere slits. "Unless someone would like to volunteer to take his place." Behind Dean, Soneschen nods and his eyes sweep over the raiders on the roof.

Utter silence settles over the men. They look at each other like they have suddenly lost the ability to speak English and need someone to translate what my brother just said. And then, one by one, they start laughing. The sound grows, like a wave rolling in to shore, until it reaches an overwhelming pitch.

I look up at the roof and my eyes are instantly drawn to one person. He stands as still as stone in the midst of the laughing raiders. His mouth moves, two simple words I can't hear, and the raiders around him stop laughing. And then the raiders around them stop laughing. It spreads, this non-laughing, until all the raiders on the roof are silent once again, and all are looking at one person. Kevin.

Soneschen walks out into the courtyard until he is standing in the grass below Kevin, looking up at him. "Did you say something?"

Kevin nods. "I said, 'I will.'"

"You will what?"

"I will take the kid's place," he answers, head held high and shoulders firm.

Soneschen nods and looks at my brother, then me. I wonder if he is blind to the family resemblance. "It seems," he says, his eyes locking on mine, "that Solomon has weeded out the one who loves you most."

Ten minutes later, I stand in an empty room with a broken and barred window. It overlooks the courtyard. I have been told to watch. Told to see the fate that has been taken from me and given to Kevin. He won't die today, Soneschen assured me before he locked me in here. He is just giving Kevin a preview of tomorrow's death, so he can think about it and decide whether or not he *really* wants to take my place. If Kevin does, he dies tomorrow. For me. In my place. And if he doesn't, I will die tomorrow.

"Jack. Come to the window." It is Soneschen's voice. My feet hardly work, dragging against the ground as I go to the broken window. Kevin is in the courtyard, walking beside Dean toward the tree. Walking beside my brother.

At the tree, Dean takes the rope I was bound with, which is still tied to the branch, and begins tying the dangling end to

Kevin's wrists. Kevin doesn't fight it, doesn't even look upset as he willingly holds his wrists out. While my brother binds Kevin, his lips barely move. After a minute, the rope is pulled taut and Kevin's stretched so tight he can barely stand on his tiptoes. Dean, with a quick glance at me, jogs to the glass doors leading into the building and goes inside.

Kevin hangs there, spinning in a slow arc, and nothing happens. My heart starts to pound as I stare at him, because I know I am waiting for something awful.

A dog howls and then barks. A man screams from somewhere inside the building. Kevin just dangles in sunlight slotted with shadow. Another dog starts barking, and I hear the sound of a door slamming.

Nothing happens.

I stare out the window at Kevin, waiting. And each second that passes, the air seems to get heavier, until I want to start screaming and kicking and punching. When I think I am going to die from waiting, the door Dean left through is opened and I see my brother look out. He props the door open and pushes a cage out—a huge kennel. The kennel is jumping and jolting from whatever is being contained inside.

Dean's muscles bulge as he takes a chain thicker than my wrist from the top of the kennel. He hefts a few feet of it back inside the building and attaches it to something. The other end of the chain leads inside the kennel.

Dean goes back into the building and then shuts the doors as much as he can, with only a few inches open where the chain comes out. And then the front of the kennel slowly begins to rise up, like a miniature automatic garage door. Before the door has risen six inches, the animal inside shoves its head out, its white teeth snapping.

When the door is a little more than halfway up, the animal drags itself out and, without so much as sniffing the air, tears across the courtyard, dead grass flying from its hind paws, to the prey hanging from the tree. Kevin screams and flinches as the dog lunges for him. When the beast is mere inches from Kevin, the chain pulls taut with an audible clang, and the creature is jerked backward by its own momentum. I gasp and clutch the metal bars blocking the window, pressing my face between two of them.

The dog is a German shepherd with matted fur. It is the biggest German shepherd I have ever seen, with massive muscles in its neck and hind legs. It rolls to its feet, snarls, and walks toward Kevin until the chain is pulled tight again. It stands there for a minute, and I forget to breathe as I watch. When it lunges for Kevin a second time, I jump away from the window. It tries a third time to get to him, and then a fourth, scraping a hole into the ground where it digs its claws into the earth, but the chain holds it back every time. When it realizes it can't reach its prey that way, the creature sits and watches Kevin, as if trying to decide what to do next. Kevin, poised on the tips of his boots, loses his balance and starts spinning.

The movement is the invitation the dog needs. It lunges again, at the exact moment Kevin swings his legs to try and turn so that he can face the dog. The dog's teeth latch onto the hem of Kevin's pant leg and it yanks.

Kevin's arms and shoulders bulge and strain as he tries to pull away. The dog starts whipping its head from side to side. It digs its paws into the ground and gives one huge, hard heave. The pant leg tears, the dog tumbles backward, and Kevin screams.

He starts spinning again, and only one of his feet is on the ground. Something about the way he's hanging looks wrong. His left shoulder appears too narrow, and he's moaning.

I cover my mouth with my hand. And then I step away from the window. A wave of emotions thunders through me, knocking me to my hands and knees. If Kevin agrees to take my place, I will be set free, Soneschen said, and made to watch Kevin die. With that thought, my throat tightens and my eyes start to burn. A small circle of black seems to open inside of my stomach and slowly spread through me, until I am filled with so much darkness that I can hardly breathe. I press my forehead to the cold, gritty tile floor and start to sob.

No matter what happens tomorrow, I will lose something precious.

CHAPTER 34

The door opens and someone is shoved inside. His feet tangle and he falls to the ground. I stare across the room at Kevin for half a minute, so shocked to see him that I don't know what to do. And then I whimper, crawl across the floor, and wrap my arms around him.

His bleary eyes focus on my face. "Jack." His voice is a hoarse whisper. With the hem of my shirt, I wipe a smear of blood from his lip, and his right hand covers mine. "I'm cold," he says, burrowing closer to me. He feels like a rock—cold and hard. A sheen of icy sweat coats his entire body and has soaked through his hoodie. He convulses once and then his jaw starts to rattle because his teeth are chattering. "My left shoulder's dislocated," he whispers.

As gently as I can, I roll him onto his back and take his left hand in mine. My throat constricts. Just below the sleeve of his sweatshirt, thick, bloody grooves are gouged into his wrist where the rope was tied. My gaze travels up his arm, to his shoulder.

When I was sixteen, I watched my dad fix Steve's shoulder after he dislocated it by trying to hoist himself over the fence in our backyard, so I have a general idea of what to do. But I don't want to do it. I might mess up. And I know it will hurt Kevin before it helps him. The embroidery hanging above the living room fireplace pops into my head. *To Be Brave, You Must First Be Afraid.* I am afraid.

"I need you to sit up," I say, and push on his good shoulder until he's sitting. "I'm so sorry, but this is going to hurt." Kevin nods. "Now, you need to relax if you can. It will make your shoulder go back into the joint more easily. Are you ready?"

"No," he says, but he takes a deep breath and visibly relaxes. Holding his wrist, I bend his arm at a ninety-degree angle, then slowly, millimeter by millimeter, start pulling his wrist away from his body, careful to keep his elbow tucked firmly against his ribs.

Kevin grimaces and I keep slowly pulling. His breathing speeds up and I keep slowly pulling. He drops his head, closes his eyes, and grunts; his muscles tighten; and I keep slowly pulling. Then he screams while I pull harder, as hard as I can, and his scream fills the entire room. Until he goes silent, like he's been knocked unconscious. His chin drops against his chest, and his body slumps.

"Kevin?" I say, panic in my voice.

"That feels so much better," he whispers, cradling his left arm. His eyes open. "You are amazing."

I try to smile but can't. Finally, I ask, "Have you changed your mind?" I pull my legs against my chest, making myself as small as I can, and hold my breath.

"Changed my mind about what?"

"Trading places with me," I whisper. "Now that you know what you're up against." *Now that you know you'll be torn to shreds.*

Face placid, he studies me for a long time. Slowly, he kneels in front of me, rests his hands on my bent knees, and says, "I haven't changed my mind."

I hug my legs even tighter and press my forehead to my knees, against his hands covering them. My ribs tighten, my eyes fill with tears, and my shoulders start to shake with sobs that I can no longer hold in. "I'm sorry," I gasp between sobs. "I'm so sorry you have to die for me."

"Don't be sorry. The only thing tying me up out there did"—Kevin whispers, his mouth beside my ear—"the only thing Soneschen proved is that my taking your place is the right choice."

My heart feels like it is being torn in two. "Are you sure?"

"I have only been surer of two things in my entire life."

I lift my face and look at him through tear-blurred eyes. "What?"

"That I would do everything in my power to make up for my sister's getting my dose of the vaccine and turning into a beast," he says, voice filled with so much conviction that it makes me shiver. "And that I love you."

My heart seems to sew itself back together and then tear in two all over again.

His gaze flickers to my lips. "And if it wouldn't risk giving away your secret, I would kiss you right now."

I grab his face and pull it to mine, pressing my lips against his. His hand cups my cheek, and he kisses me for half a minute before pulling away. Water glistens in his eyes and he blinks, spilling it down his cheeks.

"Those aren't tears," I whisper. "Your eyes are just watering because that kiss hurt so much."

He shakes his head. "No. This time they are tears. This is how much I'm hurting inside at the thought of never seeing you again. Or my sister. Or my grandpa." He presses my hand to his damp cheek and closes his eyes.

Fresh tears fill my eyes, and I say, "If it's possible for a person to fall in love when they've only known someone for a few days . . ."

He opens his eyes, stares into mine, and stops breathing. "I love you."

CHAPTER 35

The sun sets, turning the room a hazy gray. My back is against the wall, my butt is asleep, and the cement floor is seeping coldness through my pants and into my legs. I shiver.

Kevin's head is resting in my lap, and his left arm is cradled across his chest. His quiet snores almost drown out the occasional howling and barking of dogs. But not quite. And every time I hear them, I think of what they will be eating for breakfast and get hit with a fresh wave of sobs.

I'm exhausted, but sleep won't come. I don't know how Kevin can sleep when he is about to die, and I don't know what's worse: the thought of him being killed by the dogs or of me having to watch it. I trail my fingers through Kevin's tangled hair and stare at him, silently cursing the growing darkness for hiding him from me. I am trying to memorize everything about him, since I will never have the chance again.

When there's no light left outside the window, I close my eyes and lean my head against the wall and listen to the sounds he makes when he sleeps. They *say* they will set me free tomorrow—right after they force me to watch Kevin die in my place. I don't believe it, but at least I will live and have a chance to escape.

I wonder what Bowen and Jonah are doing right now. Hopefully they've found the cure and gotten out of here already. If it wasn't for me walking into the raider's hands, they'd probably all be on their way back to the shelter by now, and Kevin wouldn't be standing on death's threshold. If only I had stayed on the mountain, none of this ever would have happened. I am sick of making stupid mistakes!

I take a deep, unsteady breath, and time seems to stop moving. A stillness settles over me—an awareness—as if my mind has suddenly opened up and is absorbing more things than it has ever absorbed before, and I am hit with a revelation that steals my breath: if I let Kevin die for me, it will be the biggest mistake of my life, the one I will never recover from.

My head sags forward as shame overwhelms me. I have been content to let him take my place with the dogs. Worse—I've been *relieved* that he is taking it, *grateful* even. That I was willing to let him take my place at all, that he *volunteered* to do it, proves who the better person is. And the better person does not deserve to die. Especially when I am the one who got us into this mess in the first place.

Me. It has to be me in with the dogs tomorrow.

Doing the Right Thing Is Always Harder Than Doing the Wrong Thing. Mom embroidered that the day the vagabond—Kevin—came to our house the very first time. She cried while she sewed it but refused to tell me why. Now I understand what she meant. I lean forward and bury my face against Kevin's shoulder and start to weep. My tears soak through his shirt and my entire body begins shaking with sobs.

Kevin shifts and pulls me down, hugging me to him. "Don't cry, Jack." His voice is raspy from sleep. "I want this. I *want* you to live a long, happy life."

I press my face against his chest and cry harder.

I breathe in the smell of Kevin and press my hand over his beating heart, and fill myself with the knowledge that it will be beating for a long time. Moving my hand to my own chest, I feel the beating beneath fabric and skin and bone. *I'm sorry, heart,* I say to myself. It is slow and strong under my hand and not ready to be done beating.

I curl my body against Kevin's and lie limp and exhausted and completely defeated, with my head on his shoulder. If he wasn't holding me so close, I would fall away from him and lie limp on the cold, hard ground, staring up at the black ceiling.

Tomorrow I die.

⬡⬡⬡

I don't sleep—I'm certain of this fact—but when the door opens and two dark shapes slink inside, I wonder if I am dreaming. The door shuts and whispers fill the darkness. A light flashes on and I squint against the glow. Kevin jumps away from me and stands as I crouch on the balls of my feet in the corner of the room and wish for a weapon.

The light swoops over the floor and then flashes on the faces of the two men who have just entered. One is a grizzled bearded man who is pressing his finger to his lips. He's the guy who made chili for the raiders the afternoon I was captured—the old man who kept staring at me. He is staring at me again, furrowing his scraggly gray eyebrows. The other man is . . .

"Jonah!"

"Zeke, please tell me you're getting us out of here," Kevin says, turning toward the old man.

"We're doing our best," the old man—Zeke—answers. He holds something out toward me and I stand. It's my knife. I cross the room and take it from him, cradling it against my chest. "You're going to need to hide that," he says. "It's not going to be much defense against the dogs, but it might tip the scales in your favor long enough for you to survive."

My eyes grow round, and I wonder how this stranger knows my secret thoughts, knows that I have decided to take my death back from Kevin.

Kevin steps up beside me and reaches for the knife, but I move it before he can take it. "She's not fighting the dogs." He reaches for the knife again, and I step away.

"Yes I am, Kevin." Tears start welling in my eyes again. "I can't let you die for my stupid mistakes."

"Yes you can." His voice is hard and mad.

I shake my head. "No."

He grabs my arm a little too tightly and reaches for the knife, but I hold it as far away from him as I can.

"Actually, there's been a change of plans. Soneschen's orders," Jonah says. Kevin lets me go and turns to Jonah.

"Change of plans? Does Hastings know this?"

"If he does, he hasn't done anything about it," Zeke says. "You are *both* going into the courtyard at dawn."

"What? No!" Kevin's voice is trembling. He grabs the front of Zeke's shirt. "You've got to get Jack out of here! That's why you're here, right? To smuggle her out?"

I hold my breath and look between Kevin and Zeke.

"No rest for the weary tonight," Zeke says. "All watches have been tripled. Every exit, every window, and every chimney has at least three men guarding it. Soneschen's got a feeling something big is about to happen." He chuckles. "He's right, too. Just not what he's expecting. Let's get a move on, Jonah."

Jonah rolls his shoulders and opens and closes his hands a few times. "Kevin, you're a good man. Sorry for this." He balls his hand, pulls his arm back, and slams his fist into Kevin's chin. Kevin's entire body seems to soften and freeze, as if time has paused and the air has condensed around him. And then he crumples to the ground, mouth sagging open, eyes closed.

I fall to my knees beside Kevin and pat his cheeks. He doesn't so much as flinch. "What did you do that for, Jonah?"

"I'm trading places with him, and I don't have time for him to argue about it," Jonah explains. He peels the sweatshirt from Kevin's limp body and pulls it over his head, puts the hood up, and turns to Zeke. "What do you think?"

Zeke shines the light on him. With Jonah's face shadowed, he could pass for Kevin. At least in the dark.

"Sag a little. Slouch. You're too tall and the shirt doesn't fit right," Zeke says. "And pull the sleeves down over your electromagnetic cuffs." Jonah slouches and pulls the sleeves of his sweatshirt so they cover the half inch of metal cuffs peeking out. Zeke nods. "It might work long enough to get you in with the dogs, and once you're in, they won't be getting you out. Help me get Kev into the other room."

Jonah bends down and lifts Kevin into his arms like Kevin doesn't weigh any more than a child. He walks out the door with him and is back in half a minute. "We found the cure," he says, looking at me.

This news should make me glad. It should make me excited, even. I can barely muster up a weak "Oh."

"I would have gotten here earlier, but we've been using it."

"Wait. What? You've been using the cure?"

"Yeah."

"On the raiders' beasts?"

Jonah shudders. "We've injected all their beasts. We've also been using it on the dogs."

I stand a little taller. "The dogs we're fighting? They won't be beasts anymore?"

"No, not them. We couldn't get to them. They're under lock and key and being guarded by ten raiders. We've got an hour before dawn. Are you ready to fight?"

I shake my head. "Is anyone ever *ready* to face their violent death? I'm as ready as I'll ever be, but I'm scared."

Jonah puts his hands on my shoulders. "It's okay to be scared," he whispers. "It is better to be scared of doing the right thing, than to regret doing the wrong thing for the rest of your life." His words almost echo my own thoughts. He squeezes my shoulders. "When I woke up after being a beast, I swore to myself I'd never lift my hand in violence again as long as I lived. Even against an animal."

I look at his dark silhouette. "Then why are you doing this? Why did you trade places with Kevin?"

"Because I would never forgive myself if I watched you die when I could have possibly prevented it. I'm stronger than Kevin. I'm stronger than every man in this place. And I'm your best chance for survival. So go out there and fight as if it is your choice!"

"It is my choice," I whisper.

He wraps me in his arms and holds me close. He's solid beneath Kevin's sweatshirt, as if he has no flesh and blood, only bones and electromagnetic cuffs.

I put my arms around his rock-hard ribs and rest my head on his chest, listening to the slow, even throb of his heart. A heart that might not be beating in an hour. Because of me.

My heart starts to ache. The ache grows until I hurt so badly that I'm certain my broken heart is now bleeding.

They come for us at sunrise, when the black sky has lightened to a pale, blinding blue. As they enter the room, I focus on Jonah's scarred hands and wrists, and the sweatshirt that doesn't quite hide the electromagnetic cuffs. He tugs the sleeves down, but they come right back up.

Once again, the raiders overestimate their own prowess. They don't frisk me. They don't frisk Jonah or look inside the hood shadowing his face. They just herd us out like we're mindless cattle, smacking their baseball bats into their palms like that's the scariest thing ever. It's not.

The walk is short. Before I have time to dwell on the fact that a pack of raiders is escorting me to my violent, bloody death, I am at a glass door, looking at the courtyard. I stare at the tree where Kevin and I were tied the day before. The ground around it is scraped bare of dead grass from the claws of the dog. Those claws will be scraping me soon. I have known a lot of darkness in the past four years, but nothing has ever compared to this. I am in the darkest moment of my life, and time seems to have stopped.

As if in slow motion, the glass door is pulled open and I step outside. Cool air washes over my taut face, sunlight stings my swollen eyes, and I blink. My heart thuds in my chest. Air moves in and out of my lungs. I thrust my chin forward, put one foot in front of the other, and stand tall as I walk toward the tree. Sweat beads on my palms, so I wipe them down the front of my pants in anticipation of clutching the hilt of my knife.

I get to the tree and stand in its long, dead shadow, and all of a sudden, time no longer moves too slowly. It starts to zoom.

The air fills with cheering and I look up. At least twice as many raiders as yesterday are standing on the building's flat roof and looking down into the courtyard. I squint, searching for a familiar face. My brother, mouth in a tight frown, meets my gaze. He is at the very front of the building, with the rising sun at his back. On his right sits Soneschen, in a black office chair, white shirt gleaming with morning sunlight. Soneschen's gaze locks on me and his lips pull back into an eager smile. On

Dean's left stands a man whose face is shadowed by a cowboy hat, but I know who he is. Flint. The former king of the raiders. Succeeded by my brother.

"Go for the hamstring first, and the throat as a last resort. We don't want to kill the dogs." Jonah's voice, barely audible over the cheering crowd, jars me back to reality.

My jaw drops open and I gawk at him. "What are you talking about? *We don't want to kill them?*"

He shakes his head. "Trust me, Jack. There's a bigger picture here than just you and me fighting some biologically altered dogs. Much bigger. There are more important things than us at stake."

I want to punch him, to tell him I beg to differ. What can be bigger than me dying?

"Please trust me, Jack."

"Okay. So, I don't kill the things trying to kill me." He nods. "I'll do my best."

The crowd grows silent. I squint against the bright sky and look up. Flint is holding a hand up in the air and all eyes are on him.

"Today is a monumental day! You are about to see your newest weapons being put to use against human beings," Flint says. He clasps my brother's shoulder. "You all know my successor had the brilliant idea to start injecting dogs with the bee flu vaccine." The crowd nods and hollers. "He started with three dogs. It has been ten months. You already know they've been biologically altered. What you don't know is that for five months, he has been breeding an entire army of these biologically altered

animals, and they are all starting to turn." The raiders look at my brother, eyes wary.

"Why do we want a whole army of them when we can barely control three?" someone calls.

Flint takes off his hat. His gray hair is matted to his head, and his eyes are sharp. "You all recall that the possession of guns by civilians inside the wall is illegal, right?"

"So what?" someone calls. "It's not like we can get past the militia."

"Well," Flint continues, "we are going to set the dogs loose in the militia's tent cities. When they've killed the militia, we will let the dogs into the walled city. The citizens of the city won't be able to defend themselves. Hastings has trained the dogs for a special purpose." He glances at my brother. "Why don't you tell the boys about your pets?"

Dean nods and yells, "I have trained the beast-dogs to listen to no one but me, and to kill only men. They *hate* men. They will be brutal toward men. When the men are gone from the walled city, we will shoot the dogs and you will have your choice of women. You will get to rule. You will be the founders of a new society!"

The response nearly flattens my eardrums. I wonder if the roof holding the raiders can handle such a ruckus. They are jumping, stomping, screaming.

A gunshot rumbles, mixing with the raiders' noise. The men quiet down, but their bodies are tensed with pent-up energy. "We want women!" a raider standing behind Flint yells. My brother turns and grabs the man and puts him in a headlock. He starts pounding the guy's face and I am seeing the volatile, violent Hastings I have heard about. I am seeing the raiders' way of life.

The raiders whoop and holler at my brother and make vulgar gestures. They are like a plague, destroying everything they touch. I look at my brother, still beating the man, and know I am right. Dean would not let me die like this if the raiders hadn't poisoned his mind. He would be trying to save me.

Dean stops pummeling the raider and shoves him back with the others. He wipes his bloody knuckles on his jeans.

Flint waves his cowboy hat in the air and the raiders tone down their excitement. "And now, let's celebrate this news with a little entertainment! Gentlemen, meet the secret weapons Hastings has been creating for the past ten months: Speranza, Futuro, and Fede."

I gasp and look at my brother. I know those words, those names.

Dean gives someone a hand signal and a pair of double doors leading to the courtyard are opened. And so it begins.

CHAPTER 36

My family has a motto. It has been part of our heritage since my mother's Italian grandparents immigrated to the United States and my great-grandma embroidered it onto a piece of white linen. *Fede e Speranza per il Futuro.* It means *Faith and Hope for the Future.*

My heart starts to flutter with hope. And faith. For my future. I glance up at my brother again and his eyes meet mine. He nods, the slightest bob of his head.

I squeeze my knife hilt and grit my teeth. As if they can sense my resolve, three dogs come tearing out of the open doors—the German shepherd that tried to eat Kevin yesterday, a Doberman, and a husky. I am ready for them. Ready to fight. And then Jonah steps in front of me, blocking my view. Something flashes in his hand, metal and glass catching sunlight— and I expect to see a knife.

He is holding a syringe.

Jonah doesn't wait for the dogs. He digs his feet into the ground and runs. He's inhumanly fast, running at the Doberman. He leaps the last few feet and rams the needle into the animal's sleek black neck, wrapping his other arm around its head. They hit the ground and skid on the dead grass.

A massive weight slams into me and I face-plant into the dirt that was dug up by dog claws the day before. I roll over and swing my knife at a pair of forelegs. The knife hits, but the German shepard is oblivious to it. It jumps onto me, knocking me flat on my back. My head snaps against the ground and pain blurs my vision. I blink and my sight clears just in time to see the German shepherd's dilated pupils and sharp teeth as it lunges for my neck. I scream and throw my right arm in front of my face, and the animal's mouth closes over it.

"Imporre!" I shriek. *Lie down!* The dog growls. *"Goccia!"* *Drop!* The dog doesn't respond.

My arm feels strange—like I have an itch deep inside that I can't reach. I look at it and want to faint when I see the animal's teeth sunk deep into my flesh and my blood mixing with foamy drool. My hand goes numb, and the knife slips to the ground as I wait for the creature to snap my bone and swallow my wrist and hand whole.

But then something happens. The German shepherd's nostrils flare. It eases its teeth out of my skin and sniffs me. The animal's pupils shrink. Trembling, I pick up my knife from the ground with my left hand and stand, ready for the next attack. The shepherd crouches and then lunges toward me. I lash out with my knife, and air and dirt whip against my skin. But the dog doesn't touch me again. It soars over me. I turn and watch it sprint toward Jonah.

On the other side of the tree, Jonah is pinned to his back, struggling against the husky and Doberman. Two empty syringes gleam on the dead grass beside him.

My gaze moves beyond Jonah to the open door the dogs came through. I could run. I could leave. I could live. Relief spills through me like a waterfall. I take a step toward that door, and then force myself to stop. A sob rips at my throat. Freedom is so close that what I am about to do physically hurts. Turning back to Jonah, I clench my teeth, tighten my hand around the knife hilt, and run to his side.

He's barely visible beneath the pile of dogs. I stand a foot away from him, staring, not knowing what to do. He swings his forearm into the Doberman's face, and the animal yelps and falls to its side, dazed.

"Jack! The German shepherd," Jonah gasps. He thrusts his blood-covered hand out of the mass of snarling dogs. He is clutching a full syringe. I take it from him. The glass is slippery with blood—his and mine. I ram the needle into the shepherd's thigh and depress the syringe, injecting clear liquid into the animal. The dog doesn't notice. I drop the empty syringe to the ground with the others.

"Is it done?" Jonah asks. He's got his hands wrapped around the snout of the husky, keeping the animal's teeth from his face. The Doberman, still dazed, stands beside Jonah, shaking its head. The German shepherd's teeth are clamped around Jonah's forearm, and I'm terrified it will chew his arm off—until

I remember he's wearing the electromagnetic cuff. The dog's teeth don't sink in.

"Yes! It's done!" I say, wondering why he even cares when he's being thrashed by massive, viscious dogs. Jonah knees the German shepherd in the side, throws the husky off him, and lays his head down on the brittle grass. Peace softens his scratched face, and I realize he's resigned himself to the fact that he is going to die today.

"Jonah! Get up! Fight!" I yell. His eyes meet mine and he shakes his head a tiny bit, as if it's all he can muster. And then all three dogs lunge at him.

I stand and hold up my knife. "Come and get me!" I scream. "*Venire!* Get me!" The dogs don't even flick their ears in my direction. Jonah's eyes are closed. I step into the brawl and start kicking and slashing at the dogs. I might as well not exist—the dogs are so intent on Jonah.

"Why won't the dogs attack him?" It is Flint's voice, carrying over the noisy raiders. "I thought you said these dogs attack everyone but . . ."

Except for the sound of the dogs, the courtyard goes dead silent, and all eyes focus on me.

"The dogs attack anyone but a woman," Soneschen states.

"But the dog attacked him at first," says Flint, studying me.

"Until it got a good smell of her." Soneschen rubs his chin, and a slow smile spreads over his face.

My hands slowly fall to my sides, and I hold my breath while my eyes sweep over the men standing on the roof. I never thought this morning could get worse. I was wrong. The raiders are staring at me like . . . well, like I'm a woman. The only woman alive on the face of the earth.

Flint laughs and rubs his hands together. "I think we've had the wool pulled over our eyes, boys!" He turns to my brother. "Call off your dogs and get them out of here. We've got ourselves a female in our midst."

"*Vieni!*" Dean yells. It means *come*. The dogs pause and look toward the voice. Slowly, muscles bunched beneath their fur, they back away from Jonah. With their lips peeled back from their bloodstained teeth, they trot toward the building Dean is standing on. Dean's eyes meet mine. He knew all along—Dean knew they wouldn't attack me.

I crouch beside Jonah. His clothes are damp with blood and shredded in places. I press my hand against his cheek, and he groans and rolls onto his side.

"Gentlemen," Dean calls. I shade my eyes and squint up at him. "Take a good, close look at these dogs. They are made to tear men to pieces. They listen to no one but me. They are an unstoppable weapon—it takes a bullet straight to the heart to slow them down, and more than one bullet to kill them." He smiles—a real, true smile. "I have made them for a *very* special purpose." Soneschen and Flint both step up to the edge of the building and peer down at the dogs. Dean looks at the two men and his smile grows wider, making his eyes mere slits. And then he puts a hand on each of their backs. And shoves.

CHAPTER 37

Flint and Soneschen land with an audible thud, side by side on the courtyard grass twenty feet away from me. A blanket of silence seems to smother the world. The raiders stare down at the two men. Even the dogs freeze and focus their black eyes on them. Flint groans and rolls onto his side. Soneschen springs to his feet and starts to run to the nearest door. The dogs' hackles bristle, and their bodies bulge with tensed muscles. And then they start running, dead grass flying under their feet, until the Doberman gets Soneschen by the arm, and the other two dogs pounce on Flint.

Flint's cowboy hat falls from his greasy head, and he curls into a ball as the dogs tear into him. I cringe and look away. When Flint screams, I plug my ears.

A shadow falls over me, and icy hands clasp my wrist. I

swing my knife up, ready to fight, and find myself staring into a pair of dark-blue eyes.

"Dean." The word barely comes out of my constricting throat. He nods and shoves me at the nearest door. While I walk in a daze toward the exit, Dean runs to Jonah and lifts him to his feet. Jonah can barely stand. Blood covers both of his hands, and there are claw marks gouged on his cheek and neck. Dean loops Jonah's arm over his shoulder and they stumble across the courtyard.

"Jack, open the door!" Dean orders.

I put my hand on the door and shove. It leaves a red print on the glass. "Zeke! Help him." Dean unloads Jonah's massive body into Zeke's waiting arms. "We got Bowen out with the backpack—he won't leave until he knows Jack makes it out alive. You. Get her out of here now!" Kevin steps out from behind Zeke. "I'm going to let the rest of the dogs out to finish this!" Dean thrusts something into my hands—a folded piece of paper—and then goes back to the courtyard and starts propping open the glass doors that lead into the building. On the other side of the courtyard, all three dogs are intent on Flint, but Soneschen is gone. Sickened, I turn away and am pulled against a hard chest.

"I thought I'd never see you again!" Kevin says, holding me tightly. Dazed, I look up at him. His bottom lip is split and swollen, and on his belt are two guns—his Glock and my dad's Glock. "Come on. We have to run!"

I turn and look over my shoulder. Men are jumping off the roof, into the courtyard, weapons in hand, their attention focused on me. In their effort to reach me, they're throwing each other down, trampling each other, and hitting each other out of the way with baseball bats. The first raider reaches the door I am standing behind, and his dark eyes lock on mine. It is Striker. He smirks and licks his lips, and then he lifts his blood-covered baseball bat to smash the glass.

Someone slams into him, taking him down to the ground. "Get her out of here *now*!" Dean shouts, wrenching the baseball bat out of Striker's hand and swinging it at his head. Kevin yanks me away from the door just before the bat makes contact.

We take two steps away and pause. "Look," Kevin says. I turn and peer over my shoulder. All the doors leading into the court-yard except the one I am standing behind have been propped open and big dogs are pouring into the open space. The animals lunge for the raiders, pulling them down to the ground like prey. I look at my brother, standing in the courtyard with the dogs, and whimper. Kevin pulls me away. "You don't want to watch," he says.

We run down the hall behind Zeke and Jonah, to a pair of glass doors that lead to the parking lot. Zeke shoves them open. There are three four-wheelers in the parking lot. Two are empty, and Bowen—wearing the backpack filled with the cure—is sitting on the third. Zeke helps Jonah onto a four-wheeler and climbs on in front of him. I step through the doors, into fresh air, and dig my feet into the ground. "Where are we going? We can't leave my brother in there!"

"Jack, it's what he wants." Kevin tries to pull me away from the doors but his fingers slip against my bloody skin. "You got bit?" I nod and two deep creases form between Kevin's brows.

"How hurt are you?" he asks, lifting my arm for a better look. Blood is dripping down my arm and splattering on the ground beside my foot.

"I don't know," I say.

He takes Dean's folded note out of my bloody grasp and starts poking and prodding my arm. My stomach roils and I close my eyes. It is one thing to look at other people's wounds. But when they're on my own body, the sight is too much.

Kevin sucks a breath of air in through his teeth. "You're losing a lot of blood. If the dog hit an artery, you could die. We need to stop the bleeding." He guides me to the third four-wheeler.

"Is she all right?" Bowen asks.

"I don't know, and I'm not going to risk her losing too much blood," Kevin says. "I'm going to put coagulant on her wound and then we'll be right behind you."

"You sure you don't want us to wait, Kev?" Bowen asks.

"No. Get the cure out of here! This won't take me more than a minute or two. Zeke, you remember how to get into the tunnel through the wine cellar?"

"Of course I do," Zeke says. "Let's get moving!"

Bowen revs the four-wheeler, and as he peels out of the parking lot, I look at the giant backpack on his back. The cure— what's left of it after using it on the dogs and the raiders' beasts. Zeke cranks the other vehicle, and he and Jonah follow Bowen.

"Climb on," Kevin says, straddling the four-wheeler.

"But my arm . . ."

"We need to put a little distance between us and the raiders first."

I climb up behind him. We drive two blocks and then Kevin pulls the vehicle into a gas station with rusted gas pumps. He climbs down and gets his backpack and rummages through it until he finds a small square packet of coagulant.

Even this far from the raiders' compound, I can hear the sound of dogs barking and men fighting. I squirm in the seat of the four-wheeler and try to ignore the sounds. "Why did we use the cure on the dogs?" I ask. "If the raiders are just going to kill them, why go to the trouble? Why waste it if it's so precious?"

"If a single infected dog got loose, it would terrorize the city, preying on anything that moved. It would kill lots of innocent people before it was stopped because the dogs are nearly impossible to kill." He tears the coagulant open and pauses. "This will hurt. Are you ready?"

I nod and watch as he sprinkles tiny white coagulant beads onto my bleeding wound. My blood starts to bubble and then turns hot like it's on fire. The pain is bad but not *that* bad. Until the coagulant seeps down into my arm, reaching the deepest spot where the teeth sank into my skin. It burns like I've put my raw flesh into a pan of boiling oil. The coagulant starts to expand, so each puncture wound feels as if it is getting a flaming briquette of charcoal wedged into it.

I scream. I scream and scream, and Kevin holds me in his strong arms. Sweat beads over my entire body. The pain reaches a plateau and then starts to fade, and as the pain eases, my body begins to quiver and tears pour down my face.

"There. All done," Kevin whispers, gently wiping the tears from my cheeks with his callused thumbs. Something moves behind him, and ex-governor Soneschen steps out from the shadowed side of the gas station. His face is splattered with blood, and the left sleeve of his white shirt is torn off. His left arm is dangling lifeless at his side and so bloody I can't tell if there's any skin still on it.

"Get off the machine and I won't kill you," Soneschen says.

Kevin whips around and backs up until his body is pressing against my thigh. He takes his gun from his belt, but the governor is inhumanly fast. He sprints to us before Kevin has his gun aimed. A blood-streaked hand slaps the gun from Kevin's grip, sending it skidding across the parking lot, and Soneschen's right hand cinches around Kevin's neck. Tremors wrack the ex-governor's body, and purple veins pop out on his neck and forehead from the effort. Slowly, Kevin's feet come up off the ground. Kevin thrashes and claws at the ex-governor's hand, but the man doesn't loosen his hold.

I jump off the four-wheeler and kick Soneschen's knee, trying to knock him down, but his leg feels like steel against my bare foot. He doesn't even look at me. And then I think of the blood that was on his teeth, and the beasts kept at the compound. He's been drinking beast blood. He's as strong as Jonah.

I grab the governor's arm that is holding Kevin and pull, but the man kicks me squarely in the stomach, sending me flying backward. I slam into a gas pump and slide down to the ground. Cement collides with my head, and I stare up at the rust spots on the metal roof that shades the pumps. I lie there and stare up, trying to force movement into my aching, exhausted body while I listen to the sound of Kevin's thrashing. My eyes shift and I can see him. He is still clawing at Soneschen's hand, and his face is changing color—going from pale to red to a bulging, swollen purple—and I know he's slowly suffocating to death.

I force movement into my body and don't think—just act. I stumble to the gun Soneschen knocked from Kevin's hand and wrap my bloody fingers around it. For a split second I pause and stare at the thing, so familiar in my grasp. I am holding my father's gun.

Without wasting another second, I stand. Soneschen has his back to me. Kevin looks at me over Soneschen's shoulder and mouths the word *run*. But I'm *sick* of running, and there is no way I am going to watch someone I love die when I have the power to stop it. I shake my head and lift the gun, but because of my wounded arm, I can't hold it steady. So I trade hands.

The gun feels awkward in my left hand. I raise my left arm and grip my wrist with my right hand to steady it as much as possible. If I'm off, even a little, I will kill the wrong person. Bracing for the recoil, I aim at the middle of Soneschen's back. On an exhale, I gently squeeze the trigger, and my entire body lurches a step backward as the bullet leaves the chamber.

Soneschen drops Kevin, and they both crash down onto their hands and knees. I don't breathe as I stare at the two of them, identically posed, both gaping at the ground and gasping for breath. And then, like an answered prayer, a tiny red circle appears on Soneschen's white shirt, slowly expanding like a flower opening to sunlight. Soneschen's body starts to tremble, his nostrils flare, and he glares at me. A deep, guttural rumble starts in his throat, and he climbs unsteadily to his feet.

"You," he says, looking at me like I'm trash. "You're the dentist's daughter." He starts staggering toward me.

"Yes, I am," I say, "and if you were as smart as King Solomon, you never would have underestimated me. I am smart, and I am brave." I lift the gun. And shoot. The governor topples backward and lays still, his bloodstained white shirt glowing stark against the grimy cement.

Kevin stands and hangs his head like it weighs too much. He's still gasping for breath. I lower the gun and run to his side, drape his arm over my shoulders, and guide him to the four-wheeler. After I help him up, I climb on in front of him. Kevin wraps his arms around my waist and leans his head forward onto my shoulder. I turn the machine on and floor it. And then we speed away, with me too shocked to speak, and Kevin still gasping for air as if his throat is half-crushed.

"Dean always said you were a good shot," he rasps, lips beside my ear. I tuck my father's gun into my belt and lean back against Kevin. He pulls me close and we drive west.

CHAPTER 38

We hide the four-wheeler in a dense patch of brittle shrub high up in the foothills. The other two four-wheelers are already there, but Bowen, Jonah, and Zeke are long gone.

"Put these on," Kevin says. He pulls something out of his backpack and hands it to me.

"Socks?" I ask.

"I don't want you hurting your feet," he explains. "We have a little ways to walk, and these will help a bit."

Instead of going to the shelter, we walk to a two-story house that is surrounded by a ring of brown pine trees—the house with the telescope.

"Why are we here?" I ask. It feels like weeks have passed since I ran from this house, down the mountain and into the raiders' hands.

"If we're being followed by anyone, they'll have a harder time finding the shelter if we go in this way," Kevin explains. His voice is still weak and raspy, and his neck is swollen and turning blue.

The front door is locked. Kevin takes a scrap of wire from his pocket and sticks it into the keyhole and the lock clicks. We go inside, shutting and locking the door behind us, and go down to the wine cellar. He opens the hidden door and we step into darkness.

"I used to have a flashlight," I say. "But *someone* smashed it into the ground and broke it."

Kevin laughs a hoarse laugh and wraps his arms around me, holding me close. "Yeah. I'm lucky you didn't kill me. Your bite is a *lot* worse than your bark." He lets me go and I can hear him unzip his backpack. Something clicks and a flashlight flickers to life. "I guess it's a good thing I brought my own. Can you hold this?"

I take the light and he puts his backpack back on.

"Here." He pulls a folded paper out of his pocket and swaps it for the flashlight.

The paper is glued together with dried blood, and I can't open it, since my right hand is throbbing and practically useless. I hold it back out to him. "Can you unfold it for me?"

Kevin puts his flashlight into his mouth, takes the paper, and removes a pocketknife from his belt. Easing the blade under the folded edge, he gently pries it open. Brown flecks rain down from the paper, catching the gleam of the flashlight like falling ash. When he's gotten it all the way open, he glances at it and passes it back to me. "It's kind of ironic I'm the one giving this to you."

"Why?"

"I've been passing notes for Dean for nearly a year and a half."

I stare at Kevin. "What?"

He nods. "I'm his delivery boy. His own personal pony express."

"For my brother?"

"Yeah. Think of the first time I came to your house."

He'd been gone a month and a half. When I stood in the front yard, or on the roof during my watch, I always stared down the road leading north— the road Dean left on. I knew deep down in my heart that he would come back. It was inevitable. When he left, he took a piece of me with him, and it seemed to grow until I felt so empty that I could hardly get out of bed some mornings.

He needed to come home so he could give the piece of me back, so I could feel whole again.

I stood in the yard, facing north, breathing in the smell of sun on dead grass and the plastic-tainted smell of lacquered wood burning, courtesy of the elderly Mr. and Mrs. Pearson, who caught the bee flu and died when I was thirteen, leaving a house filled with antique hardwood furniture.

The air stirred, making long-forgotten wind chimes sing. I closed my eyes, remembering the sound of green leaves rustling. Instead, I heard one of the dogs growl. My eyes popped open, and I stared north.

A bearded man stood in the middle of the road, more than a block away. My heart raced with hope. Surely this was Dean, come back to give me my missing piece. I took two steps forward and paused with my toes touching the sidewalk—the line I was "never to cross again!" The last time I crossed it, I almost got my neck snapped by a cowboy.

The person took a few slow steps toward me and then paused again. His hands came up over his head, like a surrendering criminal's. Not a good sign. With that tiny gesture, I knew I was not looking at my brother. This person was a stranger.

I took two steps back, and without taking my eyes from the stranger, yelled, "I need backup!"

In less than sixty seconds, Steve and Josh were beside me. Thirty seconds later, Uncle Rob took his place on the roof.

"What do you want?" Uncle Rob hollered.

"I need to see the dentist." Distance made his voice quiet, but we still heard him.

"Are you a raider?" Uncle Rob called.

"No."

"Do you have the mark of the beast?"

"No."

Steve turned to me. "Jack, go inside."

"But—"

"Just do it! Tell Dad to come out here." Steve waited until I was in the house, with the door shut, before calling, "Come closer and show us your hands and arms."

Instead of getting Dad, I stood in the living room and parted the blinds, watching. The man wore fingerless wool gloves and was still holding his hands overhead. Slowly, he walked toward my brothers until he stood on the road directly in front of our house. The wind blew, pressing his tattered clothing against his broad chest.

"Very slowly, show us your hands and arms," Chris said. The man took one small step forward and stopped just beyond the reach of the dogs. He lowered his gloved hands, but I couldn't see anything. Steve was blocking my view.

"All right. Put this on over your eyes." Steve tossed a red bandana at the man and stepped back.

The man put his gloves back on and tied the red bandana around his scraggly, filthy hair. As he approached the front door, guided by Steve, I turned and ran to Dad's room. He was already awake, sitting on the side of his bed with his Glock in his lap, waiting. "I'm needed?" he asked.

I nodded. "A man wants to see 'the dentist.'"

He stood and walked out of the room. When he got to the front door and opened it, the blindfolded stranger stood framed in the doorway. "How can I help you?" Dad asked, holding his finger on the Glock's trigger.

"You're the dentist?" the man asked.

"Yes. What can I help you with?"

"I need to speak to you alone." The man's teeth were the color of moldy cheese and so plaque-covered that the spaces between each tooth looked nonexistent. "Restrain me if you'd like. But this is important."

"Cuff him," Dad said to Steve. The stranger was only a couple of inches taller than Dad, which to anyone else wouldn't be all that tall, but to my five feet, one and a half inches, he seemed huge. The man put his hands behind his back and bowed his head.

"Do you have a name?" asked Dad.

"I'm the vagabond." Mud caked the man's grizzled beard and was splattered over his ragged clothing. I shuddered and took a step farther away from him.

"Jack, stand watch at the workroom door. Steve, you and Josh double up on the front yard," Dad said, leading the man to the workroom.

"Yes, sir," we all replied at once.

I followed Dad and the vagabond to the office, then stood at the door, tense and ready to shoot, until my head started throbbing. Finally, almost an hour after they went in, the door handle twisted. Out strolled the vagabond, no longer blindfolded, uncuffed, smiling, and chatting with Dad. Dad's eyes were red-rimmed, as if he'd been crying. But maybe it was because he'd been awakened too early.

At the front door, Dad held his hand out to the vagabond and they shook. And then the vagabond held his gloved hand out to me. I put my hand into his and tried not to squirm at his touch. "Nice to meet you, Jack," he said with a twinkle in his eye. He didn't let go of my hand. The twinkle in his eyes turned into something else—an expression I knew well. Hunger. Want. Need. This man probably didn't have enough food.

I pulled my hand out of his, unzipped the bottom pocket on my tackle vest, and pulled out a container of applesauce. I stared at him and gouged the plastic sides of the applesauce container with my thumbnail while I mustered up the willpower to give it to him. It physically hurt, holding that applesauce out to the vagabond. Tears filled my eyes, so I blinked them into my eyelashes before they could trickle down my cheeks. He frowned and his face filled with wonder.

"You're giving this to me?" he asked. I gritted my teeth and grabbed his gloved hand, putting the applesauce into it before I could change my mind. "Thank you. I will treasure it," he whispered, and strode out of the house and to the street.

Dad put his hand on my shoulder. "You're a good kid, Jack," he said, and then he kissed the top of my head. Dad stepped out onto the front porch and took a deep breath of nearly warm air. "You are never to harm that man," he called loud enough for Uncle Rob, Steve, Josh, and me to hear. "He's a friend."

As we walk through the food-storage room, I think of my Dad's red-rimmed eyes. He *was* crying the day he met the vagabond.

"My dad has known all along about Dean joining the raiders, hasn't he? You told him about Dean."

"He knows the *real* reason Dean joined them."

"Which is?"

"To destroy them from the inside out."

I think of the saying my mom embroidered the first day the vagabond came—*Doing the Right Thing Is Always Harder Than Doing the Wrong Thing*—and stop walking. "My mom has known too," I whisper. Kevin nods and shines the flashlight on the paper in my hand. Even with the flashlight illuminating it, I can barely make out the words through the bloodstains.

> Jack,
>
>   Sometimes we do things that we hate to help the people who we love. By becoming a raider, I have helped save over one hundred women from the raiders' hands, and freed nearly fifty from their camp. At first, I did this for you. And now, I am doing it for my newborn daughter. Trust Kevin. He's the one who recruited me.
>
>   With love,
>   Dean
>
> P.S. Boys do cry. I'm living proof.

I sink down to the floor, too tired and sore and overwhelmed to keep standing, and reread the letter twice before asking, "My brother has a *daughter*?"

"Yes, he does," Kevin says, sitting down beside me. "She's probably about one month old now and as beautiful as her aunt."

"How? Who is the mother?"

"He fell in love with one of the raiders' women and killed any man who so much as leered at her."

"And the raiders didn't think that was odd?"

"No. A lot of them had 'favorites' and fought over them. Dean's the only one who was never beat. Which is how he became their ruler."

I scratch my head. "And how did this poor woman feel about that?"

"Well, she fell in love with him."

"But . . . I mean . . ." I bite the side of my cheek. "Where *is* his daughter?"

"She's at the colony in the mountains. Dean and I, with the help of a few others, broke all the women out of the compound. The woman and her child are safe. I'll take you to see them if you'd like. We can leave as soon as you feel well enough to make the trek."

A smile jumps to my face. A real, true smile. I'm an aunt. I look back at the paper. "Dean says you recruited him."

"Not quite." Kevin lifts his shirt and shows me the bullet wound scar on his ribs. "Your brother shot me. I guess injuring me upon first contact is a family trait."

My smile widens a little bit. "Why did he shoot you?"

"I thought Dean was a raider trying to bring Fiona's mom to their headquarters, so I tried to steal her away from him. He thought I was a raider trying to steal Fiona's mom, so he shot me. When we got things figured out, I brought them to the shelter—well, he sort of carried me, actually, since I was bleeding to death—and they patched me up. While we were in the shelter waiting for me to heal, and waiting for the snow to melt enough to take Abigail Tarsis to the colony, he told me all about his amazing little sister who loved to cook and was a better shot than any of her brothers.

"After a couple of weeks in the shelter, Dean got tired of waiting for me to heal, so he followed my map and took Fiona's mom to the colony alone. I never thought I'd see him again. I thought he'd stay there with her. But he came back. And he had a plan. He said because he loved his sister *Jacqui* so much"—he tilts my chin up, and now I know who told Kevin my name— "he wanted to give all women a chance at survival, wanted to help me in my quest to help others get away from the raiders. He really recruited himself."

"So, is what you said when you tied me up a lie? Did you go to my house to see me, or was it really to pass notes to my dad?"

"At first I went to your house to give your dad Dean's messages. But it was seeing you that made it worth it. Even though I disgusted you." I flinch and he laughs. "But after a while I started coming every couple of weeks whether I had a note to deliver or not." His fingers sweep over the side of my face. "Because I fell in love with you."

He has that look in his eyes again—hunger. Want. Need. And now I understand what it is that he hungers for, because I'm starved for it too. I put my left hand on his cheek. "I love you, too," I whisper.

"I know—I can tell by the way you look at me. I just can't believe it," he says. He slides his hands under my tackle vest and gently moves them over my back. They are warm and firm with only my T-shirt between them and my skin. And they're trembling. I close my eyes and kiss him, feeding our hunger.

After a minute, he pulls away from me. "Stop distracting me," he whispers with a grin plastered to his face. "We need to get moving."

We walk in silence, hand in hand, to the end of the food-storage room. "Did you really find all of this food by scavenging?" I ask.

"No, of course not! That would be impossible. My grandpa stored it. He is a major conspiracy theorist who had more money than he needed, so he spent it on things like top-secret bomb shelters, extreme vacations, and food storage. He had been storing food down here for decades, long before the honeybees started to go extinct. And then, when everything died, he was finally justified in his eccentricity."

We get to the pathway in the cave and deep voices carry on the air. Kevin steps in front of me and turns off his flashlight. The cave goes black.

"Please say that's you, Kevin," someone calls.

"Zeke?" Kevin turns his light back on and shines it down the path. Jonah, Bowen, and Zeke are sitting on the ground in the dark.

"We were starting to worry about you two," Zeke says, frowning. "What took you so long?"

"We had a run-in with Soneschen," Kevin explains, touching his neck. "What are you guys doing? Why didn't you go on to the shelter?"

Bowen claps Zeke on the back and says, "The old man forgot to bring spare batteries with him." Zeke chuckles and holds up a dark flashlight.

"I needed to take a break anyway," Jonah says, his voice weak. He's no longer covered with blood—just a whole lot of scratches and gouges. He's obviously been cleaned up. A lot.

"How are you doing?" I ask, crouching down beside him.

"I was doing all right until Zeke thought it would be a good idea to patch me up a bit with some coagulant." He shudders. "The stuff nearly did me in."

"Yeah, but you're not bleeding anymore, and coagulant sanitizes wounds. You won't be dying from blood poisoning," Zeke says.

Zeke and Bowen help Jonah stand, and together we finish the walk to the shelter. Zeke, the only one of us who isn't injured in some way, crouches down and removes the cans of flour from the shelter's entrance. "I'm here with four strong, healthy kids and I'm the one doing all the work," he grumbles. But there's a smile on his face. He pushes the cupboard leading into the shelter open and yells, "Don't shoot me!"

"Who are you?" Fo's voice rings out strong and clear.

"Fiona!" Bowen calls. "It's us! Don't shoot!" Zeke backs out of the cupboard and helps Jonah through. When he gets to the other side, Fo gasps, and I hear Jonah's quiet, sweet voice say, "It's as bad as it looks, but remember how fast I heal. I'll be all right."

Bowen goes through the cupboard next, and I follow right behind him and watch as he stands. Fo shrieks and throws herself at him, wrapping her legs around his hips and her arms around his neck. Her hands tangle in his hair and then they start kissing so passionately that I go back out of the cupboard, into the cement hallway.

"I think they need a minute alone," I say, unable to stop the grin that's plastered to my face.

"I think they need a honeymoon," Kevin says with a laugh.

CHAPTER 39

For the first time in more than three years I am not wearing my vest in front of non–family members. It feels scandalous, having only a T-shirt and a sports bra between my flesh and the air. Every time Kevin looks at me, I can't help but blush.

I am in the shelter, sitting on the tweed sofa, leaning over a chess board. I have been staring at the pieces for a long time. Kevin is beside me, studying my profile and holding a jumble of wire, and Jonah is sitting in one of the leather chairs on the other side of the coffee table, waiting for me to make my move. It is the ninth game of chess we have played in the four days since our return. I haven't won once.

I take a sip of my orange-flavored drink and try not to cringe when I think of one of the ingredients—Fo's spit. She made two gallons of the drink, with lots of spit added for healing purposes, right before she and Bowen left to have a honeymoon at Kevin's house.

Jonah takes a sip of his orange drink and leans back in his chair. Between the drink and his own natural healing abilities, he looks great. All his bites and scrapes have scabbed over, and his bruises are already fading. He seems more at peace, too, as if risking his life to save mine has eased some of the memories haunting him.

I glance at Kevin. His bruised throat is almost back to normal. He must feel my eyes on him, because he pulls his attention away from his latest wire sculpture—my face—and looks at me. His eyes warm, and he trails his hand over my back.

In the other chair, Zeke is sitting with Vince in his lap, reading an illustrated encyclopedia to the child. Vince's black eyebrows are pulled together, and he is studying the pages. He still doesn't talk, but he's started smiling when he is smiled at.

"Just so you know, Jack," Jonah says, "no matter what move you make, you've already lost, so you might as well get it over with."

My shoulders slump. "Okay, fine. You win again. But when we get back out there"—I point up—"I am challenging you to a target-shooting competition."

Kevin laughs. "Jonah, you better enjoy beating her while you can," he says. I smile and lean against him, and that is when I hear a soft laugh from the kitchen. Zeke stops reading. Kevin, Jonah, and I stand and go into the kitchen just as Fo crawls out of the cupboard. Bowen follows. When they see us, their eyes light up, and both of them look at me.

"You need to go to the house, Jack," Fo says. "There's something there that you need to see." She hands me her flashlight.

My heart starts pounding. Kevin grabs his gun. I grab spare batteries and shove them into my pants pocket and scramble through the cupboard as fast as I can. Kevin follows, and together we run through the passageway, the cave, and the food-storage room, until we get to the wine cellar. Without making a sound, we creep halfway up the stairs and pause.

It is sunset. Peachy light is slanting in through the west windows, making long rectangles of light across the wood floor. Kevin takes his gun from his belt and signals for me to hang back. He walks up the last few steps. "Hands up, sucker," he says. And then he does this thing. This *laughing*. And someone else starts laughing with him, a deep, rumbly laugh that I have been waiting a year and a half to hear.

I leap up the stairs and run into the room that has the leather sofa. Dean is there, leaning against the wall. He stands tall and blinks at me for a minute, like he doesn't know who I am. But that's not why he's blinking. He's blinking the tears out of his eyes. And then he holds his arms out.

"Come here, Jack. Come give your big brother a hug."

So I do.

CHAPTER 40

I shrug my shoulders out of my backpack, and Kevin takes it and sets it down. We have been hiking the last leg of the journey to Ward, Colorado—to the settlement— since four thirty a.m. All of us—Fo and Bowen, Jonah, Vince, Dean, Zeke, Kevin, and me. And now, we are on the side of a mountain, gathered on a boulder the size of a small building, which overlooks a deep, shadowed valley.

I sit down and press my frigid hands on the boulder. "The ground is warm," I whisper. "Is it from the fire?" A mile ago, we crossed the line from the dead world to the *burned* world. All the tree skeletons, brittle shrubs, and dead weeds are gone, leaving the ground an eerie, boulder-marked black beneath the light of the moon.

"The ground can hold heat for a long time after a fire," Jonah whispers, sitting down beside me. The closer we've come to Ward, the quieter he's gotten. He puts the backpack with the cure in front of his feet and rests his arms on his bent knees. I reach a tentative hand out and pat his back. I know why he's not talking. He is scared to be reunited with his mom.

"Are you hungry, Jack?" Dean asks. I hear the rattle of calorie tablets.

"No, I'm fine," I say, just as my stomach growls. Dean laughs and puts the calorie tablets away.

Kevin sits beside me, and I press the side of my body against his and shiver. The morning mountain air is freezing.

Fo unzips her backpack and pulls out a water bottle, taking a long drink before passing it to Bowen. "Why are we stopping?" she asks. "Aren't we almost there?" She sounds eager to the point of breathlessness.

"We're very close," Kevin says, his voice full of energy. "But we're going to wait until sunrise to go in. That way no one will get shot."

"Shot by whom?" Bowen asks, handing the water bottle back to Fo. From the corner of my eye, I see him lift his rifle to his shoulder.

"There are guards posted around the perimeter, but as long as they see us coming, they won't shoot you because you're with me."

"So, if we're almost at your colony, why is the ground burned to a crisp?" Bowen asks.

"If you burn the earth where the pesticide has been sprayed, it removes the toxins so new things can grow again," Kevin explains.

"Yeah . . . if there are bees to pollinate it," Bowen says, voice skeptical. He and Fo sit side by side, right beside Jonah. Fo puts her arm over her brother's shoulders, and I can't help but wonder if she knows that he's scared to see their mom.

We sit until the eastern horizon grows fuzzy with the coming dawn. "Listen," Kevin whispers, and everyone holds still. There is no sound. Confused, I look at him.

"I don't hear anything," Fo says, her voice disappointed.

"Listen harder." There is a smile in Kevin's voice. He kisses my cheek, and then puts his arm around my shoulders.

I close my eyes and hold my breath. At first I hear only the quiet swish of Kevin's breathing, the nearly inaudible sound of my heartbeat, and the small sounds of the people around me. But after a minute I hear something else. A tiny ringing. "Wind chimes?" I ask.

"Listen harder," Kevin says, his voice no louder than an exhaled breath.

I turn my head to the side, and my heart starts hammering. "Birds?" I ask, my voice trembling.

"Yes!" he says. Fo giggles.

I close my eyes again and sit perfectly still, just listening to the sound of birds. When the newly risen sun shines bright against my eyelids, Bowen starts to laugh. "Fiona, look," he says. She gasps.

I open my eyes and peer down, and my heart doubles in size. Tears fill my eyes, and the world nestled in the valley below blurs to every shade of green imaginable, with patches of warm gold in between.

"Come on. Let's go down," Zeke says.

We stand and put our backpacks on, and then start the walk

down the steep slope of a mountain. After a few minutes of walking, the burned ground is replaced by wildflowers as tall as my waist and aspen trees with gleaming white trunks and leaves so bright a shade of gold, they look like fire. I stop dead as another sound reaches my ears—the quiet, deep drone of bees. They're everywhere, just like they used to be, poking their heads into the bright blossoms. I start running, careening down the hill. Kevin runs with me. I trail my fingers through the flowers and laugh as tears stream down my cheeks. Bowen whoops and grabs Fo's hand, and they run with us.

Nestled in a pine and aspen valley below is a large group of wooden buildings. Cabins. A creek runs through the middle of the settlement, with a wooden bridge built across it. When we get to the bottom of the mountain, where the ground levels off, armed men wearing camouflage step out of the bushes and glare at me as they point their guns at my heart. I screech to a stop, my feet skidding on loose gravel. The men see Kevin and lower their guns. Smiles jump to their faces. One of the men, a blond teenager, starts laughing and runs over to me. I shrink away when he throws his arms around my shoulders. "Jack!" He lifts me off my feet and twirls me around. When he sets me down, I look at his face and gasp.

"Gabe?" I look at Kevin and back at Gabe. Kevin was there the night Gabe kissed me. The night Gabe announced that his family was leaving to find the Wyoming settlement. I look at Kevin again. "You brought Gabe's family here, didn't you."

He grins and nods. Dean comes down then and shakes Gabe's hand.

Others start coming out of the colony—men, women, and

children approach us with slow steps and wary eyes. A woman with braided gray hair shrieks and presses her hands to her heart. Tears start washing down her cheeks and she smiles. I follow her gaze and find Zeke walking into the valley with Vince on his shoulders.

"Woman," Zeke says, lifting Vince from his shoulders and setting him down. He stops in front of the woman and kisses her cheek. "Your old man's home for the winter." He leans down and whispers something into her ear. She nods, wipes the tears from her face, and hustles back toward the town.

Another woman makes her way to the front of the crowd and freezes. Her eyes grow wide in her narrow face. She looks hardly older than me and is holding a baby wrapped in a faded blue blanket. Dean gasps and rushes past me and throws his arms around her and the baby. When he lets her go, he cups her face in his hands and gently kisses her lips. He takes the baby from her and peers into the blanket, then brings the baby to me, pressing her into my arms.

My arms can do many things. I am strong and capable. But when that tiny life is placed into them, they suddenly turn awkward and uncertain. I freeze and peer down at the tiny face, at a pair of blinking blue eyes framed by perfect, tiny eyebrows.

"Jacqui," Dean says, "meet my daughter, Jacqui." The baby's mother steps up beside me. She studies me for a moment, as if she wants to say something, but instead of talking she throws her arms around my shoulders.

"Jacqui, this is Brenna," Dean says.

"I feel like I already know you." She smiles and wipes tears from her eyes. I return the smile and carefully—and a little awkwardly—hold baby Jacqui out to her.

That is when I realize Fo is standing beside me, fervently scanning the faces of the people coming out to greet us. Jonah is not here. I turn and look at the mountain we just came down and see him slowly making his way toward the valley. His hood is up, his head is bowed, and his hands are in his pockets.

In a trembling voice, Fo asks, "Is there a woman named Tarsis here?" The crowd parts and everyone turns toward the town. Zeke's wife is walking toward us with another woman. I squint against the bright morning sun, and my stomach drops into my hips. It is her—Jonah and Fiona's mom. When she gets to the outskirts of the gathered group, her eyes slowly scan over us newcomers. And then, when her eyes rest on Fo, she stops walking. Her gaze travels over every inch of Fo, and her eyebrows draw together in a frown, as if she can't believe what she is seeing.

"Mom?" Fo says. Mrs. Tarsis gasps and covers her mouth with her hand. Fo slowly walks toward her, and then throws her arms around her mother. Mrs. Tarsis wraps her arms around Fo and starts crying and laughing all at once.

"Fiona! My baby girl!" She pushes Fo to arm's length and studies her. "You're cured."

Fo nods. "They found a cure for the beasts."

Everyone breaks out in excited whispers. It is then that Jonah finally reaches us. He stops beside me and stares at his mom. It is as if Mrs. Tarsis can feel his eyes on her. She looks away from Fo and focuses on Jonah, her gaze traveling up from his feet, over his tall body, and resting on his shadowed face. He sighs and pulls the hood from his head. Mrs. Tarsis stands frozen, staring at his face. She takes two unsteady steps toward him and then falls to her knees. Jonah is beside her in the blink of an eye, lifting her from the ground. Mrs. Tarsis lifts a trembling hand and touches Jonah's scarred face.

"Jonah?" she whispers.

"Yes. It's me." He hangs his head. "I'm sorry, Mom. For everything. For Dad."

"Oh, Jonah." She sniffles. "I forgive you. I forgave you four years ago." She throws her arms around him and squeezes. He buries his face in her shoulder and his body shakes with sobs. "I love you, son."

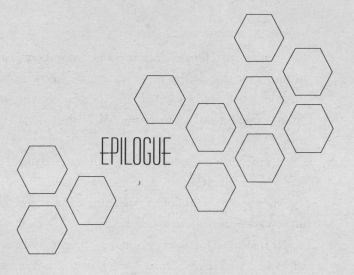

EPILOGUE

Kevin and I walk into the town. Every log cabin has the remains of a massive vegetable garden in the yard, with cold-weather plants, like acorn squash and gourds, still in the dirt. Ears of corn and baskets filled to overflowing with potatoes are sitting out on front porches, as if no one is worried about them being stolen. And I guess no one is. If a person has enough to eat, he doesn't need to steal food.

One log cabin has tall wooden boxes in front of it, and I can hear the quiet vibration of bees when we pass them. "What are those?" I ask.

"Beehives," Kevin explains. "My grandpa's."

I can't help but smile. Bees! I stop walking for a minute and listen to them. "Where is your grandpa?" I ask.

"Zeke's wife says he's at the fortress."

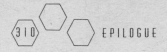

"The fortress?"

"You'll see." He takes my hand in his and we keep walking to the other side of the town, to a huge, rectangular building made of weathered logs. The air changes, growing heavy with animal smells, and I am reminded of the zoo. I wrinkle my nose. "What is this place?"

"It's the fortress—where we keep the tainted ones. The beasts. It is where my sister is."

My legs slow without my meaning to let them. "Wait. How do you keep them from attacking people?"

"If they're well fed, they're not as violent. We keep them in cages and feed them. Once a week or so, they're sedated and washed, and their cages are cleaned." Kevin pulls me toward the building. He opens a thick wooden door, and I can't help but put my sleeve over my nose and mouth to try and dull the smell.

I am standing in a huge room with knot-covered wooden columns supporting the ceiling and metal bars blocking the windows. There are more metal bars, which rise from floor to ceiling. Behind these bars are individual rooms, divided with thick wooden walls that are covered with dents and scratches, and inside each room is a beast. I look from cage to cage, counting. There are twenty beasts.

A disheveled, white-haired man is standing in the room, pressing pieces of hard, flat bread into the cages. "Grandpa," Kevin calls.

The old man turns and looks at us, and a grin wrinkles up his face. He strides over to Kevin and throws his arms around him. He looks at me over Kevin's shoulder, and his grin turns to wonder.

"Is this Jacqui?" he asks, letting go of Kevin. He puts his hands on my shoulders and takes a thorough look at me.

"Yes. This is Jacqui. And this"—Kevin takes his pack off—"this is the cure."

The old man's hands fall from my shoulders. He and Kevin both walk over to a cage on my right. Inside is a girl with tangled auburn hair that reaches her shoulders. Her hands are wrapped around the bars of her cage, and there is no tattoo—no mark of the beast—on them . . . but she's staring at us with unblinking, wild eyes, and drool is dripping down her chin.

"Jack, meet my sister, Tessa," Kevin says, and unzips the backpack.

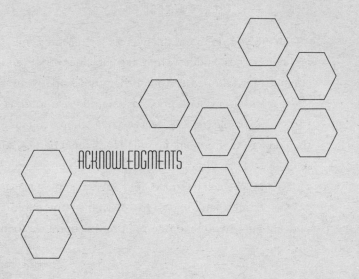

ACKNOWLEDGMENTS

I must first thank my four young children for going to bed by eight p.m. every night (not always by choice), because without my evenings free, there is no way I could write books! Now, if I could just get you to sleep past seven a.m. . . . And my husband, Jaime, who might as well have a wife who works nights even though I'm sitting in the house, typing and talking to people only I can see and hear. Thank you for your support!

Michelle, Bonny, and Kristin, thanks for being fast beta readers! You three are my go-to girls, and I couldn't do this without you.

Again, I must thank Marlene Stringer for being an agent who responds to my e-mails in mere minutes and knows exactly what to say.

All the wonderful people at Walker books, especially Emily Easton and Laura Whitaker, thank you for believing in me.

Thank you, Jonny at Silencerco, for teaching me about guns and ham radios, and how to make gasoline work even if it's been stagnant for four years. You're the guy I hope we have around if the world ever does come crashing down around us!

My incredible friends deserve a huge thank-you for everything they do for me, from baking bread for launch parties, to watching my kids so I can write, to feeding me lunch once a month. Jennifer, Kristin, Meggan, Tamara, and Sherstin, you guys are the best!

Last of all, thank you to my first fans—my parents, in-laws, and siblings—who read my manuscripts and love them.